ADVANCE READING COPY

UNTETHERED

Armida Publications is a member of the Independent Publishers Guild (UK),
and a member of the Independent Book Publishers Association (USA)

www.armidabooks.com | Great Literature. One Book At A Time.

Summary:
Cara, Lillian and Emilia are three women of a certain age who have one thing in common – a love of
animals. Sadly, on the Mediterranean island they call home there is appalling animal cruelty and after
learning of a puppy's death in a cardboard crushing machine, the three friends decide to do something
about it – they then find themselves responsible for one of the most intriguing, and in some quarters
celebrated, crime sprees in modern Cypriot history.

[1. Crime 2. Animals 3. Literary 4. Contemporary British Fiction 5. Animal Welfare 6. Women]

Cover image:
Photo by Avi Theret on Unsplash

Backcover image:
Photo by Birgith Roosipuu on Unsplash

1st edition: March 2022

ISBN-13 (paperback): 978-9925-573-94-3

UNTETHERED

Andrea Busfield

a novel

This book is dedicated to Blister, Alfie, El Disco Bastardos, Walter Pickle, Bonnie, Target, Lucky, Mina, Sundance, Mango One-Eye, Magic Tiger, Hissing China, Scraggy Ann, Fluff, Harley Baz, Jigsaw, Button Moon and the memory of my beautiful boy, Achilles.

(Shine bright, Boo).

Prologue

Somewhere in the hills, about a mile from the nearest town, the light from a single bulb seeped through the slats of two wooden shutters on a close-to-derelict drinking den that was once the area's most popular taverna. A unique take on an old classic, *kleftiko* cooked in *zivania*, had brought the restaurant fleeting fame in the 1970s; a time when people seemed to enjoy their lamb marinated in an alcohol most commonly used to sterilise wounds. Then, as the years passed by, tastes changed, along with a catalogue of names and owners, until, four decades later, the Astraea Taverna was a crumbling ruin of its former glory and called Nicos. Somewhat surprisingly, the metal trellis at the head of the driveway remained in place, but where it had once welcomed tourists with Moorish lanterns lighting up the vibrant hues of snaking magenta and orange bougainvillea it now supported only rust. Underfoot, courtyard tiles that had fallen victim to the extremes of weather and neglect, were little more than fragments within a scrubland of weeds and spiny shrubs, and only a sprinkling of cigarette butts at the end of a gravelled pathway revealed the taverna continued to attract custom, though the damage inflicted on the once-solid walnut door gave some indication as to the type of custom the place now invited. In short, the Astraea Taverna, now known as Nicos, was a shithole.

Immediately behind the battered front door sat eight circular tables, suggesting some kind of dining area. A number of cardboard boxes, worn carpets, broken fridges and punctured bicycle tyres at the back of the room suggested a skip. Walls and ceilings that were once painted white were now nicotine yellow, and the lingering smell of cigarette smoke hung in the air like a monument to the national determination to defy modern thinking on such traditional pastimes as the inhalation of carcinogenic chemicals.

In the middle of the room, between the dining area and the skip, was a counter that appeared to serve as a bar. To the right of it, a glint of light crept along the edges of the kitchen door, beyond which three voices could be heard. They were all female and they appeared to be debating the shape of the planet.

"Well, that's just nonsense," said the woman sat in the middle seat of a row of three chairs.

"Maybe, but go and stand anywhere, at any height, and the horizon will always be at eye level," replied the woman to her right. She had a slight American accent though the inflection in her speech was eastern European.

"And that's your proof?"

"Not my proof. I'm just telling you what other people believe."

"That the earth is flat?"

"That the earth is flat."

Lillian stared at Emilia, unsure as to whether she was having fun at her expense. The Romanian was hard to read at the best of times, but with a balaclava covering her face it was nigh on impossible to work out what was going on. She turned to Cara. "Have you heard of this?"

"I've heard of the Flat Earth Society," Cara admitted. "I don't know much about them, but they've been around for a while. Apparently, we're all drifting through space on the back of a giant disc. Kind of like a Terry Pratchett novel, minus the massive elephants."

"Oh, this is absurd," Lillian replied testily, her exasperation compounded by the mention of elephants. She turned to Emilia. "Who the heck believes in this stuff? And how can anyone believe it's true when photos from space clearly show the earth is round as a ball?"

"Actually, it's not that round. It's more like a ball squashed at both ends and as for explaining, I explain nothing," replied Emilia, employing a studied indifference that occasionally set Lillian's teeth on edge. Most of the time, however, Lillian liked her enormously, though she was still unused to the company of ladies bearing tattoos and piercings.

"But the photos?"

"Look, I'm with you, Lillian; the flat earth conspiracy is bullshit. But those people who like to believe in this bullshit say the photographs are lies – lies made up by the 'Round Earth' conspiracists."

"Oh, give me strength."

Emilia laughed. Though it felt unfair at times, she enjoyed toying with Lillian; she was so very British and a child of a certain age still harbouring a sentimental belief in an empire long dead. A lot of the Brits were crazy like that, or at least the ones she'd come across.

"Look, it's like this; anyone who doesn't believe that the earth is flat is a Round Earth conspiracist," Emilia explained patiently. "As for the photographs taken from space, they are supposedly fakes created by NASA and other government agencies."

"And NASA shoots anyone who tries to climb the wall," Cara added, causing Lillian's head to spin left with the kind of speed usually seen in Hollywood exorcisms.

"What wall? What are you on about now?"

"The 150-foot wall of ice that surrounds the earth. You probably know it better as Antarctica." Cara raised her feet onto the front spindle of her chair, conscious of the urine creeping along the cracks in the tiled floor.

"It's this wall that stops the oceans from emptying over the edge," Emilia added.

"Oh, come on now, this is just silly." Lillian shook her head. "No wall can hold back an ocean. And why would NASA, or anyone else for that matter, bother denying the earth was flat if it was true, let alone shoot people over it?"

"Because the beliefs of the Round Earthers discredit the Bible," Cara replied.

"What's this got to do with the Bible?"

"In the Bible it says the earth is flat, stationary and built on pillars. Or at least that's what they say it says. I've never read it."

Lillian raised her hands to her eyes, barely able to cope. The lack of faith these days astonished her. Nobody believed in God anymore and yet people were quite willing to believe they were hurtling through space on the back of a giant frisbee. "Well, I have read the Bible," she finally said, "and I can't say I remember anything about the earth being flat. However, I do recall the Prophet Elisha sending two she-bears out of the forest to kill 42 children for calling him 'baldy' and I'm not sure that's anything we should take too literally either."

"Nice prophet," remarked Emilia.

"The Lord works in mysterious ways," replied Cara.

"Like mass infanticide?"

"If you don't mind," Lillian muttered, and her friends, aware of her faith, shut up. "Anyway, how do you know so much about this Flat Earth thing, Cara?"

As she spoke, Emilia's eyes widened. "No names, we said!"

Lillian winced and immediately spluttered an apology. "Do you think he heard?" she asked, the panic evident in her voice.

The three women turned their attention to the man in front of them.

Nicos, the owner of the taverna, was wiry, middle-aged and casually dressed. He was also tied to a chair. His weak chin had long ago slumped to his chest and a line of spittle had formed a bridge from his mouth to the second button of his shirt.

"I think he's gone," Cara said.

"Poke him with your gun," Emilia suggested, and Lillian shuddered.

With a weary sigh and with one eye on the urine at her feet, Cara got up from her seat, took hold of Nicos's hair, and lifted his head. The eyes were closed, the mouth was slack and his head felt as heavy as a sack of bricks. If he was listening, he was a far better actor than he was a restaurateur.

"Yep, he's gone," Cara informed the others, "so we better go too. To be honest, he's starting to smell."

Lillian raised a gloved hand to her mouth. "Come on," she mumbled, "let's get out of here." Getting to her feet, she reached into her bag, pulled out a black felt tip pen and handed it to Cara.

"Where? Over there?" Cara asked and Emilia nodded.

Walking over to the white Formica table taking up space in the middle of the room, Cara drew four circles above a fat looking triangle. After filling in the shapes, she stood back.

"It should have claws," Emilia remarked.

"Nicer without them," Lillian replied.

"As terror signatures go, 'nice' isn't normally the desired reaction," Cara said before handing the pen to Lillian. "Have you got the chocolate?"

"I've got it." Emilia passed the truffle to Cara who placed it next to her artwork. She then handed the empty box to Lillian.

"Why do I have to carry everything?"

"You have the bag," Emilia replied.

"Not to mention the evidence," Lillian retorted.

"Give it here then, if you're uncomfortable. I'll take it home and burn it."

As Emilia reached for the bag, Lillian pulled away. "You can't," she said. "It's a Louis Vuitton and my passport is in it."

"You're kidding me." Cara's eyes rolled within the sockets of her ski mask. "You've brought your passport to a crime scene? Why would you even do that?"

"In case of emergency," Lillian answered feebly.

"The same reason I carry a condom," Emilia joked.

As the two women giggled, Cara stared at them until they noticed and quietened down. Once she had their full attention, she gestured, with some exasperation, towards Nicos.

"Finished?" she asked, and Emilia and Lillian nodded. "Come on then, let's go. It's a hell of a walk to the car."

"Oh God, the car..." Emilia dropped her head, reminded of the fatigue she had been fighting and trudged through the back door, held open by Cara.

Once Lillian and Emilia were outside, Cara glanced at the paw print drawn on the Formica table before turning to the unconscious figure strapped to the chair.

"Serves you right, you evil bastard," she whispered.

She switched off the light, shut the door and followed her friends down the gravel pathway leading away from the taverna.

Chapter One

Eighteen months earlier...

It was at a charity quiz night at The Dreamers Inn in Dromos that Cara, Lillian and Emilia initially joined forces. As first meetings go it was a fairly innocuous affair with most of the drama coming from Table Eight.

"It's Heracles."

"No, it's Hercules."

"They're the same man."

"I can only go with what's on the card and the card says Hercules."

"But that's the Roman name, not the Greek. You asked for the name of the Greek hero."

"Card."

Cara, Lillian and Emilia stayed out of the controversy, partly because they were strangers to the quiz scene, but mostly because they had gone with Hercules. As they were in the infancy of their friendship, they were also a little shy around each other.

It was only a week ago, on a bright, January morning, that Cara had met Lillian. Ambling towards the nearest kiosk, through a maze of white holiday villas and expat bungalows, she had seen a blue Toyota Rav4 emerge from a housing complex and proceed, at some speed, towards a well-dressed woman carrying two bags of cat food. Though the driver swerved at the last minute, the woman lost her balance and fell backwards into a wall. Naturally, Cara rushed to assist, and this is how she met Lillian; as a witness to an attempted hit-and-run.

"It's not the first time," Lillian revealed, her fine-featured face pale from shock and excess powder. She brushed herself down and picked up her bags.

Intrigued as to what this woman, with her neat floral dress, flat shoes and woollen cardigan, could have done to incur the wrath of someone with such alarming regularity, Cara asked.

"I feed the cats," Lillian explained. "Not everyone approves. Some think they're vermin."

"And their answer is to run you over?"

Lillian smiled, wincing slightly because she had bruised her cheek in the fall. "I'm not sure anyone would actually do it, though this guy comes close at times. I think he just wants to scare me into stopping, or stop me from doing it near his house. I don't know. Anyway, he won't win. I've had alarms fitted at mine and I usually wear a GoPro strapped to my head. Thing is, I've just had my hair done and, well, you know how it is."

Cara was shocked, partly because it was the first that she had heard of such dangers in the four years she had lived in Cyprus, but also because Lillian didn't look the type to be into action cameras. She wrote down her phone number, in case Lillian wished to take things further – "and may I suggest that you do" – and bid the older woman a safer day than she'd so far had.

On arrival at the local kiosk, a little later than anticipated, it might have been fate or really bright graphics, but Cara's eye was immediately drawn to a poster taped to the door advertising The Dreamers' Inn quiz night 'in aid of Tala's Monastery Cats and the Stray Haven dog shelter'. Despite having no one to go with, having done her best to avoid making friends since moving to Cyprus, Cara was taken by a strange compulsion to attend. For some time, she had wanted to give something back to the rescue community, and though it had taken a while, she was finally growing bored of her own company.

Cara initially moved to Cyprus on a whim, nursing the kind of disappointment that comes from loving the wrong man. She arrived shortly before the economy tanked and in time to witness the Cypriot government deal with the crisis by raiding people's savings to rescue the teetering banking sector.

"Can they do that?" her mother asked over Skype.

"I assume so as they've just done it," Cara replied, and her mum muttered darkly about Greeks bearing gifts, which made no sense at all under the circumstances.

As it transpired, the raid on the rich worked pretty well for the national economy, which must have been comforting to anyone holding bank shares rather than the euros they had worked hard for, saved for and, in some cases, laundered. More out of habit than design, Cara had kept her money in the UK banking system.

After viewing a dozen or more properties ranging from one-bedroom flats to five-bedroom villas, Cara bought a traditional one-storey stone cottage, with title deeds, on the outskirts of Dromos, a large village in the western region of Paphos. It was a sweet and basic hideaway with two bedrooms, a small garden and a courtyard. The neighbours were a mix of English and German, and far enough away so as not to be seen, but close enough to help should she need to scream. At that point in her life, the isolation appealed to Cara. After a lifetime of cities, she was done with living on top of people. Or even near them. In recent years, life had become claustrophobic and she yearned for space. It might have been her age or a deeper malaise, but she had grown sick of the world with its rising intolerance and lack of humanity. But she also needed time to recover, to find herself again, and the stone cottage in Dromos afforded her that time.

With enviable sea views, Cara's home had solar-powered hot water, wooden beams and a lemon tree in the garden. The air was clean, save for the occasional sandstorm or wildfire, and the noise was minimal. On the downside, there were mosquitoes, venomous snakes and Cyprus Tarantulas. The first time Cara saw one of those, she screamed so hard the Germans came over.

For the first month in her new home, Cara did little more than settle in and wait for the phone to ring, which she then ignored. It was petty and childish, she knew that, but she was heart sore and angry, and she wanted Tom to hurt for a while. She needed him to feel the pain of their separation so he might find a way to salvage their relationship. Cara needed Tom to fight for her. Unfortunately for her, Tom must have interpreted his unanswered calls another way entirely because, eventually, he simply stopped ringing. Cara then tried to deal with this new disappointment by earning a living.

Although Cara had bought her home outright, with savings to spare thanks to the money generated by the sale of her London flat, she hadn't counted on the cost of Cypriot electricity nor the cash-collecting vagaries of the government, so work was not only a distraction but a creeping necessity. Of course, having chosen to live in Cyprus to distance herself from people, as well as past love, she hardly relished the thought of having to deal with them to pay her bills. So, she compromised and chose her targets wisely, a wedding planner here, a tour guide there, and a beautician; exactly the kind of chat-friendly professionals that expats and tourists flock to. From experience, Cara knew these professions were a goldmine for stories, which made them ideal contacts for feature writers, such as Cara, and as wages were not what they ought to be on the island, no hard sell was needed. Cara offered a 15% commission on any stories or interviews that she managed to get published.

As Cara half-expected, this working relationship got off to a slow start, partly because non-journalists struggle to identify potential stories and partly because they actually have jobs to do. However, after a few successful hits, the arrangement started to work, meaning her contacts enjoyed some tax-free beer money and Cara could pay her bills without dipping into her savings. The money also came in handy when she unexpectedly found herself with another mouth to feed.

Within six months of arriving in Cyprus, Cara's solitary lifestyle came to an end when she discovered a puppy dumped in one of the communal bins. Barely three months old, the dog had, literally, been thrown away like rubbish. This was Cara's first indication that animal rights might not be high on the national agenda.

After balancing precariously on the lip of the bin, Cara managed to grab hold of the black and tan dog without joining him. The puppy was filthy, half-starved and covered in ticks. Even so, she held him gently in her arms as he started to shake, either from cold, fear or shock, or a combination of all three. Cara was no expert, but the long ears and velvet coat suggested the puppy was a hunting dog or at least a hunting dog mix, and she knew that if she had passed by an hour or so later, the bin men would have done their job. The thought of that haunted Cara for the rest of her days.

Having no idea of what she should do, Cara took the puppy to the local vet. There, they cleaned him up, told her "this is Cyprus", and tested him for all manner of diseases she'd never heard of and, thankfully, he didn't have. As they worked, she asked about shelters only to be told she could try ringing, but the good ones were usually full.

"What about the bad ones?" she joked.

"You'd be better off leaving him in the bin," was the reply.

So, once he was jabbed and beautified, Cara took the puppy home and named him Cooper.

In her 43 years on the planet, Cara had never owned a dog, which meant she was totally unprepared for the impact Cooper would have on her life. Yes, there were accidents requiring bleach and restrictions regarding restaurants, but from the moment she rescued him, nothing was more important to Cara than Cooper. Unaccustomed to the concept of unconditional love, both in terms of receiving it and giving it, Cara's world suddenly took on a strange and brighter hue. At last, she had found something to truly live for, to nurture and protect. It was liberating to love and never consider that love as some kind of betting chip that needed to be seen and raised. She loved Cooper. She loved the way he crept onto her pillow at night and slept with his nose pressed against the back of her neck. She loved the way he watched her every move and the sight of his gums flapping in the breeze as he rode shotgun in the car with his head out of the window. She even loved that she could smell his farts and find them comforting. In all the years she had lived with Tom, not once had she thought of his farts with any kind of affection, and she wondered whether this was actually a sign that should have been heeded. Still, what was done was done and though she was more alone than she had ever been, she was surprised to find she was happy; Cara genuinely enjoyed the company of her dog, which was fortunate because four months after she rescued Cooper, she took in Peaches.

Peaches was a tiny, sandy coloured Kokoni dog and Cara almost cried when she first laid eyes on her. She was emaciated and nursing a broken jaw and burns to her back, most likely from scalding water. Found by the side of the road, and as close to death as it's possible to be without dying, a couple of passing tourists folded her in a blanket and took her to the nearest shelter they could find. The shelter's Dutch volunteers then brought Peaches to their favoured veterinary practice, which happened to be the very place where Cooper was getting his anal glands squeezed.

"Will she live?" asked the tall, blond man who had brought her in.

"I don't know. Maybe. Hopefully," the vet replied.

"Doesn't sound great."

"Maybe, maybe not. We'll need to keep her for a week or so. We'll know more once she's x-rayed. Can you find a foster to take her while she recovers?"

"Possibly," the man replied. "I guess she'll need special care and meds?"

"For the burns, yes. The jaw can be set, though it could take between six and eight weeks to heal and she may require a feeding tube."

"I'll take her."

Having quite forgotten that Cara was standing in the corner of the room waiting for Cooper to recover from the recent exploration of his anus, both men turned to look at her with surprise.

"You want to take her?" asked the vet.

"You want to foster?" asked the shelter guy.

"Yes, I'll take her and, yes, I'll foster her if you want, but if you don't mind, I'd rather keep her."

Chapter Two

Emilia Branza was born some 37 years ago in a village close to the city of Sibiu in Transylvania. Her family wasn't rich, but neither were they poor, and she attended a decent school where she obtained good enough grades to earn her a place at university to study law.

For a while, everything in Emilia's world was fine. Until one day it wasn't.

Perhaps it was the looming reality of long hours, people in suits, and praying for the weekend that caused her to think about what she really wanted from life. And, after thinking about it, she decided she was so far off the right path that she might as well kill herself. It wasn't that Emilia didn't have an aptitude for a legal career, it was more the wrong attitude. In short, she was easily bored.

Boredom, or the fear of it, was a state of mind Emilia couldn't shake off. She recognised it as a potential problem and, after some research, she discovered it was a problem with a name; thaasophobia. Still, recognising it and dealing with it was not the same thing, and try as she might, it followed her everywhere, infecting everything she did and everyone she met until eventually people did their best to avoid her. In many cases, it was wrongly assumed that Emilia was ungrateful for the gifts that life had given her, or that she was simply rude, given her tendency to look through and past people during conversations. However, Emilia wasn't unappreciative of anything she had, not in any way, but there was a constant and relentless urge to keep on looking for what was coming next, whether it be a job, a boyfriend or a new kind of experience, because whatever state she was currently in, she worried it might be 'it'. This would be her life until the day that she died.

"Childish, teenage angst," was her stepmother's diagnosis, but her stepmother was a fool. Why else would she marry a man still in love with his dead wife?

Perhaps unsurprisingly, and part-way through a three-year internship at a Bucharest legal firm specialising in maritime law, Emilia decided it was time to leave Romania. She felt the need to travel and, for the next 15 years, she never stopped. After taking a bus to Hungary she hitchhiked through Austria, skied over the Alps to Italy, got on a boat to Greece and then took a flight to Cyprus. Along the way she held down a number of jobs, some of which she kept for a few years, some only days. In Salzburg, she acted as PA to a well-known fashion designer; in Milan, she worked as a croupier; in Athens, she became an extra in a film about refugees; and in Cortina d'Ampezzo, an ancient mountain town in the Dolomites, she took a job as a chalet maid. Emilia also took a number of lovers along the way, without ever losing her heart. This was another of her peculiarities; she didn't fully appreciate love or the dramas that went with it. All over the world, men and women were pining for people who didn't like them enough to stay with them, or they were compromising lifestyles and life choices for a happiness that remained largely elusive. If this was love, it was lost on Emilia. At least until it found her.

It was while Emilia was living in Dromos and holding down a job as a surly waitress in one of the village's less popular restaurants that she discovered true love, and it was tethered to a stake driven into the ground in an area of scrubland running alongside the coastal road. A bay-coloured horse with a black mane framing his handsome face, he had a white mark in the shape of India on his forehead. He also swallowed air, a habit that Emilia assumed was due to boredom. However, it was the eyes that struck Emilia most; beautiful pools of chocolate brown that pulled her into a soul she somehow knew. Emilia was no Buddhist, but she felt an unmistakable connection that felt like a past life so, when she eventually tracked down the owner, she bought the horse for far more than he was probably worth. She then named him Adonis.

Adonis was a four-year-old thoroughbred, according to the papers that came with him. Originally destined for the racetrack, he had failed to make the grade, but as he came from good stock he was handed to a government official who then gifted him to his son. Unfortunately, when Adonis failed to make the grade as a horse suitable for an overweight 14-year-old boy, a chain was slung about his neck and he was left to exist, and do little more than that, on a diet of stale bread, an occasional armful of straw and a bucket of water. Emilia's heart bled for the animal. While her knowledge of horses wasn't extensive, she had ridden as a child and she knew that horses needed company, preferably of their own kind, and they also needed a proper diet of hay, clover and grains. Dry pita simply wasn't sufficient.

Emilia couldn't explain it, but she felt compelled to save him. Of course, having never counted on becoming a horse owner, she had nowhere to put him and no food to feed him so, after fashioning a makeshift halter out of rope she bought from a hardware shop, she walked Adonis three miles to the only stables she knew of in the area. Under the burning noon day sun, it felt like a joyous and heroic march to freedom, until they arrived at their destination.

Greeted by a locked gate, Emilia called, banged, rattled and shouted for attention until it came in the form of an older woman dressed in beige breeches, a white t-shirt and a brown baseball cap. She reminded Emilia of a Frappuccino.

"Sorry, this is a private yard," the woman replied tersely when Emilia said she was looking for somewhere to stable her horse. "You can't bring him here."

"But…"

"There are no buts. There are no exceptions. This is my home, not a business."

"But please…"

"Sorry, no."

And with that the woman promptly turned on the heel of her Italian leather boots and walked away. No doubt she would have continued walking had Emilia not screamed.

Julia Watson would later say it was one of the most agonising sounds she had ever heard come out of a human mouth, so much so it set the hairs on the back of her neck on end. When she turned around, she found the dark-haired woman at the gate now on her knees with the horse standing next to her, gently nuzzling the side of her face. Julia felt her resolve crumble. Any other horse, let alone a thoroughbred, would have been on its hind legs at such an unholy commotion. But not this guy; he simply didn't have the energy. Slowly, she walked back to the gate.

"Are you injured?" she asked.

Emilia shook her head, not bothering to look up. "Not injured, just desperate."

It was only meant to be a temporary stay because Julia had made it crystal clear from the start that her yard was a private yard. She also wanted €300 a month for livery, leaving Emilia with nothing from the pittance she earned at Zorbas once she'd paid her rent and the various bills that went with it. Thankfully, it only took a fortnight for Julia to thaw because some people don't know they're lonely until they're forced to have company.

In spite of herself, Julia was touched by the care and devotion Emilia lavished on her horse. When Emilia wasn't working at the restaurant, she would be at the yard; grooming, washing and generally pampering Adonis. After Julia lent her a head collar and lead rope, she would take Adonis for walks down to the Sea Caves and, after a while, she permitted them to use the arena to free school. When Julia watched them play, because this was no kind of free schooling she knew of, she was reminded of a child with a puppy.

Not that it mattered. It was clear the two of them had found a rare happiness in each other's company. Unfortunately for Emilia, Adonis was not only handsome, but also a windsucker, a vice rarely welcomed in most stables. Julia understood it was a habit borne of stress, and it was as addictive as smoking when learned. She also knew that Adonis would be prone to colic as a result, and Emilia would need someone around who knew what to do when it struck.

Almost from the outset, Julia saw that Emilia and Adonis had found each other at the right time, in much the same way they had found her. And though she couldn't say why, she let them stay, telling Emilia that if she helped around the yard, her horse could remain at the yard, rent free. When Julia made the offer, Emilia assumed the older woman was a lesbian. Not that Emilia had anything against lesbians; she simply couldn't see why anyone would be so generous for relatively little in return. The woman only had four horses so there wouldn't be that much work to do. A year or so later, when their friendship had reached the point where delicate issues could be discussed with no offence taken, Julia laughed like a drain.

"Christ, if I was a lesbian, I'd hardly choose a pierced little punk like you," she told her.

"Why is it Americans only ever say 'punk'?"

Julia was in her mid-50s and came from Tallahassee, Florida. She wasn't the usual type of foreigner the island attracted; expats were mainly made up of retired Britishers, high-rolling Russians and economically-challenged Romanians, although the Chinese were starting to make an impact on the housing market in return for a backdoor entrance to Europe. But the Americans, not so much. In fact, Julia was the first American Emilia had met in Cyprus.

Julia moved to the island 20 years ago, after enjoying a successful jumping career on the international stage where she fell in love with a Cypriot guy, an equestrian who also achieved better-than-average success abroad. Even so, it wasn't enough to earn them serious money. Though the two of them possessed talent and a passion for the sport, they recognised their limitations and so, after building their reputations, they retired to his homeland and opened a livery yard for a select number of clients looking to compete internationally. They also made a handsome living from tutorials, private lessons and schooling. It was a fantastic partnership and a true meeting of minds and hearts, until, ten years into their marriage, Julia's husband was killed by a drunk driver on the highway from Ayia Napa. Julia was inconsolable.

As the couple never had children, because they believed they had plenty of time, Julia felt her husband's loss all the more keenly when she realised there was nothing left of him to hold. Her family begged her to return to the States, but she refused to step away from the ground in which he was buried. Indeed, it took her a long time to recover from his death and though she retained her passion for horses, she no longer had the stomach for people. So, she closed the business. She hardly needed the money. And she continued to walk through life, one day at a time, getting by with the help of her horses.

From the moment she found Adonis, Emilia could think of little else, but she still needed to work so she kept her job at Zorbas, which is where she came into contact with Lillian.

Emilia knew of Lillian long before they met because she used the restaurant's leftovers to feed the cats in the area. Though she usually came in the mornings, one Monday Lillian was running late and arrived midway through Emilia's afternoon shift. With a polite knock at the back door, Lillian popped her head into the kitchen where Emilia was piling plates by the sink. When she explained who she was, Emilia was surprised; Lillian was different to how she had imagined; more groomed and curiously uptight, even for the English. When the kitchen staff talked about the 'crazy cat lady', Emilia had pictured someone older and cuddlier. But Lillian was a well-presented woman in her fifties with razorblade cheek-bones and a fine head of auburn hair. She was also polite enough to answer Emilia's questions despite being in a hurry.

Lillian told Emilia she used the scraps from the restaurant to feed the colony of cats that congregated at the back of the village church.

"I thought I'd seen some there," Emilia said as she bagged up the leftovers.

"I'd be surprised if you hadn't. The cats have been there for about five years. Before that, we fed them in the car park a little further down the road, but people kept poisoning them."

"You're kidding?"

"Unfortunately, not."

As the two women continued to talk, Lillian let slip that she was looking for volunteers to cover a couple of feeding stations dotted around the village. The woman who used to help had recently re-turned to the UK. Well, the stars might have been in alignment or it could have been the talk about poison, Emilia couldn't be sure, but she suddenly had an urge to protect Lillian's homeless cats.

"How much do you pay?" she asked.

Lillian winced. "Well, nothing. We have no money to pay any-one, it's just a few of us volunteers. We buy all the food and look for scraps, we just need help to…"

"Relax, I'm joking," Emilia eventually told her.

"Oh, I see."

"Sorry."

"No, it's fine."

"But you pay the social, yeah?"

Confusion again clouded Lillian's eyes until it dawned on her that the younger woman was having another joke at her expense. Though she tried to smile, she actually found such humour ex-hausting, and she wasn't sure she could cope with it on a daily basis. In fact, if they hadn't already agreed to meet at the church the following day, she might have drifted quietly away, being careful to only return to Zorba's in the mornings.

As Lillian left the restaurant with her plastic bags loaded with the cold remnants of half-finished dishes and half-chewed kebabs, Emilia half-regretted her teasing. She guessed Lillian to be the same age as Julia, or thereabouts, but there was a beaten look underneath that well-preserved exterior. A few days later, when she started feeding Lillian's cats, she understood why – people were shits and they were especially shit to cats.

"The cats here are dying in every way possible," Lillian explained. "Burned alive, beaten, chopped up, kicked to death, run over... I've seen it all. For more than ten years I've fed the cats here and, in all honesty, they have been the hardest ten years of my life."

"So, why do you do it?"

"Because if I don't, who will?"

"Ah, Lillian. She's a funny one, but her heart is in the right place," Julia said when Emilia revealed her latest commitment to the island's unwanted animal population. "I don't know her well, but I've donated to her cats and met her on a few fundraisers."

"She's typical British," Emilia replied.

"Well, yes and no. She's a bit stuffy, which fits the stereotype, but she tends to keep away from all that expat drinking and meddling."

"I think I make her uncomfortable."

"You surprise me."

Julia nodded to the wheelbarrow in front of them. "Right madam, go and get those stables finished and I'll bring you a coffee."

"A biscuit would be nice."

"I'm sure it would."

Julia smiled, Emilia scowled, but they both knew there would be biscuits coming with the coffee.

Looking back on that day, as Julia often did in the years to come, she would occasionally be surprised by the small details that stuck. She recalled watching Emilia push her wheelbarrow up the aisle of the stables and noticing the sun's rays bounce off her jet black hair, like light on polished stone. She remembered switching on the sprinklers to water the arena and finding a half-eaten lizard by a cavaletti jump. There were two pigeons overhead, balancing on an electrical wire, and she wondered whether they might be to blame. She recalled sighing as she entered her home because she'd left on the aircon, and though it was always nice to step into a cool room, it was wasteful and bad for the planet. She debated whether to make real coffee or instant and went with the latter after glancing at the clock and realising Emilia would have to be at Zorba's in an hour. The coffee was made and she chose a red mug for Emilia and a yellow one for herself. Only just remembering to grab a packet of Hobnobs, she tucked them under her arm and walked back to the stables, wondering what saddle pad and bandage set to put on Apache. She called Emilia's name, but it sounded distant in her ears. Turning the corner, she glanced up the aisle of the stable block and saw a familiar boot sticking out from under one of the gates. 'She's with that damn horse again,' she half-laughed to herself until she remembered Adonis was in the paddock. She called again. Nothing. She walked up the aisle, feeling the world slow down as the blood started to charge through her veins. There was something wrong. She set the mugs on the floor and ran.

When Julia reached Adonis' stable, she found Emilia on the floor with her head jammed against the wall. Julia crouched down carefully, startled by the tears rolling down Emilia's flushed face.

"I can't move," Emilia whispered.

"What do you mean you can't move?"

"I can't move the left side of my body. Help me, Julia. I think I'm paralysed."

Chapter Three

Of the three, perhaps unlikely friends, it was Lillian who had lived in Cyprus the longest, coming up for eleven years.

Despite a lifetime of wishing for the sun, it actually took Lillian and her husband more than twenty years to emigrate for a number of reasons: finances, they couldn't afford the gamble; concerns about the children's education; and Lillian's unwillingness to leave all she had known and loved. Her husband Derek, on the other hand, appeared to harbour no such sentimental ties to either the UK or his children, but Lillian found herself paralysed by pending grief. However, when Derek was offered a job abroad, he issued a 'now or never' ultimatum, pointing out that Dan and Lucy were no longer children, but young adults; little birds who had flown the nest some time ago to start their own fledgling careers in construction and nursing.

For most of his working life Derek had been in the oil industry, in one form or another, and when the opportunity arrived to earn serious money as a risk analyst, assessing wells and de-gassing stations from an airconditioned office in Qatar, it seemed too good a chance to pass up. Derek seized the day and the immense pay packet that went with it and after a little more cajoling he and Lillian got packing. Of course, coming from a generation that occasionally mistakes prejudice for a rational distrust of Muslims, they agreed that Qatar was probably not the best place for a Western woman, no matter how sunny the climate.

"What about Cyprus?" Derek suggested. "You've always liked the place."

And indeed, during the few holidays they had enjoyed there, Lillian had been very taken by the island, not least because everything was so British; from driving on the left to the number of

Marks & Spencer outlets. Even so, Lillian struggled with the idea that she would no longer be in the same country as her children and if it hadn't been for Skype, she would probably have remained in rain-lashed Cheshire. But there was Skype, and there were cheap flights every day between Stansted and Paphos, and so a villa was rented, and during the weeks that Derek was away, Lillian found company among the island's stray cats.

Because Derek had agreed a four-week-on, four-week-off contract, it meant that Lillian spent a lot of time alone, something she had initially felt trapped by. In her previous life, she had never given much thought to finding ways to pass the time because there was none; as a housewife and a mother, life had filled the hours for her, often leaving her wanting more. Even after Dan and Lucy had grown up and moved out, Lillian had kept busy, with what she couldn't quite recall, but there was never a still moment that she could recollect, not until they moved to Cyprus where Lillian was suddenly confronted by this huge, intimidating number of hours to fill, in a place where there were no kids, no friends and, for much of the time, no Derek.

"You'll make friends," her husband assured her, but socialising was his field of expertise, not Lillian's. A robust man with a personality to match, Lillian used to watch Derek work a room with something close to astonishment, and she often wondered what it was that he had seen in a wallflower like her. In fact, looking back on their life together – all 32 years of it – it struck Lillian that most, if not all of her friendships had been instigated by Derek, in one way or another, be it a work do in which she had met other wives or a BBQ he'd organised and invited the neighbours to. Indeed, the only person she had ever come into regular contact with, unprompted by Derek, was her gynaecologist.

In the first few months of her life as an expat, Lillian concentrated on setting up home. There were the usual headaches to contend

with – residency forms, internet connection, insurance coverage, hiring a pool man and dealing with ants in the kitchen – and
then, once the formalities were over, there was the daily shop to
keep her occupied thanks to the local fruit and vegetables having
a maximum shelf life of two days. As a result, Lillian visited her
local supermarket almost daily and, in order to eke out the time
that little bit more, she would often read the free ads glued to
the window. Most of them were posters for various tribute bands,
which appeared to be something of an epidemic in the area, but
there were also items for sale as well as invitations to join cultural
societies, language courses and charitable enterprises. There was
one advert that immediately caught her eye and it read, 'Got too
much time on your hands? Then get in touch. Me and the cats of
Dromos could do with your help." And this is how Lilliam came
into contact with Primrose Merryweather.

As well as possessing the prettiest name Lillian had ever heard,
Primrose was a true eccentric with a heart of gold. Although her
age was never discussed, Lillian was quite capable of judging a
book by its cover and she placed Primrose somewhere between
late 60s and early 70s. Primrose was, in fact, 82 years old.

Their first meeting took place at the steps leading to a small,
white church in the village. It was a glorious June day and as Lillian
followed Primrose along a gravel pathway that skirted the church,
the sound of singing cicadas was gradually joined by a chorus of
cats congregating in a nearby car park. There must have been more
than twenty – of various colours, sizes and hairiness – and they all
came bounding towards Primrose with their tails held high and
their eyes expectant. Under her wide-brimmed straw hat, Primrose smiled.

"There's always a welcome with a hungry cat," she said. "Ring-
worm too, occasionally."

Seeing Lillian's face change, Primrose laughed. "Wash your
hands before you eat, you'll be fine."

Of course, Lillian did far more than wash her hands, and for the first few months, she turned up at the feeding stations armed with gloves and bacterial wipes. Although Primrose thought her neurotic, she didn't say anything because people had their ways and she needed the help. Primrose fed three colonies of strays in the village, twice a day. As she supplied the food, the only cost to Lillian was time, which happened to be the one commodity Lillian had in abundance. So, it was a win-win situation; Lillian felt busy and useful, and Primrose was able to devote more time to the cats' medical needs as well as the trap-and-spay programme she ran with a few other British ladies.

Although it might have surprised Primrose to hear it, Lillian felt hugely inspired by the older woman's dedication to the village's unwanted cats. It wasn't only the feeding and the medical care that was impressive, but the fact that Primrose had names for them all. Her devotion was touching. She worked tirelessly to keep them healthy and she cried bitterly when they turned up beyond her help or they simply disappeared. It was rare to find an old cat in any of the colonies.

"I can't bear to think about what happens to them," Primrose told Lillian. "I've heard too much and I've seen too much."

After spending close to two decades feeding the island's feral cats, there was little cruelty Primrose hadn't witnessed and even less she didn't know about it. Brought to Cyprus in the 4th century, the cats were introduced to the island by St Helen to rid the place of snakes and vermin. According to Byzantine legend, the cats answered the call of two bells; one that summoned them for meals at the monastery and another that sent them out to hunt for snakes in the nearby fields.

"Nowadays, the snakes are people, and the cats don't stand a chance," Primrose stated one morning as she placed the bodies of two poisoned kittens in the boot of her car. Two days after she buried them, Primrose also died.

Though the two incidents were unrelated, from that day on whenever Lillian came across an injured cat, and there were too many to count over the coming years, she often heard Primrose's bleak assessment of the local population. "People are snakes." Though Lillian agreed, she also thought they were psychopaths.

For a number of years, Lillian fed the cats she had inherited from Primrose unaided. She nursed them, wormed them, moved them from the car park to the back of the church, gave them names and even stopped wearing gloves. In short, she became a bona fide crazy cat lady.

Even when Derek said they needed to tighten their belts, Lillian made sure the cats never suffered. And, to her immense relief, he never once moaned about it. Clearly, Derek had no understanding of the depth of her devotion or how the cats had given her life purpose when she was floundering in the dark, but she didn't need her husband to understand. Lillian was simply grateful that he didn't interfere or try to take over. And when his rota changed to six-weeks-on, three-weeks-off, she didn't make a fuss. What could she say? In this day and age, she knew she ought to be grateful that Derek even had a job. It was the same when he revealed there would be less money coming in due to a change in his tax-free status.

"We're in a global recession, Lil', and even the oil industry is feeling the burn. I wish it were different, but it isn't." As Derek spoke, Lillian saw how uncomfortable he was and her heart ached. Derek might have lost much of his hair and there was a lot more padding on his once-athletic build, but she loved him nonetheless. She had always loved him. But more than that, she knew they were far better off than many people. They enjoyed a more than comfortable existence. They retained and let their home in Cheshire and they also owned an apartment in Valencia, bought in 1998 to rent out as an investment. So, while the pocket money might have tightened, the recession had no great effect on their standard of

living, only the time Lillian and Derek spent together. At first, that
was hard, but gradually Lillian started to make friends. Her own
friends.

As a fully paid-up member of the crazy cat lady community, Lillian
came into contact with a number of voluntary feeders, all women,
mostly over the age of 50, but surprisingly varied in their nation-
alities. There were Brits, Germans, Norwegians, Romanians and
even Cypriots, which surprised Lillian because the common per-
ception among most expats was that the locals didn't give a fig
about animals or their rights. As time went on, this conceit was
further quietened by tales of Brits returning to the UK without
their pets, some of whom loyally waited at the only home they'd
ever known, for the only owners they'd ever known, until they
were either rescued or joined the rest of the animal debris that littered the streets, hills and shelters of Cyprus.

One of the main challenges facing Dromos' cat population was
the level of copulation; the volunteers couldn't neuter them fast
enough to control the number of new arrivals. So, after flying solo
for five years, Lillian called in reinforcements. The first lady she
found was an older woman from Birkenhead. She and her husband had recently retired to the island, but then, six months in,
they realised that living 2,000 miles away from their grandchildren
wasn't really for them and promptly returned to the UK. Lillian
wasn't especially surprised. She empathised to a degree. So, she
resumed her search for another helper, which is how Emilia entered her world.

From the get go, Lillian found Emilia hard work. It wasn't because she was Romanian, a lot of people were on the island, and
it didn't have so much to do with the jet black hair, tattoos and
piercings, though it struck Lillian as an odd look for a 35-year-old
woman. No, it was the darkness of her personality, even when she
was joking. Emilia wasn't exactly morose, but she was dour and

sometimes difficult to deal with. There were days when she would come and go with barely a word said. Sometimes, she wouldn't turn up at all, though this was rare and usually accompanied by a text. But then occasionally, and usually at a point when Lillian was just about done with her, Emilia would perform an act of kindness wholly unexpected. On one such occasion, on a cold January morning, Emilia brought Lillian a flask of soup made from onions, garlic and ginger.

"It tastes like shit, but it will clear your cold," she said. And she was right on both counts.

On another occasion, after Lillian had survived her second hit-and-run that year, Emilia downloaded a couple of pages from the internet about GoPro cameras.

"They're expensive, otherwise I'd have bought you one, but people might be less willing to try and kill you if they're being filmed."

As Lillian and Emilia saw each other most days it was perhaps inevitable that they would start to exchange cards and small gifts on each other's birthdays and at Christmas, but it wasn't until they met Cara that they began to think of themselves as friends. Given the direction that friendship took them in, it is perhaps fitting that their first encounter as a trio took place at a quiz night in aid of Tala's cats and a local dog shelter.

Lillian had actually been in two minds about going that night as she wasn't really a drinker, she had a headache and her general knowledge was poor. But because Emilia had suggested a night out, and such suggestions were few and far between, Lillian felt obliged to support the younger woman's effort to be sociable. In turn, Emilia nearly pulled out after returning from the stables so utterly exhausted that the slightest movement was a chore let alone small talk and trivia. But she knew Lillian rarely went out and that she was lonely without her husband so Emilia took a cold shower, slapped her face and got going.

By the time the two of them arrived at The Dreamers Inn, the tables were filling up fast. There was a heady scent of floral perfumes and musky aftershave clogging the air and, as Lillian's head felt thick enough already and Emilia always had one eye on the exit, they agreed to take the table nearest the door. After ordering a rum and coke and a pint of Guinness, Cara walked in. She was dressed in tight blue jeans and a white shirt with her long black hair pulled into a high ponytail. The bright red lipstick she wore might have looked like a fashion statement, but it was really a ploy to distract attention from the spot that had appeared between her nasal bridge and left eye socket.

"Cara!" Lillian called out.

Cara turned to face the two women sat at the table nearest the door. Instantly recognising the older one from the hit-and-run the week before, she did her best to hide her surprise that she had a goth-metal friend.

"Are you on your own?" Lillian asked, and Cara confessed she was. She then found herself explaining that the quiz was in aid of the shelter that had rescued her dog Peaches so she had come to support them.

Though she wasn't a shy person, Cara was relieved when Lillian invited her to sit. She also assumed the two women were as good a team as any to join, but as the night wore on this proved to be wrong. They were actually quite appalling. Though they didn't come last, they didn't come close to bothering the leader board, not even in the pop round, and they were among the youngest in the room.

"Professional quiz goers," Lillian explained. "The same lot win all the time, but it's OK, it's only a bit of fun and all for a good cause."

"Yes, it's no big deal," Cara agreed, sitting back from the table once the quiz was finished because the goth among them kept glancing at the spot on her face. Deciding this was either extremely rude or an indication that something massive was happening, Cara excused herself and went to take a look. When she saw herself in the mirror, she sighed; it was bad, but without a scalpel to lance it there was little that could be done.

When Cara returned to the bar, she found Lillian and Emilia discussing the Chinese and their fondness for dog meat.

"They really are a disgraceful race," Lillian muttered.

"Well, that's a little unfair," Emilia replied. "The Yulin Festival is fucked up, for sure, but not every Chinese eats dogs. I was speaking to Lin about it last week, that girl who works at the Nail Place, and she said her family always had dogs in the house. She was vegetarian too until she married a Cypriot. Her mom and grandmother as well. Only the father ate meat. She also told me that when one of their dogs died, a huge dog, sixty or seventy kilos, her father was so scared their neighbours would find out he waited until three in the morning to bury him deep in the forest. And then, because it was winter and minus twenty, so the ground was like a refrigerator, he checked on the grave for more than a month until he was sure no one would rob it and eat their dead dog."

As Cara sat down, she cleared her throat. "Sweet story," she said, and Emilia laughed like a drain, which was a surprise.

Though she couldn't say why, Cara instantly warmed to Emilia that night, and after a few rums had loosened up Lillian, she found she liked her too. It was a feeling that appeared to be mutual, because as they parted ways shortly after midnight, they all agreed to meet up the following week – and in that one evening, at a charity quiz night in Dromos, their fate was sealed.

Chapter Four

After a couple of phone calls and some brief discussion via text message, Cara, Lillian and Emilia chose Valentine's Day to meet up, mainly because no one had anything better to do; Emilia was currently "between lovers", Lillian was "without husband" and Cara was not only in between and without, but totally indifferent.

It had been more than four years since Cara last felt a man's breath on her face and though she had missed the feeling at first, she had not missed it for a while. Even so, there were occasional moments, like a song or a smell or a phrase she'd hear that could have come straight from his mouth, and the ground would open up beneath her feet. Though such moments had become rare, they hadn't entirely ceased and there were days when Cara felt like she was rusting from the inside out; struggling with a toxic grief that would slowly corrode every layer of muscle and tissue until one day she would disintegrate entirely, leaving nothing behind her but a body-shaped stain of iron oxide on the bedsheets. Most of the time, however, Cara was fine and after giving the matter serious thought, in the third year of her life without Tom, she discovered there was a direct correlation between Rusting Cara and Prosecco Cara. It was at that point that she more or less gave up drinking; reserving alcohol for special occasions only, such as hosting her first dinner party.

Cara had offered to cook for her new friends because it saved having to explain that she was vegan. She had been vegan for a couple of years. It was a Facebook video showing a boy hugging a chicken that finally did for her and, to her surprise, she made the transition from flesh-eater to plant-eater with relative ease. But now, for the first time since changing her diet, Cara had an audience to impress, and she hoped to do so via a selection of dips followed by sticky shiitake mushrooms on a bed of sushi rice and chocolate mousse for dessert. She also made sure to buy plenty of wine because women will forgive anything if the wine is plentiful.

The morning of the dinner, Cara bought her own body weight in cashews, which she then blended into all manner of dips and faux cheese concoctions as sporadic gunfire echoed in the hills around them, a reminder that the hunting season was upon them. When Cooper and Peaches became increasingly agitated by the sound of hounds baying in the distance, Cara put a Mark Lanegan track on the stereo, because nothing says Valentine's Day like a former drug addict wondering where his girl might have slept last night.

Ten hours later, Cara's guests arrived and Lanegan was replaced by Pergolesi, which seemed more apt for a dinner party. By the time her guests had ploughed through three courses of vegan deliciousness, four bottles of Prosecco and half a bottle of Cyprus brandy, they were singing Abba's Waterloo. Even Lillian. In fact, as she sang, her auburn hair shining in the light of a halogen heater, Cara was reminded of Frida.

"I have to say, I'm not totally convinced by the lyrics," Emilia said, breaking away from the group to smoke out of the window.

"Which part?" Cara asked.

"All of it, right from the opening."

"Napoleon surrendering at Waterloo?" asked Lillian.

"OK, that's the one bit I accept," Emilia admitted, "but the rest of it, all that meeting their destiny in a similar way. It's insane. I mean, as far as I know, Benny and Bjorn were never defeated by the British, forcing them to abdicate their role as predominant Swedish popstars before heading into exile."

"What about the two girls?" Lillian asked.

"I don't think they died in exile either."

"No, I mean, why mention only the boys."

"Because they wrote the songs, didn't they?"

"Ah yes, you might be right."

"Actually, the blonde one kind of went into exile," Emilia said. She paused to blow smoke out of the window. "I read somewhere that after the band split, she chose the company of horses over people. I can only respect that."

"Wise woman. Give me my cats any day," Lillian responded, before quickly apologising. "Present company excepted, of course."

"Of course," Cara smiled. "Actually, it's interesting, the relationship between women and animals. Do you think it might be an age thing?"

Cara walked over to the stereo and turned down the volume. As the music died, a sleepy Cooper sighed while Peaches, who was sat by his side, kept her eyes trained on their guests, watching their every move.

"Might what be an age thing?" asked Lillian.

"The whole animal thing?"

"Wow, you two are articulate after a drink, aren't you?" noted Emilia dryly.

"You know what I mean," Cara replied.

"Yes, I do," Emilia said with a smile. "And in answer to your thought-provoking question, I think, yes, it probably is an age *thing*. To my mind, a compassion for animals goes beyond a nurturing gene. I also think it reaches its zenith at a point in women's lives when – following years of inequality, humiliation, sexual and physical abuse, intimidation, name calling and all the rest of the patronising bullshit that's endemic in a patriarchal society – they say, 'you know what, fuck you, World. I'm out of here'."

Emilia flicked her finished cigarette into the garden and shut the window. Cara glanced over at Lillian who was stood near the kitchen, clearly struggling with aspects of Emilia's theory.

"Well, I'm not sure that's quite the case with me," she finally said, the edges of her high cheek bones rosy from wine and the liberal application of rouge. "I honestly can't recall having been so badly treated in my lifetime."

"Even though a Russian man tries to run you over at least twice a year?" Emilia asked.

"Well, yes, but that's not because I'm a woman."

"Isn't it? Would he try to intimidate a man in the same way or would he worry that a man might take a crowbar to his fat, stupid ass face? I tell you, Lillian, men treat women badly, even when they think they are treating them well."

"Not all men," Cara interrupted because even though she thought Emilia had a point, she also thought it extreme, not unlike the t-shirt she wore emblazoned with the band name Anal Vomit.

Emilia cocked her head for a second, allowing her fringe to fall over one eye. The other one, unmolested by her jet black hair, looked vaguely conniving.

"So, tell me Cara, why are you no longer with your boyfriend?"

The directness of Emilia's question caught Cara off guard; she had never once mentioned an ex-boyfriend, though it was probably safe to assume that, like most single women, she had one somewhere. Put on the spot and perhaps influenced by Emilia's previous observations, Cara found herself struggling to recall all that was good about the man she once loved, perhaps still loved. Instead, all that came to mind were the times he had let her down, like the evening he told her he never wanted kids or when he said there was no point in them buying a house together in the current financial climate or the occasions when he was sharp with her, either privately or in company, or when he criticized her for not looking quite right or the way he stole her confidence, little by little, piece by piece, until she felt less of the person she had been before they met. For so long she had fooled herself into thinking she was in a relationship built on compromise, but her relationship with Tom was never one of compromise, it was one of submission, and after a while she became too angry to ignore it. She had no choice, but to leave. And yet even this felt like an act of supreme selfishness, that by leaving she had betrayed him. Tom had done nothing to ground her and yet, when she flew their nest, she blamed herself because underneath the scowls and the silences he wasn't a bad man. In many ways he had been extremely good for her and at no point did she ever feel that Tom didn't love her. So, in the end there was only one answer Cara could give to Emilia's question.

"We weren't right for each other."

Once the alcohol ran dry and Lillian had recovered from the knowledge that the mousse she'd eaten was made from the juice of canned chickpeas, Cara led the way into the kitchen where they all wrapped their fingers around hot mugs of instant coffee while pointing their feet towards the one halogen heater in the room. Contrary to popular belief, even the 'Sunshine Island' experienced winter for a few weeks of the year, not that the construction industry considered this to be reason enough to install fanciful extras such as central heating in houses. Most of them hadn't even grasped the concept of cupboard space. Still, for Cara, the fact that there were four very clear seasons added to the island's charm.

"At one point my *ex-boyfriend* and I were thinking about moving to Qatar," Cara revealed, emphasising 'ex-boyfriend' for Emilia's benefit. "Tom was – is – a TV news journalist and there was an offer on the table from Al Jazeera. They were recruiting heavily in those days. Anyway, we went to take a look, but the place was so beige neither of us thought we'd be able to hack it full-time, tax-free perks or not."

"Not that they lasted long, did they?" Lillian responded.

"What didn't?"

"The tax-free perks. Because of the financial crisis."

Cara shook her head and laughed a little. "I can't see anything affecting the petro-dollars of places like Qatar, Lillian. Not even global economic meltdown. As far as I'm aware, wages are still tax free."

Maybe because they were drunk, no one noticed Lillian's eyes dilate a fraction or the fact that she lost the thread of their conversation for a moment.

"So?" Cara asked, and Lillian was startled to see her two friends looking at her.

"I'm sorry?"

"I said, do you miss England?" Cara laughed gently and Lillian grabbed hold of the question like a much-needed lifeline.

"I miss Dan and Lucy," she admitted, "but England? Not so much. In fact, I'm not sure I could live there again. Every time I go back it seems less of the place I left; harder in some ways."

"At least the English are better to their animals," Emilia said.

"Not all of them," Cara replied. "There are plenty of horror stories in the UK; dog fights, horse stabbings, cat poisonings. No country is immune from cruelty."

"Well, Romania is a disgrace," Emilia replied. Before she could expand on the statement, Lillian slapped a hand on the table.

"Did you read that awful story in the Cyprus Mail about the puppy thrown into a crushing machine?"

"Bloody hell, yes, at the hotel near the coast." Cara put down her mug.

"Horrific way to go. Poor little thing."

"Which hotel was it?" Emilia asked.

"The paper didn't give a name, just said it was in the Paphos area," Lillian told her. "But I was speaking to Janet and Marion who feed the cats down by Tala Road Kiosk and they said it was the hotel up from the Sea Caves."

"The Kaliteros?"

"Yes, that's the one."

"How do they know?" Cara asked.

"Marion knows someone who works, or rather worked, in the reception. A young Russian girl. She resigned in disgust."

"Good for her."

"Is this the same hotel that puts poison on the path next to it? The path where people walk their dogs?" asked Emilia.

"I'm not sure. I wouldn't be surprised though, not following this latest incident."

"And it's *definitely* this hotel that crushed the puppy?" Cara asked.

"Yes, some tourists saw it happen. They were the ones that informed the girl on reception. They then went to the police, possibly the newspaper too, who knows."

"That is so sick," Emilia mumbled, and all three women paused for a moment, their eyes subconsciously looking for Cooper and Peaches.

"Sometimes I feel there's no hope for this island," Emilia eventually said.

"Me too," Cara agreed. "Things need to change. There needs to be greater punishments for animal abusers."

"Or any kind of punishment," Emilia interrupted. "When did you last hear of someone being prosecuted for poisoning an animal or for keeping their dogs locked in cages under the burning sun, left to eat their own shit before turning on each other? Trust me, it will take a seismic mind shift in the national psyche before change comes to this place."

"Then maybe we should do something to convince them," Cara said.

"By way of protests and placards and charity quiz nights?" Emilia responded. She shook her head and wiped at her eyes, knowing she would have smudged her make-up, but hardly caring. She felt so tired. All the time. "Look," she continued wearily, "there are plenty of marches that take place here, usually in the capital and usually about the retard zoos, but what changes? Nothing. These bastards get away with their cruelty time and again until they think they are untouchable because if you prosecute one, you have to prosecute them all. Like this stupid hotel bastard. We all know that people will soon forget because something worse will happen somewhere else and people will direct their outrage at that for a while. In the meantime, the tourists will come and they will continue to stay at this rancid fucking hotel that thinks nothing of crushing puppies because they won't actually know what the owner has done. It's not as if this crime will be mentioned in any of the tour brochures. It's not as if they will see the blood on his hands."

"I bet blood in the pool would stop them," Lillian joked, and Cara and Emilia turned to look at her.

Chapter Five

At 9am, and with her head banging from the previous night's excesses, Emilia texted Cara.

"Was it the drink talking or a plan?"

Ten minutes later, Cara responded: "Drink talking, but it's a great plan. What does Lil say?"

"Will text now. Hold on."

"Lillian, shall we do it?"

Within two minutes, Lillian confirmed they should. "Yes!! Already planning food for war meeting!!!"

"Lil in," Emilia texted Cara.

"Really?! Surprised at that."

"Ur not alone."

"C U later."

"xx."

Emilia slipped the phone into the back pocket of her jeans and turned her attention to the cupboard in the tack room. "This is ridiculous," she mumbled, realising her horse actually had more medicines and cosmetics than she possessed in her entire home. Taking up the entirety of two shelves were cans of topical spray, wound powder, various fly deterrents, conditioners, baby shampoos, a jar of Vaseline, a bottle of neem oil, a tube of anti-inflammatory gel, pink hoof clay and a tub of Sudocrem. In fact, the only thing Adonis didn't appear to possess was dental tape. But apparently, "horses don't floss".

"You're officially insane," Julia replied after Emilia asked whether she ought to clean her horse's teeth. Emilia had only been at the yard a few months and she knew no better at the time, but once Julia stopped laughing, she did in fact recommend, and invite, an equine dentist to visit. "Horses, like humans, should get their teeth checked once a year." A few weeks later, when the "nice man from Nicosia" arrived, he pretty much confirmed everything that Emilia had always suspected; dentists were professional sadists, no matter whose teeth they worked on. Using some kind of medieval torture device to prise open her horse's jaw, he filed Adonis's teeth with what was, to all intents and purposes, a power drill.

"I can't look," Emilia moaned, all the while holding Adonis's head in position, as the dentist smiled.

"Our horses eat hay and grain, so the jaw moves with an up-and-down motion rather than side-to-side, as it would if they were grazing on grass," Julia explained. "Over time, this creates sharp points on the teeth, which can cut into the horse's mouth. So, they need a helping hand. From a dentist."

"Or a sadist," Emilia corrected because by then the dentist was packing away his power tools and was out of earshot.

"Or a sadist," Julia confirmed.

"Do you want me to remove the bean while he's sedated?" the dentist asked. Once it had been explained to Emilia that the 'bean' in question was actually the build-up of crud in the hole of her boy's penis, she reluctantly agreed that a build-up of anything in that area was probably best removed. Even so, she ended the day thinking there was a special place in hell waiting for sadists with a hand in both ends.

Emilia rifled through the contents sitting on the shelf in front of her.

"What are you looking for? A defibrillator?"

Emilia turned to face Julia, her face blank.

"You look like death," Julia explained.

"Ah. Prosecco and brandy," Emilia replied.

"No wonder then. I guess you'll be needing a coffee soon?"

"I will, and some of that blue spray if you have it. Adonis has thrush in one hoof."

"It's the weather. Take a look in my cupboard. There's a can in there."

Julia then walked away, affecting the lightness of step often employed by smug non-drinkers.

Grabbing her grooming kit, Emilia dragged her sorry ass up to the stable block. Though Julia always groomed her horses in the tie-up area, Emilia preferred to keep Adonis in his stable so he could amble around, eat hay and bite at the flies irritating his belly. As a rule, she was never in any great rush and having him untethered allowed her to take her time, and time spent with Adonis was pretty much everything Emilia lived for. Though the past few years had been tough and she had seen her freedom curtailed in a way she could never have imagined in the fifteen years she had travelled the world outrunning boredom, life remained bearable because of Adonis. From the moment they joined forces, he had given her the best therapy she could never afford because for at least three hours of the day there was nothing occupying her mind other than him. There were no worries about how she might pay the rent or wondering whether today would be 'the day' when she would crash her moped and die. There was only Emilia and Adonis. And Emilia loved that feeling. She loved Adonis. And like a mother with a child, she spoilt him and worried about him. In the three years they had been together, there had been anxious moments such as unexpected lameness and infected cuts. There had also been at least ten bouts of colic. The first time it happened, Adonis had simply seemed a little 'off'. It wasn't nice to watch, but it was nothing Julia had been overly alarmed by; he refused his carrots, he couldn't get comfortable, he was up, he was down and then he had a crap and got on with things. However, the second time Adonis had colic, the symptoms were worse and Julia had to inject him with a painkiller.

"Colic is basically an umbrella term for any gastrointestinal condition," she explained while searching for the vein in Adonis's neck to administer his medicine. "There are different types of colic, but they all share one common factor and that is acute abdominal pain. Unfortunately, what goes in can only come out the back end.

Horses don't vomit and they don't burp. So, if something blocks the way, well you can imagine how uncomfortable that might feel and, in some cases, it can be fatal."

"Adonis could die?"

Julia saw the horror and vulnerability in Emilia's eyes, but there was little point in sugar-coating the potential reality. "Yes, Emilia, it's a possibility. It's always a possibility with any horse, no matter if they windsuck or not. Despite their size, they are extremely sensitive animals."

If Emilia hadn't been overly worried before, she certainly was after that particular lesson and every time Adonis subsequently had colic, Emilia would stay by his side until each episode passed; walking him until the injections kicked in, trying not to cry when he lay in his stable, stretched out on the floor, baring his teeth in pain, his stomach swollen like a barrel and taut as a drum, while she tried to keep the flies from the grazes scarring his handsome face. And all the while she would sing to him, so he'd know she was there. She would always be there.

Usually, after a couple of hours had passed, followed by some epic farting, Adonis would get to his feet and shake himself down like a wet dog. He would then start eating, as though nothing had happened, and Emilia would be relieved. Eventually, she would even start to forget he had been sick. Until the next time.

"So, are you riding today or not?"

Emilia spun on her heels to find Julia standing at the stable door holding two mugs of coffee.

"Jesus, you nearly gave me a heart attack," Emilia mumbled.

"I had to check there was life in you. You were in some kind of zombie-like trance a minute ago."

"I was thinking."

"Well, that probably explains it."

"Very funny." Emilia set her brushes on the floor and accepted the offered mug before sliding her back down the stable wall. As Julia was wearing pristine lemon breeches, she remained standing.

After sipping her coffee, Emilia asked Julia whether she had heard about the puppy murdered at the Kaliteros Hotel.

Julia rubbed at the tip of her nose. "Yes, I heard about it. Not much, but enough. What can I say? It's disgusting, but no worse than a lot of stuff that goes on."

Emilia looked up, unable to ask the obvious because she was too hungover to talk.

"It's not just dogs," Julia continued. "You'd be horrified by the stories I've heard about horses on this island."

"Such as?"

Julia paused, unsure whether to say more because it rarely achieved anything. "A lot of the racing here is a disgrace," she eventually offered. "There are good yards, of course, and good owners, but where there's good, there's always bad. I know of one yard on the outskirts of Larnaca that has an area kept out of public view, specifically for retired racehorses. They call it 'Death Alley' because the horses are dumped there and starved."

"Why starved? Why not put them to sleep if they no longer want them? Why torture them?"

"Perhaps it's cheaper. Who knows? Another racing yard I've heard of doesn't starve its unwanted horses; it feeds them to the lions at the Sunshine Zoo."

"You're fucking kidding." Emilia was horrified, immediately imagining terrified horses cornered and waiting be ripped to shreds by animals that knew no better. "How do you know this?"

"I've heard talk of it and I've occasionally seen horses going that way. Two at a time in a trailer. There are no abattoirs on the way to the zoo."

"God, I feel sick."

"Me too."

"No, seriously."

And Emilia got to her feet and ran from the stable, only just reaching the toilet in time to throw up.

Before Cara left the house, she kissed her dogs 'goodbye'.

"I won't be long," she lied. Then, after waiting for Peaches to leave her bed to join Cooper in his, Cara walked to the door, turning one more time to look at their sweet, expectant faces. "Don't judge me," she told them. "I do this for you."

Both dogs looked at her blankly.

Roughly five minutes from her home and close to the village centre, Cara stopped the car in front of a florist shop. It briefly crossed her mind to get out and buy something for Lillian, as it was the first time she would be visiting her home, but before she could act on the thought Emilia appeared at the passenger door window.

"I thought of bringing wine, but I'm not sure I can face it," Emilia said as she belted herself into the seat next to Cara.

"I couldn't think of anything worse. I threw up three times this morning."

"Only once for me, but it was like the cherry pip scene in The Witches of Eastwick."

Cara laughed at the image, but not too hard as she didn't want to bring on another episode. "Never again."

"Never again," Emilia echoed. "Seriously, I am that close to giving up wine." She raised a hand to show an inch of space between her thumb and index finger. "It's the ruin of middle-aged women all over the world."

"I'm not sure we're middle-aged yet," Cara replied, feeling strangely stung by the suggestion. "Lillian might be in the ballpark though."

"Sure. It's a matter of perspective, isn't it? When I was younger, I thought 30 was ancient. Now I can only dream of being that age again."

"You're hardly old now, Emilia, but yes, in my late 20s and 30s I was already feeling old and increasingly irrelevant. But when I look at photos, I can't believe how young and pretty I was. Not drop dead gorgeous or anything, but certainly prettier than I remembered feeling at the time. Maybe it will be the same when I'm in my 50s and I look back at my 40s. Or perhaps now is the time to invest in botox and fillers before I disintegrate further."

"If I had the money, I'd get it all done," Emilia confessed, "my tits, bum and both sets of lips."

Cara's head span left, and the car bounced off a kerb.

"Relax, I'm kidding. What do you take me for?" Emilia opened the passenger window to let in air, suddenly feeling nauseous.

"I watched a documentary about vaginoplasty a couple of years ago," Cara revealed. "It was bizarre. Quite disturbing."

"Of course, it was," Emilia replied. "Yet more freakish non-sense devised by men to make women feel bad about themselves. I remember reading about a cosmetic firm offering the procedure for between $3,000 and $12,000 depending on *the extent of correction required.* I mean, really? Have we messed with women's brains so much that they believe they have an *incorrect* vagina and, more than that, they'll pay a year's wages to rectify what nature freely gave them?"

"It's insane," Cara agreed before nodding ahead of her. "Is it the next left?"

"Yes, and then the first right."

Cara did as she was instructed and a few seconds later they arrived outside Lillian's home on a small, exclusive-looking estate.

"Nice gaff," Cara commented.

"Gaff?"

"Home, house, pad…" Cara explained, forgetting that English wasn't actually Emilia's first language, despite her command of it. "It's slang."

"I understood that much. Wait, hold on." Emilia reached out to stop Cara leaving the car. Her face had taken on a greenish hue. "Sorry, but I feel sick again. Give me a minute. It will pass. I just don't want to deliver the contents of my stomach onto Lillian's driveway."

"Fair enough. I'm sure Lillian is feeling just as bad," Cara replied. Then, as she tried to give a reassuring smile, Emilia threw up a little. Her hands moved quickly to keep it in her mouth, but it was all too much for Cara's hyperactive gag reflex to handle and she retched before turning away to stop her own stomach from following through. Of course, none of this was lost on Emilia who desperately dug into the pocket of her coat to pull out a plastic bag. In response, Cara made a grab for an open packet of Skittles sitting in the tray under the glove box.

Having heard a car pull up, Lillian moved to the kitchen window to look for her guests, wondering what on earth was taking so long. She then had to blink twice, hardly believing her eyes as she watched two dark-haired women of a certain age taking it in turns to throw up in the front of a silver Ford Puma. It was like watching two sopranos compete in an operatic duet, with added vomit.

Lillian shook her head, glanced at the neighbouring houses to see if anyone was watching. She then walked to the utility room at the back of the kitchen.

Outside, it took a few minutes for Emilia and Cara to regain control of their stomachs. After wiping their faces on whatever they could find, they next took their plastic bags to the nearest green bin before returning to Lillian's driveway. As they walked to the front door, Cara was struck by the resemblance of the house to its owner; neat and stylish with a few sharp edges here and there, most notably the hip-high window sills that caught Emilia as she passed by.

"Clumsy, aren't you?" Cara commented.

"It has been said."

Before either of them had chance to raise a hand to the bell, Lillian opened the door. Behind her, on the kitchen counter, stood three martini cocktails. They were supposed to be a 'welcome drink', but after watching the spectacle that had taken place at the end of her driveway, Lillian handed them a bucket instead before directing them to the dining table where a box of tissues waited.

Both Cara and Emilia mumbled their thanks and took their

buckets into the lounge, feeling more than a little embarrassed by what had happened. Cara's black eyeliner was smudged and lining the creases under her eyes, making her look older than her years. Emilia looked beaten. Her eyes were bloodshot, her cheeks were pale and her throat felt like it had been attacked by a horse dentist's rasp.

A second later, Lillian appeared from the kitchen holding a red polka dot tray on which stood three glasses. Two of them were tall and filled with ice-cold water, which she placed in front of her guests, the other was a martini cocktail.

"Cheers," Lillian said as the other two women looked at her with disbelief and a quiet respect.

"Were you drinking what we were drinking last night?" Emilia asked, and Lillian smiled. Her rose painted lips matched the colour of her cheeks, as well as the blouse she wore, and her blue eyes sparkled.

"I don't know why or how, but alcohol rarely gives me a hangover. Tequila, occasionally. But not wine."

"It's always the quiet ones," Cara mumbled, and Emilia tried to laugh, but she wasn't ready for such exertions.

Once her guests had drunk their water, and managed to keep it down, Lillian disappeared into the kitchen, reappearing seconds later with a huge wooden paddle carrying her "first ever vegan pizza".

It looked immense, and an impossible dream for both Cara and Emilia, but after a tentative start the pizza was quickly demolished and declared a "success".

"God, I needed that," Cara admitted.

"It was great, Lillian," Emilia confessed.

Lillian glanced at the buckets at their feet, feeling pleased with herself and not a little grateful that her meal hadn't ended up in them. After clearing away the plates, she suggested they take their coffees to the "seating area", which was a plush haven of plump cushions and velvet beanbags glowing in the warm light of a coal-effect gas fire. Derek called it the Marrakech Room. Lillian simply thought it 'comfy'.

"You have a lovely home," Cara told Lillian.

"Thank you. We like it. Though it really needs a pet by the fire. Unfortunately, Derek is allergic."

"I did wonder," Cara replied.

"Shame really, but hey ho. You can't have everything in life and I do what I can, as we all do. Speaking of which…" Lillian walked over to the cupboard under the stairs and took out a Louis Vuitton shoulder bag. "By the way, Emilia, did you get that information from your friend?"

Emilia nodded. She had called Constantin earlier that morning before he started his shift at the Petrolina garage and before her hangover kicked in. During the summer, Constantin worked at the Kaliteros Hotel as a barman, so he knew the place pretty well.

"Constantin told me the hotel is a shithole and the owner is an arsehole, but of course we knew that. He also told me that the arsehole hates to spend money, so even though there are CCTV signs around the place there are no cameras up and operational."

"What about intruder lights?" asked Lillian.

"No, nothing. Everything, and I mean everything, is switched off by 2am in the winter. I guess the holidaymakers there are older than the usual crowd."

"That's all very helpful." Lillian reached into her bag, feeling a tremor of excitement course through her veins. Though the original plan had been to fill the Kaliteros pool with blood, on deeper reflection this was deemed to be somewhat problematic as it would necessitate either murder on a mass scale, be it animal or human, or a blood bank burglary. So, after a little more thought they had opted for something more symbolic. Sitting cross-legged on the floor, Lillian took out a wad of paint sample cards from her bag and fanned them on the carpet. "I got these from Homebase,

Home Centre and DIY Paphos this morning. I think we should go
for the most popular brand and colour on sale, just in case. My
personal favourite is Salsa Red."

Cara asked Lillian to point it out and she picked up the card.
"It's a lovely colour," she admitted, "and very bloody. Trouble is,
it's gloss."

"And?"

"Gloss paint is oil-based."

When Lillian continued to look puzzled, Cara explained that
putting oil-based paint into a swimming pool would have no effect
at all because it wouldn't mix, only sink to the bottom of the pool.

"It would look like a giant menstrual blood clot," Emilia added, and Lillian grimaced at the crude analogy, which made Emilia
smile a little inside.

"If we're going to do this properly, we need a water-based
paint," Cara informed them. After taking a moment to scan the
cards, she selected one.

"Pillar Box Red," said Lillian. "That looks bloody enough. How
much do you think we'll need?"

"If we carry two cans each, that should do it," Cara replied.

"And how will the arsehole know this is about the puppy rather
than a random act of vandalism?" Emilia asked.

"We could leave a note," Lillian suggested.

"Or a sign," said Cara.

"Like a signature?" asked Lillian.

"Perhaps we could even leave a... "

"Paw print."

"Paw print."

"... paw print."

Chapter Six

Inspector Antoni Giagkos stood at the window with his back facing the man who was ranting at him. It was a great view; brilliant white rock set against the glittering expanse of the Mediterranean with lush, green shrubbery flowing up and towards the hotel, the wall of which was bordered by yellow buds of winter jasmine. It was a scene as pretty as any picture postcard – if you ignored the blood-red swimming pool immediately below them and the sight of fifty or more protestors holding homemade placards screaming "Murderer!" Unsurprisingly, it was this aspect of the view that had the hotel owner, Stelios Spyrou, in a fit of rage.

As the man spat his anger over a fibreboard desk, Antoni occasionally took notes, more out of politeness than purpose. People expected notes in an investigation, but it was hardly the most complicated case; a nasty old bastard ordered his people to throw a poodle into a cardboard crushing machine and animal rights activists were none too happy about it. If the truth be told, he thought they had every right to protest. It was an abhorrent way to treat a defenceless animal, yet it was doubtful that much would come of it. Rightly or wrongly, crimes involving human victims took precedence within the national police force.

"So, when will you arrest them?"

Antoni looked at Stelios. The man was dressed in a blue sweater and a pair of jeans that were too short in the leg to be considered fashionable. His dark hair was receding from a well-fed face and a number of rings adorned his fat, hairy fingers. He was not an attractive man even without the tag of 'dog killer'.

"And who do you suggest I arrest?" Antoni asked calmly.

"Them out there!" Stelios pointed to the window. "The animal rights lot will have done this."

Antoni shrugged before shaking his head. "You might well be correct, given that a puppy was allegedly killed in the grounds of your hotel and the people who vandalised your pool appear to have left you a message in the form of a dog's paw drawn on the tiles. Still, we may need more evidence before detaining anyone."

"What do you mean 'appear'? That they 'appear to have left you a message'? It's there in plain view."

"Yes, but at this stage we don't know for sure that the person or persons who threw paint into your pool are also responsible for the paw."

"Are you joking with me? Who else would be responsible? Oh wait, maybe there's a gang of crazed street artists roaming the island defacing people's properties. Or maybe you think I drew it, perhaps?"

"I'm not saying that."

"So, what are you saying?"

"I'm saying that we will investigate the criminal damage done to your property and that the drawing of the paw may very well lead us to the person or persons responsible for the criminal damage done to your property."

"May very well lead you? So, this is a joke." Stelios got up from his seat and marched to the window, rearranging the jeans around his crotch as he went. "I can lead you to the people responsible!" he shouted, before pointing to the group of protestors chanting outside his gates. "There they are! There! Now go and arrest them!"

"Well, I'll definitely talk to them," Antoni confirmed and Stelios almost melted in the internal rage that erupted in his chest, triggering beads of perspiration to appear on his balding pate.

"Yes, go and talk to them, why don't you! Invite them in for coffee and we'll all sit down and eat cake!"

Antoni took his pen and tapped it against the two stars sitting on the rank slide of his shirt; a gentle reminder to the hotel owner that he was talking to an officer of the law. Stelios reddened, but immediately quietened and Antoni smiled, which only seemed to aggravate the man's blood pressure. Slipping his notebook into the top pocket of his shirt, Antoni said he'd be in touch "as and when the inquiry demanded". He then went downstairs to talk to the special constable assigned to help him with the case; the guy who usually mans the school crossing at lunchtimes.

Like many Cypriot police officers, Antoni was laidback, but he wasn't a fool; he knew the game his colleagues were playing, and he was OK with it. Being the new boy, in terms of time served on the patch rather than rank or age, he was also the hotshot from Nicosia who needed to be grounded in the more parochial procedures of the provinces. He was OK with that too because, truthfully, he no longer cared. In less than two decades, the force had cost him his marriage, half his money and the whole of his house. Not that he cared so much about any of that either.

Reaching the entrance to the hotel and noting for the second time the useless CCTV warning signs, he made his way down the small flight of steps to the courtyard. At the gates to the hotel, he caught up with Special Constable Michalis Georgiou who was drowning in a sea of very angry women. Although there were a couple of men standing on the side lines dressed as hippies and hipsters, the protest was mostly a female affair.

"Anyone admitted anything yet?" Antoni joked, though this was lost on Michalis.

"No," he replied. "No one has admitted anything, but a lot of them seem to wish that they'd done it. Some have even said the criminals didn't go far enough and they should have…" Michalis paused to move the cigarette from his lips and check his notes, "… here we go, that they should have 'stabbed the bastard'."

"I take it that was the guy from the Animal Party?" Antoni teased, and Michalis shook his head before checking his notebook again.

"It was Maria Constantinou, age 37, from Pissouri." Michalis looked towards the crowd and nodded in the direction of a woman with dark auburn hair and a loud speaker in her hand. "I thought I better take her details and anyone else's if they uttered threats of violence. Just in case."

"Good thinking, Constable. So, where is our friend from the Animal Party?"

"He had to go, He said he had a meeting with the mayor regarding the incident with the dog and then he was speaking at a charity lunch in Giolou."

"Typical politician – always looking for a free meal. Did you call the refuse department?"

"Yes, they'll stop collections within a three-mile radius, but only for 24 hours."

"Well, it gives us time, I suppose. OK, let's go and look at some bins seeing as the clock is ticking. And though it's unlikely that there are any clear tyre tracks left in the vicinity, thanks to the protestors, we should at least look for some."

"Yes, good, that sounds good …" Michalis replied, clearly not convinced that this was a good idea at all.

Antoni sighed. It was the same old drill with the same old characters no matter the division or the unit. "You want a coffee break, don't you?"

Michalis smiled the kind of smile that teachers reserve for slower students who suddenly see the answer.

Antoni shrugged. What did he care? This was Dromos, not the mean streets of Nicosia and he was investigating a case with a man who drove a Smart car out of choice. "We've time for coffee," Antoni agreed. "After the bins."

Cara listened to the local expat radio station, as she did most days of the week, but whereas she usually kept an ear open for a news story to work on, that morning she was surprised to find she was the news story. In fact, she was the lead news story every hour on the hour.

"...Police are investigating an act of vandalism at the Paphos hotel where a dog was allegedly killed in a cardboard crushing machine. According to reports, red paint was thrown into the hotel's pool at some point in the night, causing hundreds of euros worth of damage. Although police are keeping an open mind as to the motive behind the attack, it occurred just hours before a mass protest took place staged by a number of animal welfare organisations, activists and representatives of the Animal Party Cyprus..."

Dabbing nail varnish remover on a couple of red splashes on the front of her jeans, Cara fought the urge to text Lillian and Emilia. They had agreed not to contact each other for a few days and not to meet up again until Derek had returned to Qatar. Lillian's husband was on his way home that afternoon, which is why they had needed to act quickly because husbands tend to get suspicious if their wives disappear in the dead of night.

"...Police are investigating an act of vandalism at the Paphos hotel..."

The first time Cara heard the bulletin, at 7am thanks to Cooper and Peaches rising with the sun, she was surprised on two accounts; one, that 'the event' had made the news and two, that a protest was taking place at the hotel that same day.

"Quite fortuitous," she mentioned to Peaches who was sat by her feet, her white fur glowing orange in the light of a halogen heater. Cara looked over to Cooper who had retired to his bed so he might eat his blanket. It was one of the things he did. She had tried, numerous times, to stop him, using treats and threats, but it was a battle she always lost and she was now resigned to the fact that his poos would sometimes come out woolly.

By the time the 10am bulletin aired, Cara was feeling rather smug. The report hadn't changed at all, which suggested the police had no idea what was going on. Although she had no right to feel so good about herself, given the appalling death of the dog involved, Cara did. In fact, the more she heard the news, the more fabulous she felt about what she had done. Then, approximately 15 minutes after the lunchtime bulletin, Cara took a call from the commissioning editor of one of her regular magazines. They wanted a

750-word feature on the "dog-killing hotel". Apparently, the editor
had seen it on the wires an hour ago "and loved the pool-of-blood
angle".

Cara put down the phone and turned to Peaches. "Well, this is
an interesting development."

Emilia's arms felt heavy as lead as she cleared Table 6. She was beyond tired and if she hadn't been running on adrenalin she might
have collapsed before the lunchtime rush was over. It wasn't just
the marathon night-time walk with a can of paint in each hand that
had taken its toll, it was the lateness of the hour. Lillian had insisted
they not only wait until 2am before heading to the hotel, but that
they also wait for as much cloud cover as possible to dim the light
of the moon. Cara then insisted they park at least a mile from the
hotel because she had watched some cop show in which the detec-
tives always checked for tyre marks.

"This is Dromos, not New York," Emilia had complained. "I'd
be surprised if they notice 15 litres of paint in the pool let alone
tyre marks."

Of course, Lillian and Cara's caution made sense, but it also
meant that it was 3.30am before they even got to the hotel and,
more than ever, Emilia struggled to cope if she didn't get eight
hours sleep at night. Thankfully, there had been little to do at the
stables that morning as Julia had a meeting in Limassol, which only
left her shift at Zorba's to get through. Unfortunately, the restaurant was uncommonly busy by the time Emilia arrived, but just as
she was starting to flag, she went to clear Table 4.

Adam and Gillian Rogers were regulars at Zorba's and because
they 'liked what they liked' they rarely ventured beyond 'pork
chop and chips'. In fairness, this was standard fare for most of the
English expats and Adam and Gillian were a nice couple. Unfail-
ingly cheerful, they always left a €2.50 tip even when the service
was far from cheerful, possibly because they knew that the cheap
prices were a reflection of the wages. Alan and Gillian knew this

because Emilia once told them it was so. "The owner is a pig grow-ing fat on slave labour," were the exact words she had used and Gillian had flinched slightly. But this was the economic climate. Ever since the financial crisis, it was a buyer's market in Cyprus and workers were ten a penny. But because the rent had to be paid, a horse had to be fed and there were now medical considerations to budget for, Emilia continued to work for the pig while listening out for any other opportunities. It was while she was listening that she picked up snippets of gossip here and there, usually involving the bed-hopping antics of minor local celebrities and bar owners. But that day, the main talk in the restaurant was not about the local entertainment, but about the protest taking place further down the road.

"I wish I could have seen that bar steward's face," Alan said to Gillian before turning to apologise to Emilia for his "language".

"Doesn't bother me," Emilia replied as she cleared their table.

"Well, whoever did it deserves a medal," said Gillian. "If noth-ing else comes of that poor dog's death, at least that monster will feel it in his pocket."

"Red paint though," Alan laughed. "That'll be an absolute bug-ger to clean up."

And that's when the penny dropped for Emilia, and very nearly a plate with it.

With her heart racing, and her arms full, she scuttled away to the kitchen, all the while doing her best to hide a very uncharac-teristic smile.

Lillian had spent most of the morning cleaning the house. This was partly because Derek would be home within hours, but also because it helped take her mind off things. Criminal activity was something new to Lillian and she was battling some very conflicting emotions. On the one hand, she felt bad for engaging in activity she suspected was highly illegal, on the other hand she had never felt more alive.

All her life Lillian had played by the book and done her best to be a good wife, a good mother and ultimately a good person, something which largely involved not upsetting anyone and not breaking the law. But how good a person can anyone be if they do nothing in the face of cruelty, if they only condemn and never stand up? What good are words when the authorities don't want to hear them? So, perhaps it did need a few brave men, or women, to step forward and make a difference in the world.

"And I'm sure the 9/11 Jihadis felt exactly the same way," muttered Derek a few hours later when he arrived home, tired and moody from his flight.

Derek had been listening to the news on the drive from Larnaca airport and when he mentioned the lead report to Lillian, over a cup of tea, she had felt compelled to justify the crime while doing her very best not to own up to it. Her heart ached to tell the man she had shared two thirds of her life with that she had been the one to vandalise the pool, that it was she who had withdrawn the cash from the ATM and driven to Limassol to buy six 2.5-litre cans of red paint from three different stores, and that it was her idea to dress in black so they would better melt into the night. But she didn't. Not just because of the Jihadi comment, which suggested Derek might not be overly supportive, but because she had promised Emilia and Cara that she wouldn't breathe a word of it to anyone – not even to her husband or children.

So, when Derek continued to bang on about "out and out vandalism" while blaming "kids or Communists" for the crime, Lillian stayed silent. At one time she might have agreed with him and laughed at his joke about who was to blame because no one talked about Communists anymore, but on this occasion she struggled to hide the disappointment she felt in her husband, not because of her involvement in 'out and out vandalism', but because he was failing to grasp the bigger picture; that a clean pool could never be more important than a little dog's life.

Having checked the bins as well as the mess of tyre marks in the vicinity, Antoni Giagkos relented and allowed Michalis to have his coffee break. They chose a local place where the coffee was free and the company elderly, and Michalis managed to smoke four cigarettes in the space of 20 minutes. Antoni said nothing, it wasn't his place to tell grown men how to look after their bodies, but he couldn't help thinking that if a situation arose where they had to give chase, he'd need to strap an oxygen tank to his colleague's back.

"It's one of those protestors, for sure," Michalis said with no invitation. "I'd put money on it. Who else would go to such trouble for a dog?"

Although Antoni could have agreed, after all it was the most obvious conclusion to draw, he said nothing. It was usually a mistake to solve a case before the facts had been established, and besides, Michalis was a fool whose main job involved collecting utility payments at the town hall, along with the rest of his relatives because nepotism was a thriving industry in Dromos. The man was also a hunter, which wasn't a crime in itself, but hunters and animal activists rarely made easy bedfellows. In contrast, Antoni had been raised with pets, at a time when dogs in the house weren't especially fashionable in Cyprus. He liked animals, and though he'd admit to being as blind as the next man to much of their suffering, he didn't need a hand-painted placard to feel disgusted at the killing of the dog at the Kaliteros Hotel. Then again, just because he could sympathise it didn't mean he could discount the involvement of the area's animal rights movement, so once their coffee break was done and Michalis had smoked enough cigarettes to survive the five-minute car drive to the centre of the village, he threw himself headlong into research, on Facebook.

There was actually a huge number of rescue groups and animal shelters operating across the island. Some were private individuals doing their best to home the cats and dogs they came across, others had organised into groups, many of them acquiring 'charity' status

in order to raise funds to pay for vets' bills, foster homes and flights
out of the country. In fact, the more he looked into the matter, the
more impressed he became not only by the scale of these opera-
tions, but by the amount of them and the fact that Cyprus's unwanted cats and dogs were finding five-star homes all over the world,
though mostly in the UK and Germany. It was like looking at a tree
and finding a different kind of fruit on every branch. After starting
with the Animal Party, he was led to a group of activists operating
under the banner of Cyprus Animal Defenders (CALF), which then
led to a whole host of rescue organisations and shelters with names
like Paws, Stray Haven, Cyprus Love Rescue Dogs, Tala Monastery
Cats, D.O.G. Rescue Cyprus (DALI organized group), Sirius Dog
Sanctuary. The list went on and on and on. And it didn't end in Cyprus. The links went global and Antoni found himself transfixed by
videos of dog rescues carried out by India's Animal Aid Unlimited
and QAWS in Qatar as well as heart-breaking photo-stories of love
and neglect posted by Prince Fluffy Kareem, a charity doing some
interesting work with Egypt's battered horses. For more than an
hour, Antoni found himself caught between despair and hope until
eventually he took command of his senses and began compiling a
list of possible suspects. It was as he began writing that the door to
his office opened.

"There's a reporter at the desk wanting to speak to you," a female officer informed him.

"Then show him in," Antoni replied.

"It's a she and she's British."

"A Britisher? Then, at least *she'll* be polite."

The officer smiled before closing the door. Less than two
minutes later, Cara appeared and, for a second, Antoni was lost
for words. Maybe it was the long black hair or the sun breaking
through the clouds to brighten the room at the exact moment she
walked in, but he was reminded of Mother Mary, only hotter and
wearing jeans, and he found himself sitting a little taller in his seat.

"*Melate Anglika?*" Cara asked.

"Yes, I speak English," Antoni replied.

He flashed her his best smile and invited her to take a seat.

Chapter Seven

As February melted into March, the winter winds breathed their last and any of the local wildlife that had survived the hunting season lived to flee another day. Once again, calm was restored and the hills around Dromos reverberated with the sound of birdsong, bleating goats and the gentle hiss of blunt-nosed vipers lurking in the long grass.

For the majority of residents, spring was the most welcome of the four seasons. But while the Cypriots marked the occasion with ten days of carnival followed by preparations for Lent, the expats emerged from their homes like prisoners blinking in the sunshine, albeit prisoners in bathing suits hooking a towel under one arm and a copy of the Daily Mail under the other. They then spent as many of their days as was physically possible poolside until the relentless heat of summer drove them back indoors.

For most people, spring is the most joyous, fantastic, life-affirming time of the year, the season of fresh hope and new beginnings, yet Cara found herself bedevilled by thoughts of impending death, chiefly her own. She wasn't sure what had triggered the gloom. It wasn't as though she was depressed in any way and she never typically dwelled on such matters, but somehow, for some reason, she had begun to reflect on how her life would end. Cara had no children, Tom had never been keen on the idea and she had accepted his choice, thinking her love for him was greater than her desire to reproduce, but now she was single and in the latter part of her 40s, she had to accept that her ovaries were little more than internal baubles rather than functioning apparatus. All of which meant, she would die alone.

Cara wasn't being overly dramatic, at least, not in her own head, it was merely a fact she had been paying an increasing amount of thought to. It was reasonable to believe her parents would die before her, she had no siblings and, after four years on the island, she remained resolutely single. So, given her almost solitary existence, the likelihood was that she would continue to walk the earth unaccompanied, save for two dogs who would also leave her eventually. And though there might be other pets as the years passed by, there would come a point when it would be irresponsible to indulge her need for company in a dog; a dog that might end up outliving her. All of which meant she would absolutely die alone, without even a dog to mourn for her, and possibly eat her face should she lie undiscovered for a while. But even worse than dying alone was the thought of all those years spent living alone as she waited to die. And perhaps because she had worked herself into such a frenzy about what the future promised — and it was the season of fresh hope and new beginnings — when she bumped into the policeman she had interviewed a few days earlier, and he invited her out to dinner, she said 'yes'.

"You said what?"

"I said 'yes'."

Emilia paused as she tacked up Adonis. "Are you suffering from Stockholm Syndrome?"

"Isn't that when a victim falls in love with the kidnapper?"

"Or captor," Emilia replied. "Maybe you're preparing the groundwork for our arrest."

Cara smiled, because she felt that she should and it was actually easier than sharing the reality; that she had agreed to dinner because she was a coward scared of dying alone. Besides, Antoni was dark, handsome, presumably single and roughly her age. He was also pretty tall for a Cypriot. "Have you seen much of Lillian?" she asked.

"Nice deflection," Emilia noted. She checked her horse's girth before tightening it a notch. "Yes, I've seen Lillian, here and there, wearing her GoPro, but she likes to feed the cats in the mornings while I do the evenings after work. Here, hold this for me, will you?"

Emilia handed Cara a bottle of water, she then led Adonis from the stable and down the aisle to the mounting block. After climbing the steps, she gently swung her right leg over the horse's back, placed her feet in the stirrups and wiggled.

"What are you doing?"

"Plugging into my three-point seat," Emilia explained. "Bum bones, fanny bone, firmly on the saddle."

"Sounds comfy," Cara replied.

"I guess it depends on how much junk you got in your trunk."

"Then I'm surprised a skinny girl like you can walk by the end of your lessons."

"Talking of which…" Emilia nodded towards Julia who was standing in the middle of the arena pointedly checking her watch as her perfectly drawn eyebrows pinched inwards to create a look that was distinctly impatient.

"She looks kind of fierce," Cara muttered.

"You should try having a lesson with her."

"Not likely. I don't ride anything that doesn't come with a seatbelt."

"Well, that explains while you're still single then."

Cara held Emilia's stare for a second. "You have a filthy mind."

"It has been said." Emilia pressed her calves gently against her horse's sides and they walked over to an increasingly disgruntled Julia.

As Emilia warmed up, Cara wandered to the other end of the arena, still holding her friend's bottle of water. Finding a wall to sit on, she set her shades in place and prepared to enjoy the show.

Although Cara, Emilia and Lillian had all agreed to stay away from each other until Lillian's husband left, more than two weeks had passed since they dumped 15 litres of paint into the pool at the Kaliteros Hotel and nobody was even talking about it anymore. So, having finished an interview close to the stables with a woman who apparently spent her days lounging around the Sea Caves dressed as a mermaid, she texted to see if Emilia might be up for a visit before her shift at the restaurant started. Cara was also keen to take a look inside Julia's place. Set back from the main road and obscured by huge conifers, the stables had an air of mystery that caught Cara's imagination. But, as ever, the reality was more mundane than the imagining and walking onto the yard she found there was little in the way of intrigue to be had, and more in the way of flies. She also discovered that Cypriot flies like to bite. In fact, they like to bite a lot, and if she hadn't told Emilia that she would "love to see her ride", Cara would have gone home. Horses were nice and all, but nothing she wanted to suffer for.

Although Cara loved the idea of horses, she actually found them intimidating. It wasn't simply their size or the fact that they weighed half a ton and were clearly unpredictable; it was the way they looked at her. They weren't stupid animals. They were highly sensitive, they recognised her fear, and Cara always got the impression they were plotting something; something she wouldn't come out of well. Not that this was always the case, Cara used to ride as a child, and was reasonably good at it, but then boys came along and, over time, nerves got the better of her. So even though she hadn't sat on a horse for 30 or more years, she understood a few things about riding, not that it made her any kind of expert. She merely knew how to kick a horse into walk, how to follow its movement, how to still the body, how to hold the reins to get them to stop and how to execute a rising trot. So, it was with some surprise that Cara watched Emilia go into trot, only to see her rise from the saddle and start twerking. As this was a dressage lesson, rather than a common or garden learn-how-to-stay-on kind of lesson, Cara assumed it was some kind of fancy exercise they were doing ready for a movement that other mere riding mortals had little or no knowledge of. And because she assumed this, Cara paid little attention to Julia as she walked over to Emilia.

"What's happening," Julia asked quietly, gently taking hold of the reins to stop Emilia from pulling on her horse's mouth.

"I can't control my left leg when I stand," Emilia replied honestly, her eyes welling with fear and frustration.

"OK, don't panic, just sit in the saddle, if you can." Julia tilted her head a fraction towards the top of the arena. "Does your friend know?"

"No."

"Do you want her to know?"

"No."

"Fine. OK, sit still for a minute, compose yourself, and then we'll concentrate on lateral work in walk until you feel capable of dismounting without arousing suspicion."

Emilia nodded. She then wiped her nose on the arm of her sweatshirt before breathing in deep, taking up the reins and asking Adonis to walk forward.

Lillian tried to ignore the sound of the shower as she washed the breakfast dishes, but it was an impossible task because her mind was too switched on to what she couldn't see. She listened to the water running upstairs, knowing she would be better off listening to the radio. When the water stopped, she heard the dull thump of his veined feet landing on damp tiles. She pictured him reaching for a towel, checking his face in the mirror, tilting his head back to get a better angle in the dim light and then "one... two... three..." the whine of his electric nasal hair trimmer. He'd need them for his ears soon, Lillian thought, before crossing her chest. She was being cruel. She never used to be cruel. But then again, Derek never used to be so meticulously groomed before leaving for a flight. Once the trimmer stopped, there was silence, but the images kept coming; of Derek clipping his toe nails, of him checking his ever-growing bald spot, of him cutting back his pubic hair, all of which was followed by the smell of his aftershave. Lillian was so tuned into the moment she could smell the scent downstairs and it smelled like pears and patchouli. Not that long ago, Derek would have smelled of Imperial Leather and Sure for Men deodorant.

Finally descending the stairs, dressed in his good jeans, Derek carried his suitcase with a carefulness that had become the hallmark of their relationship over the last six months. Occasionally, Lillian wondered whether it was her fault that he acted so delicately around her. Maybe she was the one putting him on edge. Maybe the distance in her voice echoed her own insecurities rather than the truth of her suspicions. And perhaps having her eyes burning into his neck whenever he turned to his phone had unnerved him, so much so that he sometimes flinched when she came into a room. In short, maybe Derek was being extra careful because he thought his wife was about to implode. And he might be right, Lillian thought; she had rarely felt so coiled. And because she could still see another possibility, and in spite of the evidence of her senses, Lillian kept her counsel. She was afraid to push, in case she was wrong, in case she was right. She was damned either way.

As Derek readied to leave, he made a lame joke about "staying out of trouble" and it was all Lillian could do to stop herself from reaching for the bread knife and stabbing him in the throat. Following a cheery, if awkward, kiss on the cheek, he walked out of the house and Lillian moved to the kitchen window to watch his car pull away. Once upon a time, she would have taken her husband to the airport, but apparently her assistance was no longer required because Derek had found a long-stay parking lot, which worked out cheaper than the petrol money it cost to have Lillian as private chauffeur.

Once Derek's car had disappeared from view, Lillian walked over to the sofa and patted the soft padding of the cushions before sitting and crying. After starting quietly, she was soon crying like she hadn't cried in a lifetime, with huge racking sobs. Blinded by tears, Lillian felt rage, disappointment and fear wash over her in a tidal wave of despair that left her struggling to breathe. And though her anguish lasted only minutes, something inside her changed forever. In some ways it felt like being reborn. Lifting her head and straightening her back, Lillian found herself oddly calm and surprised by the hysteria that had descended upon her. So surprised, in fact, that if she hadn't already gone through 'the change' she would have sworn she was menopausal. Once the tears dried, Lillian washed her face, blew her nose, reapplied her make-up and strapped on her GoPro because it was time to feed the cats. More than that, she needed to be with them.

It was a strange feeling knowing that a colony of feral cats desired her company more than her husband did, and yet it was also a feeling that left Lillian humbled. Cats took no prisoners. They would eat anything put in front of them, apart from a worming tablet, but they would only hang out with people they liked. And they seemed to like Lillian, which she found gratifying.

After packing the boot of the car with various brands of cat food, Lillian drove to her first feeding station at the back of the church. On the way she passed a tired old bungalow on the right, like she did most days. Through the chicken wire fencing and the wall of weeds, Lillian kept her eyes peeled for 'Old Boy'. And there he was, like he was every day, tied to the trunk of a tree by a metal chain. Some time ago, Lillian had stopped to check on the dog, which is how she knew his 'home' was a badly rusting oil drum. She noticed there was plenty of dog food and water filling the bowls nearby, but it was no kind of life for a dog, and her heart bled for him. The bungalow Old Boy belonged to was surrounded by the kind of bric-a-brac most commonly found in municipal dumps and Lillian assumed that the dog, who looked a mastiff mix, was there to guard the haul. After spending a few minutes checking the sores on the dog's throat from the constant weight of the chain rubbing it, the owner appeared – a local man, in his mid-50s wearing the camouflage of the weekend hunter. He was polite enough, given she was standing in his dump of a garden, and after a few niceties he allowed her to take a blanket from her car to line the oil drum and provide his dog with some kind of bed.

As she did so, she glanced at the Mercedes-Benz C-Class parked in the driveway. He must have followed her eyes because he asked, "Beautiful, isn't she?" and it was all Lillian could do to stop herself from screaming in his face. That was a little over five months ago, and there wasn't an occasion that Lillian didn't drive past the place and look for Old Boy, all the while hating herself for not doing something to save him.

When Lillian finally arrived at the church, another helper named Janet was already there, releasing a young cat back into the colony after a spaying. Naturally, the two of them got chatting, but not about anything important because Janet wasn't that kind of acquaintance and she was pretty intolerant of other people's dramas. "Life is life and you have to get on with it," was a favourite phrase. As Janet had lost a leg in a collision with a bus some years earlier, Lillian felt in no position to disagree. So, whenever she asked, "How are you?" Lillian usually replied that she was "fine", an answer that suited Janet very well. But that morning was no ordinary day, so when Janet asked, "How are you?" Lillian told her the truth; that she felt wretched. Of course, she didn't reveal the whole truth, only part of it, mumbling something about Old Boy instead.

"Well, there's not much you can do about it, is there?" Janet sniffed. She then listed a number of other things that Lillian couldn't do much about such as world peace and the fact that the municipality was cutting off the water to the dog pound.

"But why?" Lillian asked, having heard nothing about it within the rescue community.

"The pound was shut down years ago for being a craphole, but people still dump their dogs there and the mayor is sick of it. As you know, a number of volunteers go in and care for the dogs, a job that doesn't get any easier if they cut the damn water off. Still, I'm told there are only five dogs in the pound right now, so I'm sure everyone will do their best to prevent them from dying of dehydration."

"But how can this happen?"

"This is Dromos," Janet said with a shrug, as if that was reason enough.

"Dromos my arse," muttered Cara when Lillian mentioned the municipality's decision some ten hours later during a drink with Emilia at the Pig and Poke. Though Cara's comment made no sense, whatsoever, everyone nodded in agreement.

The three women had chosen that evening to get together because Derek would be in Qatar by then. Even though there had been little reason to be careful as the initial excitement surrounding the Kaliteros Hotel had died down in a matter of days, the insider information provided by Cara had made them all cautious. The police were not only continuing their investigation into the puppy murder, but also hunting the "vandals responsible" for the damage caused to the hotel pool.

"Antoni doesn't hold out much hope that they'll be caught," Cara said with a wink.

"I can't believe you had the gall to interview the policeman in charge of the case," Lillian whispered over the rim of her gin and tonic.

"Neither can I," Cara agreed.

"I can't believe you've got the gall to date him," Emilia joined in, aiming a mischievous smile at Cara before turning to gauge Lillian's reaction. It was instantaneous. The eyes grew wide, the cheeks flushed furiously and bewilderment revealed itself in every strand of lightly curled hair. Lillian was shocked. She was also firm in the belief that this "wasn't very good at all."

"Relax," Cara replied. "I've only agreed to have dinner with him, it's hardly dating and it hasn't even happened yet. Anyway, as the saying goes, 'it pays to keep your friends close and your enemies closer'."

"Like in your vagina?" asked Emilia and Lillian nearly spat her gin and tonic across the table.

"Now, please," she protested, but Cara was giggling and it made Lillian feel prudish for denying the joke. For a second, she thought of Derek and what he might make of the company she now kept, but then the thought of his face made her mood sour, so she catapulted herself back into the here and now by changing the subject.

"So, can we do something or are we just going to let those dogs in the pound die?"

Cara and Emilia were momentarily stunned by the question.

"Well, I'm open to suggestions," Cara joked. "Have you got any?"

And maybe because Lillian felt obliged to offer something, she said, "Well, yes. I might have, actually."

Chapter Eight

Like many of the roads in rural Cyprus, St. Andrew's Street was tarmacked up to a point. Beyond that point, which lay about 40 metres north of the last house, it became a winding track of rubble and dirt used only by hunters, goats and, on this occasion, Lillian.

Parked on the grass verge, well back from the street's only light, Lillian's dark blue Pajero painted an indistinct smudge in the gloom thanks to the heavy cloud cover blocking the moon. She thanked God for that. It was twice He had given them the luck of the weather. Most of the time, clouds were less common on the island than sightings of Elvis.

Lillian looked at the time on her phone. A little after four in the morning. In an hour and a half, the sun would rise, and so would the locals. Looking towards a driveway that was the size of a small lane, she raised the phone's microphone attachment to her lips. "How's it going?" she whispered, placing a hand over her left ear to better hear Cara's reply.

"Getting there. One more to go. All quiet your end?"

"Yes, very quiet."

"Roger that."

"Roger, Roger, over," Lillian replied, before dropping the microphone from her lips.

Placing the phone on her lap, Lillian kept the call open as agreed, in case she needed to sound the alarm, but there was no movement to cause concern, no noise, no light, no nothing, and she was struggling to stay awake. Being the look-out was actually quite exhausting, especially as she had grown accustomed to Cara breathing in her ear and the occasional tinkle of broken glass. Earlier in the day, when she had imagined herself in this very position, Lillian assumed adrenaline would be enough to keep her alert.

Now she wondered whether she ought to have packed a flask of coffee and a packet of Modafinil.

As there was nothing better to do than watch the dark get lighter, Lillian's mind began to wander, meandering along the usual nooks and crannies concerning chores to be done, bills to be paid and Skype calls to be made, until it arrived at an increasingly familiar and unsettling dead end.

"Lord, give me strength," she muttered, not realising she had spoken aloud until she heard the panic in Cara's voice, wanting to know what was wrong. "Sorry, nothing, just mumbling to myself," Lillian replied. "Roger, Roger, over."

Lillian shook her head and pinched the bridge of her nose. Embarrassed by her mistake, her cheeks burned with a heat intensified by feelings of shame and inadequacy. Lillian felt silly and weak, and strangely soiled, as confusion and pain overwhelmed her for a second or two. She knew it would pass, like it had passed before, but when she called on the Lord to help her it wasn't a phrase trotted out without thought, it was a genuine prayer. There was no one else for her to turn to; she simply wasn't ready yet. But God, well, He already knew the truth, unlike Lillian, and that made Him more than qualified to guide her. Right now, she felt so lost it was all she could do to drag herself out of bed in the mornings. While she rarely went to church these days, her faith hadn't waned and she continued to resolutely believe in God and the power of good, which is why she had always tried to live a life that was not only without sin, but also without sinful thought. Unfortunately, having recently floated into unchartered waters, her thoughts had been less than charitable of late, and they often involved a sharp knife and her husband's penis. Lillian shook her head in frustration, dislodging the earpiece for a second. She then crossed her chest and tried to take her mind off her husband's possible failings by thinking of Dan and Lucy.

Despite a few, admittedly forced, Sunday school attendances, neither of her children were believers. Dan robustly dismissed the

Bible as a collection of "morally-questionable fairy tales". Lucy, who had always been the more thoughtful child, had dabbled with Buddhism for a year before concluding that all religions had some nice ideas, but were "essentially nuts". As for Derek, he had never openly dismissed Lillian's beliefs, but he was an atheist at heart and always had been.

For many years, her family's lack of faith had worried Lillian, not that she mentioned it much because nobody took her concerns seriously. Still, it was difficult to look forward to an afterlife devoid of those she loved, especially as all the signs pointed to them spending an eternity in hell. There could have been hope for Derek because the Bible said the unbelieving husband could be sanctified through the wife. But the Bible was also pretty clear on adultery; marriage should be honoured and the marriage bed kept pure. "For God will judge the adulterer." Yes, God will judge. The adulterer.

Lillian shuddered as she tried to still the contents of her stomach. She had no proof, only a feeling; a terrible, cold, ache of a feeling deep within her. Let God be the judge, she reminded herself, but even that was hard to accept because the thought of God's judgement left her terrified and grief-stricken. She was worried for Derek's eternal soul, whether he believed in it or not, and she was broken hearted at the thought there might be no place for him in heaven. Yet, there was also a part of her that hated the thought of Derek living a long and fruitful life, while merrily dishonouring the marital bed, and only paying the price at death. Whereas she, his honest and faithful wife, had to suffer the torment of his sin in this life. And what if Dan was right, and God and heaven and all the rest of it was make believe? There would be no paradise for Lillian and no retribution for Derek, and Lillian wasn't sure how she felt about that. She had to admit, if only to herself, that deep down, if everything was true and Derek was cheating on her, then she wanted him punished, in this life, in the afterlife, in whatever life. And that wish for revenge also worried Lillian.

A little ahead, coming into view under the one and only street light, Lillian spotted the shadowy form of a couple walking towards her. Given the hour and the way they were stumbling, they were clearly drunk, bouncing off one another before embracing like two lovers caught in a storm. Lillian's heart ached at the sight as she tried to shrink into her seat. Once the couple reached the lamplight, Lillian noticed the man wore a smart, if dated, suit and large, dark-rimmed glasses. The woman was kitted out in a suede tasselled mini dress and knee-length boots. As Dromos was a relatively small place, the two of them were not unknown to Lillian, but then just as she was about to pull her black woollen hat completely over her head and plant herself face down on the passenger seat, the couple shared a passionate kiss before turning left to go up a side alley. As they disappeared into the night, Lillian kept her eyes fixed on the road ahead, unable to think because her heart was beating so loudly in her ears. She then dropped her phone.

"Flipping heck," she mumbled, and scrambled to retrieve it from under the driver's seat. Bringing the mic to her lips, she whispered. "You still there?"

"Yes, are you OK? What's going on?" Cara asked.

"Nothing, well nothing now. Sorry. I dropped my phone when Roy Orbison and Cher appeared."

"Roy Orbison and Cher are here?"

"Not now, they've gone. The coast is clear again."

"OK. Roger that."

Cara hooked the phone back onto the belt of her black jeans and looked over at Emilia who was staring at her intently, unable to hear what was going on because she only had a pay-as-you-go phone.

"Roy Orbison and Cher were here," Cara explained in a whisper.

"Sonny will be furious," Emilia muttered, and Cara almost laughed until she remembered not to. She looked at the window in front of her, stepped back and tipped her head at Emilia.

"That's the last one done," she said.

"Great. Let's go," Emilia replied before remembering something requiring an expletive.

"What is it?" Cara hissed, dropping to her knees only to find Emilia still standing.

Emilia rifled in the pocket of her jacket, pulled out a marker pen and waved it. "On the front door?"

Cara nodded as she got back to her feet. "It needs be somewhere obvious for this clown."

Edging along the pathway that skirted the property, being careful not to step on the gravel, they made their way as quietly as possible to the front door. Once they were within touching distance, a welcome light tripped on, emitting a beam so bright it wouldn't have been out of place mounted on the walls of Alcatraz.

Both Cara and Emilia froze before hitting the deck, staying there until the light went off, roughly eight seconds later. The two of them then remained where they were, not daring to move as they listened for any sounds coming from inside the house, something made all the harder for Cara by Lillian whispering loudly in her ear, demanding answers.

"What's going on? Is everything OK? I can see a light. Wait, it's gone. Are you there? What should I do? Cara? Cara? Cara, can you hear me?"

Cara motioned to Emilia, making a beak of her fingers and thumb. She then opened and closed it to illustrate Lillian talking in her ear. Unfortunately, it also illustrated just how sensitive the welcome light was. Once again, Cara and Emilia froze. In the end, the tension became too much for Emilia who was tired, taut and starting to tremble down the left side of her body. She got to her feet, snapped the lid off the marker pen and quickly drew a paw print on the white plastic frame of the front door.

"Right, let's get the hell out of here," she whispered. She dragged Cara to her feet and they ran for it, back up the lane, towards the road where Lillian was waiting for them.

Chapter Nine

Inspector Antoni Giagkos laughed as he completed his report. In fact, he hadn't stopped laughing since 8am that morning when the Mayor of Dromos, apoplectic with rage, called the station to reveal someone had superglued his house during the night, trapping him and his wife inside. If that wasn't enough to make Antoni's day, shards of broken glass had been stuck to every windowsill on the ground floor, presumably to make any attempt to escape through the windows just that little more challenging. The culprits, who could have been pranksters or criminals at that point, had also cut off the water to the house. The mayor's money was on political enemies.

"The bastard communists did this," he announced when Antoni arrived at the scene.

Now, Antoni knew the communists had their faults, like most political parties, but imprisoning minor officials using strong adhesives was not one he was overly familiar with. Of course, like most politicians, the Mayor of Dromos was convinced he was right.

Constantinos Georgiou was voted into power on an independent ticket following the financial crisis of 2013. This was a time when having no political affiliation had become the most credible position to be in after a flurry of corruption scandals had disgraced national party connections. Amid much fanfare, his appointment was believed to herald a new dawn for Dromos municipality, yet three years in, the old conventions of nepotism, corruption and cronyism remained alive, well and positively thriving. Antoni hadn't been in Dromos long enough to be disappointed in the mayor, but he knew enough about politicians to not be surprised. Nor was he surprised that he had, once again, been assigned Special Constable Michalis Georgiou to help him with the case.

After explaining to the mayor's wife how he took his coffee, Michalis went to check for any signs of blood on the window sills, in case 'the communists' had cut themselves. When that yielded no results, he checked for footprints in the flowerbeds. An hour or so later, he was in a position to confirm that as well as no blood on the premises, there were no footprints to be found on the grounds and no fingerprints immediately apparent around the doors, the window frames or the water shut off valve attached to the outside wall.

"Can you think of any other clues we might have missed?" Antoni asked Michalis as they stood in the mayor's porchway.

The Special Constable sucked heavily on his cigarette and nodded slowly, employing the steely gaze of the seasoned law enforcer. "Well, I think it's clear the suspects wore gloves."

Antoni also nodded. "So, we're looking for criminals wearing gloves. Anything else?"

Michalis smoked a little more, thought about it and shrugged.

Being a patient man, Antoni tried to help his colleague by tilting his head towards the front door. In the end, he had to walk up to it, bend down and point to the paw print that was drawn at knee height. "Ring any bells?" he asked.

Michalis glanced at the doorbell before turning his attention to the paw. "I thought it was a decoration of some kind," he confessed, "you know, like car bumper stickers."

"Interesting. And while that might be the case, don't you recall that not so long ago there was another paw print left at the scene of a crime?"

Antoni saw the light switch on behind the curtain of Michalis' hazel eyes. "The swimming pool!"

"Yes, the swimming pool," Antoni repeated, shaking his head. He then went to tell the mayor that the communists might not be to blame after all, and ask him why he might have been targeted by animal rights activists. That's when Antoni learned that a small protest had been taking place, almost daily, outside the gates of the old municipal dog pound.

"What are they protesting about?"

"Who knows what goes through the minds of these extremists," the mayor replied.

"Oh Constantinos, you cut off their water," the mayor's wife revealed, employing a healthy dose of exasperation as she entered the sitting room carrying a tray laden with Cypriot coffee cups and small plates of walnuts soaked in syrup.

Antoni smiled at the mayor before thanking his wife for the helpful information. He then turned to Michalis who was already reaching for a walnut. "I guess we know who to speak to next."

"We do?"

For a second, Antoni stared at Michalis, unable to believe that anybody could be that moronic and still hold down a part-time job in the police service. But then he remembered where he was, and that he was not only in Cyprus, but Dromos, and Michalis was the son of one of the region's biggest, and most generous, property developers. "To clarify," he said, "I guess *I* know who to speak to next."

Some hours later, as the lowering sun turned the sky a darkening swirl of deep red, burnt orange and indigo blue, Cara ran herself a bath — partly because she was cold and it was the only way she could warm up, but also because old habits die hard and a 'date night' meant shaving.

Lying on the bed, Cooper and Peaches eyed her with suspicion through the bathroom doorway. The dogs weren't stupid, and though Cara rarely went out at night, they knew that whenever she did it started with goings on in the bathroom. In turn, Cara knew that Cooper and Peaches knew something was up, and she struggled not to feel guilty about leaving them alone.

She wasn't sure when, or even why, going out had become such an ordeal; lots of people owned dogs and still managed a social life. But for Cara, the dogs had definitely become a stumbling block to any new romance, should she choose to have one, not to mention the possible complication of sex. Rightly or wrongly, depending

on one's view of dogs, hygiene and personal space, both Cooper
and Peaches had taken to sleeping on the bed at night. Though Cara
had initially attempted to keep them on the floor, she had discovered over time that she rather liked having her dogs sleep alongside
her. It might have been the weight of their bodies pressed against
her back that she found comforting or their warmth when winter
came around. Whatever it was, Cara's bed had become as much
Cooper and Peaches' bed, which made the idea of some sort of
sexual activity taking place there unappealing. If sex was to occur
it would mean moving Cooper and Peaches off the bed, at the
very least. However, should the dogs stay in their own beds, which
seemed highly unlikely, Cara wasn't sure she would be able to have
sex while they remained in the room, listening. This meant the
dogs would have to sleep downstairs, which struck her as a step
too close to eviction. Therefore, should sex occur, it wouldn't be
taking place in her house. If it was going to happen it would have
to be at his house. Not that Cara would feel happy about leaving
the dogs alone all night, so she would basically have to do it and get
out, which seemed not only rude, but shameless.

"Do it in the car," Emilia suggested when Cara called for advice
after working herself into a frenzy about the possibility of having
sex with a man whom she had yet to decide whether she wanted
to have sex with.

"I'm too old to be shagging in the back seat."

"Use the front then. Or the bonnet, though I hear that's more
of a dogging move."

"You had to mention dogs, didn't you?"

On the other end of the line Emilia snorted before finally
taking pity on her friend. "Relax, Cara. It's only a meal you're
going for. If later you like him enough to want to see him naked,
we can worry about logistics then. But all you're doing right now
is talking yourself out of free food. So, go, enjoy yourself, eat,
be merry, laugh a little and return home. He does know you're a
vegan, right?"

"Um, no."

"Oh well, problem solved. The chances are he'll think you're a hippy crackpot whose vag smells of patchouli oil and he won't want to have sex with you anyway."

"You say the sweetest things."

"I try. By the way, have you checked out Facebook today? We're famous."

"We're what?"

"Log on. Take a look. The usual sites. Anyway, got to go. The Zorba regulars are shouting for chips and chops."

Lillian stared at the screen, hardly believing her eyes as she read comment after comment under an online newspaper article headlined 'Dromos Mayor Comes Unstuck'. Though the spelling and grammar was mostly shocking, and there was some choice language in places, it appeared that the majority of readers were absolutely delighted that Constantinos Georgiou had been superglued into his home. While some of the comments mentioned 'political enemies' and 'organised criminal gangs', many of them had taken the article's lead and connected the incident to an animal welfare issue. The newspaper had even mocked up its own paw print above a caption that read 'The perpetrators left this signature on the door'. While a couple of comments speculated about a possible link to the 'Pool of Blood' at the Kaliteros Hotel a month earlier, only one comment, by 'Old Peg Leg', hit the nail on the head, claiming the damage to the mayor's home was "an act of solidarity with the poor dogs at Dromos municipality pound who have been without water for three days." It didn't take a genius to work out that the author of that particular comment must have been Janet, Lillian's one-legged fellow cat feeder. "Bloody brilliant! I whole heartedly applaud whoever did this! They are heroes in my book!" concluded Janet and Lillian got up from the table, smiling.

Antoni stepped out of the shower, patted himself dry and liberally applied deodorant to his armpits and as much of his body as humanly possible before finishing with a short blast to his pubic hair. It wasn't that he was expecting anything to come of his date with Cara other than good food and polite chit chat, but he liked to smell nice and as a police officer he knew it paid to be prepared for any eventuality. With that in mind, he also plucked the grey from his chest. Just in case.

Tonight's date would only be the second for Antoni since his marriage to Elena ended in a tiring drama of tears, accusations and legal papers. The first date had been an unmitigated disaster that had taken place ten months earlier in Nicosia after he made contact with a former girlfriend from school. Their original relationship had foundered by the fourth grade of primary school for reasons he could no longer remember, but he assumed it had little to do with the woman's now extraordinary appetite for alcohol. Although Antoni tried to be charitable, putting her excessive drinking down to nerves, it was more likely an addiction she suffered from, and for that he was truly sorry. Addiction quite often followed the lonely, but he knew he would not be the one to save her, so there was no second date.

Thankfully, from the little that Antoni had seen of Cara, she hadn't struck him as an addict of any kind, not that first impressions were fool proof. Still, all the signs suggested he was about to enjoy a nice meal with an attractive, professional woman in her late 30s who had her own teeth and no track marks running up her arms. Even if things didn't work out romantically, he knew there were worse ways to spend an evening; he could have been pulling a night shift with Michalis. As he cleaned his teeth, Antoni shook his head at the thought of his colleague. Michalis had driven him nuts that day. While he had no problem with the lazy and inept, it was simply how some people were, he did have a problem with idiots who didn't know they were idiots. That afternoon, if Antoni hadn't stopped him, Michalis would have arrested four female protestors, who had been quietly standing at the dog pound, for the criminal damage done to the mayor's house, despite the lack of any evidence placing them at the scene. Antoni had looked at the women, one of whom looked older than Methuselah while another appeared to be missing a leg, and he apologised for his colleague. He took Michalis by the arm and led him, not so gently, to the pathway running alongside the pound where a disability scooter was parked.

"Is that your idea of a getaway car?" he asked, and Michalis at least had the good grace to blush before dropping the butt of his cigarette and walking off muttering something about having had no lunch.

Antoni checked himself in the full-length mirror attached to the back of the wardrobe door. Having given the matter careful consideration, he had chosen to wear a pair of good Levis with a black shirt. His outfit was complemented by slightly battered biker boots that offered a hint of rebellion while falling shy of 'no-money loser'. His hair was lightly waxed, his fingernails were trimmed and his nasal hair had been dealt with. Not so bad, he thought. Of course, he was more handsome when he was younger, but though the face was now fuller so was the wallet.

"There's still time, there's still hope," his mother was fond of muttering, desperate for her youngest son to settle down again because having nine grandchildren clearly wasn't enough for her. Unfortunately, and despite the best efforts of a number of medical specialists, Antoni's ex-wife had been unable to carry a child past three months, and though it wasn't the reason for the failure of their marriage, it was an emotional difficulty that took its toll. As a result, and for many years, Elena was consumed with thoughts of what she could never have whereas Antoni took whatever the world wanted to offer or deny him and ran with it.

Antoni glanced at his watch; ten past eight. He had booked a table at Luigi's for 8.30pm and didn't want to be late. Taking one last look at himself in the hallway mirror, he grabbed his car keys and headed for the door.

It was part way through the main course that Cara really began to enjoy her date with Antoni. It wasn't that the evening had been bad up to that point – there was champagne, a well-received request to the chef for vegan options and the company was not only sweet and polite, but well-presented – however, it was only once she was halfway through her bowl of Ribollita Toscana that she laughed out loud. And it felt good. The champagne might have helped, but it was rare to find someone who genuinely amused her, so rare in fact that she had stayed with the last man who did for far longer than she ought to have done.

After learning that Cara had a Kokoni rescue dog, Antoni revealed that his sister had also rescued one, in as much as she had acquired the little guy from some Bangladeshi labourers who had half-adopted him after he wandered onto their banana plantation.

"Well, when she got this dog home it wouldn't eat," Antoni said. "My sister gave it every kind of food you could imagine, but he wouldn't touch it, not even sniff it. Now, for some reason, my sister was crazy for this dog, so she gave it roast chicken, roast pork, chopped liver, boiled kidney, even the best cut of steak from the butcher, raw and cooked. I'm not lying here. This dog was given the kind of food the rest of the family could only dream about, and still it refused to eat. Not one piece of it. Well, as the days went on, it was clear the dog would eventually starve to death so my sister took it to the veterinary clinic. For four days they kept it at the clinic, running test after test on the little bastard, all of them coming back clear. In the end, the only thing left to do was open him up and take a look inside to see if they could see what was going on. Of course, my sister was sick with worry, but then on the very day that the dog was going to have the operation she met one of the labourers in the supermarket. He asked how the dog was doing and she started crying, explaining that he wouldn't eat. "I've given him everything," she said, "roast chicken, roast pork even the best steak, but he would rather die." For a second, the man looked confused. He then asked how she fed him and when she told him, "in a bowl", he laughed a little and said she should try feeding him by hand because that's how the dog would eat with him and his friends. They would feed him. By hand. Like a little king with his slaves. Well, my sister didn't believe it at first, I mean what kind of dog would rather die than eat out of a bowl? But what choice did she have? She telephoned the vet, catching him just before he prepared for surgery. She repeated what the labourer had said and though she felt pretty stupid she asked the vet to give it a try. The vet agreed. Taking a can of dog food from a shelf he opened it up, stuck his hand in and offered the meat to the dog. Twenty minutes later, the vet called my sister. "You're not going to believe this," he said, "but your dog ate the whole can." Unbelievable. Six hundred euros in vet bills, not to mention wasting some of the best meat in Cyprus, and all the little bastard wanted was for someone to feed him by hand. To this day, my sister still feeds him like this."

It took a while for Cara to stop laughing, but when she did, she gaily revealed that Cooper and Peaches would eat anything put in front of them, "even their poo". As she spoke, Antoni's fork stopped its journey to his mouth, causing Cara to laugh again. And it was at this point in the evening that she began to notice Antoni's eyes; they were the colour of melted chocolate and they were beautiful.

Later that evening, after a sorbet dessert and coffee with a brandy chaser, Antoni walked Cara to the nearest taxi rank. There was no queue, which Cara found quietly disappointing, and following an awkward handshake, Antoni leaned in to kiss her on the cheek. This was also disappointing. But then Antoni asked whether they might have dinner again one evening and Cara said she would be "delighted". And with that, the two of them parted ways.

During the 20-minute journey from Paphos to Dromos, Cara passed the time reliving moments from the evening, grateful it had gone well. To her surprise, she genuinely liked Antoni; he was kind, charismatic, attentive and intelligent. When the taxi pulled up outside her house and she reached into her bag, she found another reason to like him.

"No, no," the cab driver said as she took out her purse. "Your boyfriend paid already."

It was an old-fashioned act of chivalry that Cara wasn't expecting and once she had given Cooper and Peaches a dental treat "for being big, brave babies waiting all alone in the night", she texted Antoni to say thank you. The next text she sent was to Emilia.

"OMFG! In a good way! Will call tomorrow xx"

Chapter Ten

Emilia rubbed her forehead with her right hand as her left was still heavy from another "episode". It had been two days since the last attack, and each new one seemed to take a greater toll on her than the last. Physically, it could be another two or three days before she lost the sensation of feeling unequal. Financially, it was killing her. The last "episode" had cost Emilia her job.

"This is no good. I cannot..."

"It won't happen again."

"*Kori*, you said this the last time and the time before that. Sorry, but the restaurant business is no business for clumsy girls. You must finish now. You must go."

Emilia stared at her boss. Though he liked to play the part of fun-loving 'Zorba' this was an act solely for the tourists. In real life, Zorba was called Savvas and he was a mean-spirited, tight-fisted son of a bitch.

Briefly considering whether to argue the toss, after all, how much more Greek could you get than a few smashed plates, Emilia saw little point in causing a scene. Accidents happen and they would happen again. And they would keep on happening until the day she lost the ability to hold a plate altogether.

"Fine, Savvas. I'll go if that's what you want, but I think it's only fair you give me three months' severance pay, one month for every year I've worked here." Savvas snorted through his long nose, ready to laugh in her face, until Emilia continued. "You know I have photographs of you and Kasia on my phone, don't you? Photographs I'd be happy to share with your wife."

In the space of a heartbeat, the air turned blue, the cheeks flushed beetroot and the man's eyes burned with fire and outrage for a full three minutes until, like a light switching off, he shrugged, opened a drawer and pulled out a bundle of fifty-euro notes. He threw three months wages on the desk before him.

"Take it," he told her, his top lip curling. "God knows it will be difficult for a Romanian peasant bitch like you to find work again." As Emilia reached for the money, Savvas grabbed her hand, almost crushing her bones between his meaty, hairy fingers. He pulled her towards him, close enough that she could count the open pores on his nose. "Now listen to me," he snarled, "if you come back asking for more, I promise I will snap you like a twig. Believe this."

Emilia tugged her hand away, grabbed the money and told him she wouldn't be back, hardly able to believe her good fortune. There were no photos, there had never been any photos, and she had only guessed that her boss might be up to no good with one of the other waitresses. Still, as her mother once told her, fate shines a light in a person's darkest hour and, if they have any sense, they will run to it. Six months after those pearls of wisdom, her mother died from stomach cancer, no doubt chasing her light all the way to heaven.

Emilia sighed, crossed her chest, got up from the table and wandered to the kitchen to get a glass of water. At the sink, she turned on the tap, using her right hand, before taking a glass, in her right hand, and holding it under the tap. After setting the glass on the draining board she then turned off the tap, with her right hand, before returning to the small table in the sitting room of her small apartment to resume writing. Luckily for Emilia, she was righthanded.

On a sheet of A4 paper she had compiled something of a hit list. In fact, she had titled it Hit List.

HORSES:

SUNSHINE ZOO, LIMASSOL: They feed horses to the lions (Julia).
DEATH ALLEY, LARNACA: Back of racing yard where they leave retired or injured racehorses to starve to death (Julia).

DOGS:

KIVOTOS FARM, PAPHOS: 12 dogs dead in squalid conditions, farm closed down, but operating again with more dogs (Facebook: Cyprus Dog Rescue).

BIRDS:

STELIOS LOIZOU, trapper: arrested and fined for selling songbirds to Thalassa Taverna in Paphos. NIKOS DEMETRIADES, owner of Thalassa Taverna: also arrested. Police found 40 birds boiling in the kitchen (The Mail).

(Traps kills millions of birds each year. In 2014, 2.5 million birds were killed. They are trapped with mist nets and glue sticks, sold to restaurants as ambelopoulia. It is ILLEGAL. Glue sticks are twigs, about 50-70cm long...

Emilia's train of thought was interrupted by her mobile phone ringing. Putting down her pen, she stood in order to extract the phone from the front pocket of her jeans. One glance at the display told her 'Julia' was calling.

"What's up?" she asked, trying to sound more cheerful than she felt because Julia rarely rang for reasons other than Adonis.

Lillian gazed at the two adults sat opposite her in the restaurant, hardly able to believe they were her children. It was Dan's 30th birthday and Lillian had flown to England to celebrate the occasion. Her daughter Lucy had made the shorter trip from Warwick to Cheshire to join them, while Derek had flown in from Qatar. The family tried to come together at least once a year in the UK, and though the visits tended to be short they were always sweet.

As the conversation turned to politics, Lillian found herself half listening because she had little interest in such matters and she was simply content to soak up the atmosphere. Though she knew she was biased, Lillian was often awestruck by the adults her children had become. A late starter, physically, Dan was now taller than his father, by a head or more, and the hours he spent in the gym had made him a stronger man than Derek had ever been. Perhaps that was why, as she looked at father and son sitting at the same table, laughing at each other's boyish jokes as they supped their pints, she started to see Derek for the man that he now was rather than the man he had always been. He was in his 60th year and pedalling slowly downhill towards retirement. Though he remained in good health and in fairly good shape, their son's height, width and sheer vitality made Derek look frail in comparison. And it dawned on her that if she saw this difference in her husband, so did he.

For much of his life, Derek had been a force of nature, resolutely masculine, opinionated, cheerful and for the most part charming, but whether he wanted to admit it or not, he was nearing his autumn years. Lillian wasn't blind; she saw he could no longer read without his glasses, that he found it harder to straighten his back after getting out of bed, that certain foods irritated his bowels, and that his hair was not only thinning but emerging from his ears. But none of this mattered to Lillian because she loved him. And yet, right at that moment, sitting in a restaurant that seemed to offer nothing but chicken, she also pitied him. Derek's star was fading and, in a strange way, Lillian felt empowered by that knowledge, perhaps because she had never thought of herself as being anything more than the person she was. And having come to an understanding that Derek was in denial of his own mortality, she further understood that she too had changed. As Derek had grown weak, she had emerged stronger, and it had nothing to do with the power dynamic within her marriage and everything to do with her friendship with Emilia and Cara.

If it wasn't for her friends, Lillian would not be the woman she was that day. Though she hadn't realised it immediately, it was clear she was no longer simply a housewife and mother; she was a doer, someone who walked the talk, and a woman not to be messed with. On top of that, she was a wanted criminal, a fact that had cheered her up no end during the past week in which she had endured the great British weather and forced marital jollities.

Lillian looked over at her daughter and smiled. Caught unawares and wrongly assuming her Mum was looking for reassurance, Lucy smiled back and because Lillian saw the sincerity underlining the gesture, she had to stop herself from explaining that she wasn't looking for any kind of support or comfort. On the contrary. Lillian was happier than she remembered being in a long while and, if anything, she would have loved to share the reason for that happiness with the one person who would have got the biggest kick out of it.

Being a steelier version of Lillian, Lucy had always encouraged her mother to get out and do more; to forge a life beyond that of her husband and children. Needless to say, Lillian had never heeded that advice because for much of her adult life she had no interest in anything other than her husband and children. Now, however, things were different and instead of finding her head confused with thoughts about Derek and what he may or may not be up to, or the worry and fear that had always accompanied her love for Dan and Lucy, she found herself wondering what Emilia and Cara were doing, how her cats were getting on and whether there was a way to save Old Boy from ending his years tied to a tree with a chain eating away at his neck.

"Right, I'm done," Lillian said as she pushed her plate away. "Let's finish up and go to the pub."

Somewhat surprised by such a suggestion coming from their mother, Dan and Lucy glanced at each other before grinning. Derek, on the other hand, almost choked on the last of his flame-grilled peri-peri chicken.

Cara shouted for Cooper and Peaches to "heel". Once she had shouted this command four more times, her tone becoming increasingly threatening, they finally came bounding to her side and she clipped on their leads.

"Why not let them run more? There are no goats here, no dogs, no cars. Let them be free."

As he spoke, Antoni stopped walking in order to make a 360-degree turn, stretching an arm before him, like a king presenting the extent of his kingdom.

Cara stopped to look about her. It was indeed a beautiful sight. Stood on a white-rock track that sparkled with shards of quartz, they were a few feet away from the peak of a hill, the right side of which fell away sharply. Thorny green bushes dotted with yellow and purple flowers hugged both sides of the track with only a few gaps here and there where the local goats had made their own trails. Beyond the cliff edge, Dromos could be seen in all its entirety; a sprawling collection of flat rooftops topped by solar panels and water tanks. A little further away, the great expanse of the Mediterranean Sea danced and glittered in the spring sun. It was a breath-taking spot and at first glance it appeared to be relatively unspoilt. But the three Santa dolls hanging from a nearby carob tree suggested the place was not unknown to locals and the few scraps of tissue paper discarded on a shallow ledge partially obscured by a yellow spiny shrub, suggested these locals were not only possessed of a dubious sense of humour, but a dubious sense of hygiene as well.

"People come here to take a shit," Cara informed Antoni. "That's why I put my dogs on the lead. I don't want them to eat it."

Antoni glanced at Cooper and Peaches before looking at Cara with concern. It was the third date since they discovered they liked each other in the Italian restaurant, and it wasn't the first time she had mentioned her dogs' appetite for faeces.

"Have you tried feeding them?" he joked.

"Have you tried asking your friends to use a toilet?"

"Well, as you know, we are not so civilised as you English."

Cara dropped her head. "You're right. I expect too much."

"Yes, you do, but you'll learn," Antoni said before boldly stepping forward to invade her personal space. "Of course, you'll need the right teacher."

Cara wasn't a fool, she knew a line when she heard one and so did her heart, which began thumping its interest in her chest.

"Would that teacher be you, by any chance?" she asked, sounding more flippant than she felt.

"I think it might be, yes." Antoni placed a hooked finger beneath Cara's chin and lifted her face until their lips met.

As kisses went, it wasn't the longest Cara had ever experienced, nor the most passionate, but it was warm and sweet, and maybe because it had been so long since she had felt any kind of tenderness, it made her knees go weak. 'Like in the films,' she heard her head say. And though she knew it was irrational, if not stupid, not least because they had only known each other a matter of weeks, Cara was overwhelmed by a surge of emotion that made her insides churn with hope, desire, excitement and trepidation until they combined into something that felt ridiculously like love.

"Cara," Antoni said softly in her ear. "I have to tell you something."

"What is it?" she half-whispered.

"I think one of your dogs has peed up my leg."

"What the hell?"

Julia took one look at Emilia, dropped the bucket she was carrying and came running.

"It's nothing. I'm OK," Emilia insisted trying to bat Julia away as she fussed around her head.

"But you're bleeding!"

"It's just a cut. Please, leave it, I want to see Adonis. How is he?"

Julia shook her head as she forcibly pulled Emilia towards the tack room. "Adonis is fine. He's lying quietly and over the worst of it. The injections worked, he's passing gas like a king and he'll be on his feet in no time."

"OK, good, but I still want to see him."

"And you will. In a minute."

Though the tone of Julia's voice wasn't exactly harsh, it was firm and it left no room for doubt as to what the order of things

would be. As Emilia was also starting to feel lightheaded, she followed the older woman into the tack room and gingerly sat herself on a chair. As Julia poked about in her cupboard, muttering
something about antiseptic wipes, Emilia tried to compose herself, but she knew she was only a heartbeat away from screaming.
She closed her eyes and let Julia take charge as she tried to keep a
lid on everything that was bubbling below the surface.

"Lucky for you, it looks worse than it is," Julia said after she had
wiped the blood from Emilia's forehead. "You won't need stitches."

"I told you it was nothing."

"And it might well have been nothing if you'd worn a helmet.
How many times do I have to tell you, Emilia?"

"I know. I'm sorry."

"Sorry isn't good enough, and next time you might not have the
luxury of being sorry, so just do it." Julia stood back and wiped the
hair from her face. It was rare to see her without a baseball cap and
Emilia assumed she must have been on her way out when Adonis
fell sick. In fact, she almost mentioned it, but a wave of nausea suddenly prevented her from speaking and instead she meekly tipped
her head back when Julia told her to and tried not to wince when
Betaisodona was liberally applied to her cuts. Only once she was
bandaged was Emilia finally permitted to leave, but not before answering one final question.

"Are you going to tell me what happened?"

Having had time to prepare, Emilia told Julia she had swerved
to avoid a cat. "I came off, not at high speed, and it's no big deal. It
was an accident."

"I'm aware it was an accident otherwise it would have been a
failed suicide. Anyway, you know what I think about motorbikes."

"It's a moped."

"Mopeds, motorbikes, they're all the same. They're death traps
on these roads."

"Maybe, but a moped is a hell of a lot cheaper than a car." Emilia
smiled, but she was also irritated. In the not-too-distant future it

was doubtful she would be able to afford the roof over her head let alone the expense of a car. But of course, she said nothing because Julia had given too much already, and she was too ashamed to reveal she still needed more.

After taking a sip of water from the bottle Julia handed her, Emilia went to see Adonis. As she expected, she found her horse lying flat on the floor of his stable, his stomach huge and swollen, his eyes glassy and his teeth bared. Above his eye socket and along his cheek bones, bloody grazes hinted at the extent of her boy's pain and she pictured him slamming his head against the wall as he fought for relief from the agony torturing his messed-up gut. As hot tears welled in her eyes, Emilia unbolted the stable gate to get to Adonis. Crouching beside his head, she waved her hands over his handsome face to keep the flies from landing there.

"What are we like, you and I?" she whispered, grimacing as she straightened her leg because, unbeknown to Julia, she had a bloody big hole in her knee cap. As the jeans she wore were black, the blood wasn't immediately apparent. Emilia held her breath and waited for the pain to reach a more manageable level, reliving the moment of the accident as she did so. There had been no cat. She had simply lost control of her bike, like she knew she would one day, and now it had happened she was terrified.

Emilia moved closer to Adonis. It was a silly thing to do because he might strike out with his hooves if he was caught by another spasm, potentially swatting her like a fly. But Emilia didn't care. She needed to feel him and let him know she was there. So, she lay her head on his neck and cried into his mane.

"What are we like, you and I?" she repeated. "We're like diamonds; diamonds in the sky."

Chapter Eleven

When Lillian returned to Cyprus, she didn't feel quite herself and, for once, she thought that was no bad thing. Whereas in the past, leaving the UK would have triggered a haze of bereavement lasting two or three days as she struggled to adjust to the distance between herself and her children, this time it was different. Lillian came back itching to get on with life. This was something of a surprise because up until then she had never considered she had one. If anything, Lillian had imagined herself as the glue keeping other lives together. Another key difference from previous trips away was the absence of her husband. Normally, Derek would join her at home before returning to work, to help her settle back into Cyprus living. This time he flew straight to Doha. He did offer to take extra leave, but Lillian told him there was no need. She was 'fine', she said, and in this case, 'fine' really did mean 'fine'.

Lillian realised this newfound confidence was wrapped up in her friendship with Emilia and Cara, but there was something else not so easily attributed to their alliance; a sense of freedom. The shackles that once bound her to a life of conformity had been removed, allowing her to step out of her husband's shadow and write her own story. With absolute conviction, Lillian believed she was leading a battle against evil. Furthermore, she was one hundred percent committed to seeing it through to the bitter end, whatever, wherever and whenever that might be. So, one of the first things Lillian did when she returned home, after unpacking, showering and making a nice cup of tea, was to charge up the laptop and check out her Facebook page.

Having never been one for social media, as she used to find it a bewildering and embarrassing place filled with people airing their personal laundry in the guise of inspirational quotes, she had become something of a fan in recent months. It was Emilia who had alerted her to the animal rescue pages and once she found one or two, they all came tumbling onto Lillian's newsfeed. In one respect, it was distressing because there seemed to be no end to the abuse on the island, but it was also heartening to see so many groups working to stop it. At least half of the pages were managed by Cypriots, and though Lillian had only a smattering of Greek, she found the messages familiar; anger, anguish, appeals for help, pleas for foster homes and links for donations to cover shelter costs and vets' fees. But there was also something else that kept her looking at these sites, and it fell much closer to home.

Many of the pages that were devoted to the island's rescue shelters, as well as pages covering the Paphos region and its various municipalities and communities, had running threads about the Mayor of Dromos and his wife being glued inside their home. From what Lillian could tell from the amount of laughing emoji faces accompanying the comments, people seemed to be largely in favour of what had happened. However, as Lillian read through each updated post, her exhilaration was marginally spoiled by trepidation and the fear of being 'outed'. It was this fear, rather than ego, that kept Lillian returning to each and every post. She needed to be sure that nobody had worked out who was involved. So far, everyone was fairly wide of the mark with the most common suspects being the Cyprus Animal Liberation Front or bored kids. Not one person had suggested, as far as Lillian could see, that the culprits might be three foreign women old enough to know better.

As well as providing reassurance, the posts also revealed interesting gossip. Some of it involved the police being complicit in the nefarious activities of local hunters, most of it was about incompetent and corrupt politicians. The government veterinary service didn't come out of it too well either. One comment in particular caught Lillian's eye and it came from a friend of the mayor's wife.

Apparently, Mrs Georgiou was furious with her husband for cutting the water to the old dog pound, not least because she was the
patron of a small rescue shelter in her home village of Droushia.

"Yes, I saw that too," Emilia said when she phoned to welcome
Lillian home. "Unfortunately, all the forums and web pages are
turning quiet again, like they always do."

"What do you mean?" Lillian asked. "Like they always do?"

"It's always the same on social media; lots of comments and chit
chat, then nothing. People talk the talk until they get distracted
and forget. In my opinion, something seismic needs to happen to
have a lasting effect, and I doubt you want to go that far."

Lillian felt her throat constrict and her tummy tighten as she
contemplated Emilia's words. Despite an absolute conviction that
they were firmly on the right side of morality, if not the law, she
really didn't know how far she would be willing to take things. But
eventually she said, "I don't think we should give up quite yet. Do
you?"

On the other end of the line, Emilia whistled through her teeth.
"You surprise me, Lillian."

"I've surprised myself," Lillian confessed.

"Well, if you're serious, I suppose we should devise a plan. I've
already drawn up a list of targets."

"Actually, I've had my mind on possible targets too," Lillian
confided, almost in a whisper, and Emilia laughed.

"Sounds like it's time to hold another meeting of the board."

"Sounds like a good idea. Will you speak to Cara?"

"If I can get her away from that policeman."

"That's still going on then?"

"Going on and hotting up."

As the dawn light crept through a crack in the curtains, Cara
yawned and stretched, acting feline and touching canine. At her
feet, Cooper responded by doing what he always did when he
woke up; he noisily licked his genitals. To her right, resting against

her thigh, Peaches groaned in a way that reminded Cara of her old self, when she wasn't much of a morning person either. She smiled at the sound, opened her eyes and stretched a little more before turning her head to the left, which is when she stopped breathing.

Paralysed by the kind of confusion that had remained largely unknown to her for the best part of a decade, Cara found herself face-to-face with a man's back. It was broad, tanned and a little hairier than she was used to. It was also naked. Unable to stop herself, Cara looked down and gently lifted the covers to see how far this nakedness went. It went as far as the eye could see.

Cara didn't know whether to laugh, cry or be sick. She recalled food being consumed and alcohol being drunk and now the fog of sleep had lifted she also recalled sex. From what she could remember, it had been good sex. But even though she had recollected all of this, she remained in a state of complete and utter confusion. Cara lifted her head, glancing at Cooper and Peaches, unable to work out how they had got into the room because the last time she saw them she had kissed them goodnight in their own beds, which had been strategically placed downstairs.

To her left, Antoni stirred. Cara lay there, unmoving, because she wasn't sure of the modern-day protocol. Thankfully Cooper took control of the situation in his own inimitable fashion. Getting to his feet, he checked that everything was still where it ought to be before shaking himself down and making his way to the top of the bed. After using his wet nose to prod Cara's arm out of the way, he settled into the gap and sniffed the strange man in their bed. He then licked the man's ear.

"I assume that's a dog," said Antoni, his voice deeper after sleep.

Cara laughed. It sounded forced and unnatural to her ears. Antoni turned to face her, bringing a hand over the duvet to pat Cooper on the head.

"Morning," he greeted.

"Morning," Cara replied. She reached to her side to stroke Peaches, surprised to find her so relaxed as well as on the bed.

"Look, can I ask you something?"

Antoni gave her a warm, sleepy smile that started at his eyes. "Yes, we had sex."

"I know we had sex," Cara replied, too hastily to sound cool. "I wasn't that drunk."

"No?"

"No."

"In that case, yes, we had sex and yes, you were fantastic."

"Now, I know you're lying."

Antoni laughed, and Cara wasn't sure how to take it.

"I wasn't fantastic?"

Antoni paused, understanding he was sailing perilously close to dangerous waters and the next answer he gave might have a direct impact on the chances of him ever having sex with this woman again, fantastic or not. "Well, you had some good moves, nothing too crazy, you were clean, not too loud…"

"I was clean?"

"Yes, you're no dirty girl like Christina Aguilera."

"Christina Aguilera?"

"It's a song, *kori*."

"How do you even know that?"

"Hey, come on. I'm no dinosaur."

"I'm not saying you are. It's just, well, it doesn't seem like your kind of music."

"You are right. Christina Aguilera was my sister's favourite singer, when she was younger, before marriage and Church changed her."

"The sister with the fussy dog?"

"No, another one. I have four. And two brothers. See, there's much you don't know yet."

"True. I don't even know how my dogs got on the bed. I thought I left them downstairs."

"You did, and this will be a very heart-warming story for our kids," Antoni replied, gently laughing. Though Cara laughed with

him, she was blindsided by the casual mention of kids. Mediterranean men were very different from Englishmen. "As you know
we had sex," Antoni continued, unaware of the goings on in Cara's
head. "And it was good sex, fantastic sex, the best sex in the history of sex, and then you started crying. A lot. I swear, not since
APOEL won the football championship for the fifth-year running
have I seen such tears. Anyway, you were saying how you hated
yourself for abandoning your babies and for what – and this is a
quote from you – for a 'moment of pleasure'. Now, this was not
so nice to hear because I tried very hard last night to last for at
least two moments. Anyway, after all the boo hoo hoo, you fell
asleep, like a brick on the pillow. I tried to wake you, but you were
snoring. So, because I was lonely, I went downstairs for a glass of
water and I told your dogs they could sleep wherever they wanted
to. When I came back to the bed, you were snoring and spitting a
little from your mouth, but I guess the dogs must be used to this
because they came in and went to sleep on the bed next to you."

Antoni finished with a smile and Cara was both touched and
mortified. "I was crying? Seriously?"

"Like a baby. And spitting, like a footballer on the pitch."

"Oh God...."

The board of the Dromos Animal Liberation Front, otherwise
known as Cara, Emilia and Lillian, finally found time between
horses, cats and naked policemen, to reconvene three days after
Lillian's return to Cyprus. It was Emilia's suggestion that they
meet at the coffee shop off the main road in the village, saying it
was quiet enough to be heard, but busy enough not to be over-
heard and "though the coffee is weak, the banana cake is vegan." It
was also close enough for Emilia to walk to now she was limiting
the number of outings she made on her moped.

After drinks and cake were ordered, and polite conversation
about visits to the UK and sex with members of the local con-
stabulary had been exhausted, the three friends turned their at-

tention to more serious matters. It was Emilia who started the conversation and she did so hesitantly because even though Lillian had indicated she was onside, the jury was out on Cara.

"Guys, I know we started this journey as a bit of a joke, but maybe, I don't know how you feel, but maybe it should be…"

"Something more?" offered Cara, and Emilia nodded.

"Have to say, I'm with Emilia on this," Lillian said. "Animals are dying, some of them in horrific circumstances, and they will continue to die unless something major happens. What we have done so far is important, but I've come back from England to be met by the same stories of abuse that I left, including a dog tied to a dustbin, half garrotted. It's got to stop, and I think the only way to do this is to make them fear us."

Intrigued by Lillian's descent from pastel-wearing housewife to animal rights extremist, Cara asked her to go on.

After checking no one was eavesdropping, Lillian took a sip of her *café au lait* and inched herself forward. "So far, we have made a point, but it's not enough to invite change. Hunting dogs will still be dumped, puppies will be thrown in bins, cats will be run over and shot at and, to be frank, it's time someone put an end to this nightmare, once and for all. When we did that other stuff, the impact was almost immediate, and it felt like we had done something good. But as Emilia pointed out to me, people forget and they move on because outrage is a fire that needs feeding. I'm not saying we should do anything overly extreme, but we need to keep the momentum going. People need to worry that they could be the next target."

Lillian stopped talking and gave Emilia a shy smile. She then looked at Cara, noting the scepticism in her eyes.

"So, what are you suggesting?" Cara asked. "What is it you think we can possibly do to change things? We're just three women."

"We might be 'just three women', but the enemy doesn't know that," Lillian replied, more fiercely than she intended, and Emilia couldn't help but laugh. Despite her reservations, Cara joined in.

She wasn't being deliberately obstructive, but she was trying to be realistic. Animal abuse was a huge problem – in Cyprus, in the UK, in most parts of the world – and if the authorities couldn't put an end to it, or the various charities, societies or sab groups that devote their lives to raising awareness of the issue, she thought it highly unlikely that anything the three of them did would have any great impact either. But, of course, if everyone felt that way, nothing would change, and Lillian did have a point; the largest part of any battle was psychological. As it stood, no one knew who was behind the blood-coloured pool or the glued-up residence of the mayor, which meant that the perpetrators were not only faceless, but potentially a gang of knife-wielding psychopaths. Even the police hadn't a clue who they were looking for. Naturally, Cara had been careful not to talk too much in front of Antoni, but he had mentioned the cases he was working on, probably because she had written about the first one, and he was surprisingly honest about not having any idea who was to blame. The motive was obvious, but the culprits less so.

"I hear what you're saying," Cara said, "but I still don't see what we can do that will make any great difference."

"We could make a difference if we do more," Lillian said matter-of-factly. "We need to show people this is not a game, that it's a movement. It's retribution time."

"Oh, I like it." Emilia slapped her hands on the table. "And it's more or less what I've been thinking. I've even started a hit list."

"We can't kill people!" Cara said with alarm.

"Why not?"

"Emilia, stop it," Lillian warned, shooting her a look that surprised even her. "Okay," she continued, "I know this started out as a bit of a joke, despite the anger and sadness behind it, and perhaps you're right, Cara; maybe it's wrong to think of it as being anything more than that."

"You're not wrong, Lillian," Emilia interrupted, and she turned to look at Cara. "Is she?"

Cara sniffed, took a sip of her coffee and, after giving the question a second's thought, she shook her head. "No, you're not wrong, Lillian. If we can make even one bastard think again about what they're doing, we have to keep going. But seeing as you've had a little more time to think about this than me, do you have anything in mind?"

"Well, it's funny you should ask…" Lillian replied.

Chapter Twelve

Feeling slightly foolish, Lillian inspected herself in the bedroom mirror. It wasn't the plain white t-shirt that was the problem. No, that was fine. It was the mischief happening further down that was causing her anxiety. Lillian wasn't sure what had come over her, but if she had been one of those evangelical types, she would have put money on it being the devil.

Turning this way and that, she cast her eyes over the previously unworn Jasper Conran jeans that she'd bought on a whim, not realising they were cut with a flare. For years they had taken up space in the back of a wardrobe. That morning, she had taken a pair of scissors to them.

Lillian had seen plenty of women wearing cut-off denim shorts, women of all shapes, sizes and ages. She lived on a tourist island after all and people were a lot more body confident on holiday than they were at home. Yet despite being careful not to cut too high, as her buttocks seemed to drop an inch with each passing year, she still found it a hard look to take to after two decades of caramel culottes.

Lillian glanced at her feet, or rather at the sand-coloured military-style boots she had ordered off the internet back in 2013. Like the jeans, they were another impulse buy, purchased for hiking. However, after ordering them in May, they arrived in June, and by then, Cyprus was too hot to go rambling around, with too many snakes lurking in the long grass. So, after trying them on and finding them too heavy and butch looking, they were consigned to the back of the wardrobe where they had gathered dust, until today. Now, things had changed and so had Lillian's tastes; she was at war and she wanted to look the part, in 81°F heat.

Performing one more turn for the mirror, Lillian checked her
bum. "Come on, Lillian. You're not too bad for an old bird," she
told herself. After running her fingers through her thick auburn
hair, she strapped the Go-Pro to her head and walked purposefully
to the front door, picking up three bags of cat food along the way.

It was barely 9am, but Lillian could tell that the day was going
to be a scorcher. May was traditionally an odd month, with extreme weather conditions, but this year the rain had stopped early
and there was even a hint of August humidity sucking the oxygen
from the air. As ever, and even after all these years, the arrival of
summer always caught Lillian off guard and she felt a pang of sadness for the spring flowers losing their blush and the green grass
turning to hay before her eyes. While Lillian loved the summer as
much as the next expat spending their retirement by the pool, she
was also painfully aware of how hard the season was on the island's
unwanted animals that now had to add water to their daily hunt
for sustenance.

As Lillian approached her first feeding station, a patch of wasteland in a residential area that had not yet been sold to developers,
she was greeted by Scratchy, Tyson, Pickles and Dancer all mewing
for attention. Although she tried not to, Lillian had her favourites
and Scratchy was one of them. A friendly cat, to the point of intrusion, Scratchy had a voice like a rasp. Lillian was also very fond of
Dancer; a tri-colour ball of fluff who once disappeared for more
than a month, only to return missing half of her tail. Lillian didn't
like to think about where it might have got to. The main thing was
that Dancer had returned and though she came back thinner and
shorter of tail, she was alive.

As Lillian set down her bags to better pet the cats that had come
to welcome her, a spin of wheels sent them running for the bushes.
Turning on her heels in the nick of time to jump out of the way
of a blue Rav 4, Lillian cursed herself for not being more vigilant.
Also, with her back turned, she had failed to catch the moment on
camera. She walked to the middle of the road, stood tall, stared

at the bumper of the car now fading from view, clasped her hands together, lifted them to eye level, made the shape of a gun and cocked her right thumb.

"One of these days, you nasty, little man," she muttered. Then, feeling the phone vibrate in the pocket of her denim hot pants, Lillian lowered her 'weapon' to answer it.

"Morning," she said tensely. "What? No. I'm fine. Don't worry. Are you there already? OK, I'll be with you in ten if you can hang on. I've something to ask you."

Emilia tried to blink away her tears, but it was a battle she was losing as she looked into Adonis's wary chocolate eyes.

"I know, it doesn't look pretty, but we need to do this," Julia said softly. "It should help."

Emilia nodded. She understood the reasoning behind the contraption Julia had fixed around her horse's throat, but it looked more like a medieval torture device than a solution. Specifically designed for horses that windsuck, an aluminium clasp, shaped like a nutcracker, rested against Adonis's throat, held in place by a leather strap that sat behind his ears. He would no longer be able to raise his head and open his throat to swallow huge gulps of air, but with his neck lowered and relaxed he would be able to breathe and feed normally.

"You'd think there might be something less brutal looking," Emilia said.

"It may look brutal, but it's not. And if it saves your boy's life…"

"I know. I know." Emilia nodded. She had done her reading. She knew the score. Even so, she turned her head away so neither Julia nor Adonis could see her tears fall.

Despite everything they had tried – from dietary supplements to salt licks, distraction toys and paraffin oil – Adonis still windsucked and he still suffered from colic, far more than most other horses. Colic was an umbrella term for pretty much all equine stomach upsets, but Julia had determined that Adonis's weakness was gas colic. This was why the pain eased after passing wind, and why his windsucking would not be helping.

"Sadly, we don't know what your boy has been through," Julia told her. "He could have been taken from his mother too early and placed in the highly stressful environment of a racing yard where he may have been pumped full of steroids and crap before being dumped because he failed to make the grade for whatever reason. You know, it's not uncommon for ex-racers to be riddled with ulcers brought on by the stress of their formative years. People really have no idea, or they simply don't care. These animals are super sensitive."

"I just want him to be better."

"I know you do, and hopefully he will be, Emilia. But for now, do the boy a big favour and dry those tears. Stop acting like it's the end of the world. With any luck it will be the start of a new one for little Adonis."

Because Julia was right, Emilia bit her tongue and wiped her eyes. Even so, she couldn't stop the despair from eating her insides and once Julia had disappeared, Emilia took off the collar to better groom her horse.

"Well, this is your life now, baby," she whispered into his warm neck. "I'm sorry to do this, but we are not so perfect you and me. We both need a little help here and there. But I tell you, nobody could love you more. Me and you, Boo. Against the world."

Cara had never visited a junk yard before and she found it rather depressing. Everywhere she looked she saw the metal carcasses of Audis, VWs, BMWs, Nissans, Toyotas and Suzukis. Common sense told her they were knackered old machines that had served their purpose, but Cara loved her Puma, and because there was a touch of anthropomorphism to many of her dealings with inanimate objects, she felt sad for the unwanted cars surrounding her that must have once been someone's pride and joy. When she considered all the money she had spent on her own car over the years, Cara knew the cash might have been better spent on buying a new one, but she had refused to give up on the Puma because the Puma had never given up on her. She couldn't bear the thought of strange hands dismantling her, piece by piece, until there was nothing left but an oil stain of betrayal.

When she had recently revealed her fears that the old girl might not make it through her next MOT, Antoni had laughed. "It's just a car," he said, but he was badly wrong about that. The Puma was part of her. After she shut up her heart, she drove that car all the way through Europe to the port of Patras in the northern Peloponnese and onto a ferry destined for Cyprus. It was a nonsensical expense, but it didn't matter. The Puma had been present during some of the most turbulent moments in her life and though she wasn't acutely conscious of the fact, she was aware there was a lot of Tom invested in the car. Even now, when she looked over to the passenger seat – if it wasn't occupied by Cooper or Peaches – she often saw him sat there, his face pale and tense as he complained about her driving.

"You should fit two off-road tyres the amount of time you spend on the verge," he once grumbled, and she had laughed because she thought he was being funny.

"*Boro na sas voithiso?*"

Cara span around to find a portly Greek man staring at her. He was dressed in dirty overalls, cleaning his hands with an oily rag, which struck Cara as a bizarrely ineffectual thing to do, but what did she know about the motor industry.

"Do you speak English?" she asked with an apologetic shrug.

"*Ligo.* A little," the man responded, which was enough for Cara who quietly pocketed the shopping list Emilia had written in Greek.

"What you want?" the man asked. "You want engine, gearbox, pump, alternator, windscreen, seat, light, what?"

"Do you have nuts and bolts?"

"Like screw?"

"Well, I guess so," she confirmed. Without thinking, she held out her index finger and made a circle of her thumb and other index finger to illustrate a bolt screwing into place. The man raised his eyebrows.

"I know what you want," he said, chuckling. "*Ela!* Come!"

As Cara followed, her cheeks burning, she hoped the man really did understand what she wanted, and not what she had possibly mimed as wanting.

"I can't thank you enough for this," Lillian told Janet.

The older woman waved her away in the usual gruff manner that belied a gentler soul. "If there's anything else…" she said, leaving the sentence unfinished before hobbling away to her disability buggy.

"No, you've done enough," Lillian replied as she followed, tugging self-consciously at the bottom of her denim cut-offs.

Before boarding her buggy, Janet paused to stare at Lillian, as if seeing her for the first time. "I don't know what you're up to," she said, "and it's probably best that I don't, but whatever it is, I wish you well, Lillian. Sincerely."

Caught off guard, Lillian felt strangely moved by Janet's support. As she roared away – her disability buggy colliding with the kerb as she hit a top speed of 4mph – Lillian waved after her. Not that Janet saw because she didn't look back.

After checking the water trays were full for the cats, Lillian gathered her empty bags, turned on her GoPro and headed towards Zorba's restaurant. As she walked, she ran through the list of things that needed to be done. She had gathered the majority of Emilia's bits and bobs, apart from the cushion stuffing, but that was easily sorted with a trip to the charity shop on the way home. She could drop them off later, once Emilia had finished work. Everything else she expected to find at Home Depot later that afternoon.

In her pocket, the phone vibrated with a message from Cara.

"Nuts & bolts sorted & got utility chain & huge fuck off lock!

Ready for biz this end!"

Lillian smiled, despite the language. "Got sewing stuff for Emilia. Will pop by DIY later. Excited! LOL!"

Returning the phone to the pocket of her cut-off jeans, Lillian looked up to find she was almost at the front steps of Zorba's Taverna. She took the side path to the back of the restaurant. The kitchen door was open and a young Romanian boy, who was possibly the dishwasher, was smoking outside.

"Hello, you come for food for cat?" he asked with a smile as he stubbed his cigarette out beneath a pair of worn trainers.

"If you have some that would be lovely," Lillian replied. "But I've actually come to drop some things off for Emilia."

"Emilia?"

"Yes, if that's all right."

"Emilia – black hair, tattoos, bad mouth?" the young man asked, and Lillian laughed at the basic, but accurate description of her friend.

"Yes, that's the one."

"But this girl is gone," the boy said, looking puzzled. "Finished. No work here no more."

"Are you sure? Did something happen?"

"For sure, something always happens when people lose job." The young man laughed. "But me, I don't know what. Long time she is gone now. But Savvas forever kicking people to the street."

"What do you mean 'long time'?"

"One month, maybe more. Yes, long time she not work here. OK, stay one minute. I find the food for cats."

As the young man disappeared, Lillian reached for her phone before changing her mind. If Emilia had wanted her to know she had left Zorba's she would have mentioned it by now, which meant Emilia's employment status was none of Lillian's business until her friend decided it was.

That evening, as Emilia finished her sewing and Lillian stared at the

moon pondering the meaning of life and whether she should take
a pair of scissors to the Calvin Kleins in her closet, Cara enjoyed a
sweet and sexually-charged encounter with Antoni. She had needed the distraction, he was keen to have sex, and as they lay in the
dark, their naked bodies radiating heat and happiness, Cara became aware that her initial attraction was transforming into something deeper. She knew this because she felt it in the very core of
her being, the place where love tugs at the gut and blocks the mind
of all other thoughts. She also knew it because he had more or less
told her this was the case.

It happened a little after midnight. Antoni had pulled on his
pants to go downstairs and bring up the dogs. As they all settled
into their various positions – Cooper at Cara's feet, Peaches by
Cara's side and Cara nestled on top of Antoni's left arm – the two
of them began talking about life and love and some of the highs and
lows that tend to accompany such experiences. Antoni explained
how he used to blame work for his broken marriage when in fact
the splinters had always been there. He and Elena had married
young and though their love was as real as it could be between
kids, they grew older in different ways, "like branches of a tree
moving further apart with every new year." When Cara heard the
sadness in his voice, she sympathised. It wasn't easy, giving up on
love, but sometimes there was no other choice, and to illustrate
that she revealed a little more than she had previously done about
her relationship with Tom and how she had lost herself in his life
before leaving him to reclaim her own.

"Do you still love him?" Antoni asked gently, and Cara had
shrugged.

"There will always be a part of me that loves him, but I don't
want to be with him. Not now. That ship has sailed," she said. It
was an honest response, or as honest as she was prepared to be at
that point. Of course, the full story was more selfish; she couldn't
forgive Tom for falling in love again. A few years ago, Cara had followed a trail of Facebook posts to their inevitable conclusion. De-

spite three years having passed since they split, when Cara found out just how far Tom had moved on, a part of her died that day. She no longer saw Tom as more than he was. He wasn't a movie star hero. He was a man; a man who had once loved her, before deciding to love somebody else.

"Tom was no Heathcliff," Cara told Antoni, and because Antoni had no idea what she was on about, and she rightly assumed he was about to ask, she changed the subject. "So, what made you give up the big city?" she asked breezily only to feel Antoni's body tense beneath her. Cara looked into his face to find the moonlight caught in his eyes. He looked more beautiful than she had ever seen him and she almost told him so.

"There's too much shit in the big city. I'd had enough," Antoni replied. He then glanced down to see the light of the moon dancing across Cara's cheeks and he wondered whether he should tell her how beautiful she looked. Before he had a chance to make up his mind, she pressed him on 'the shit' he had experienced and the moment was lost.

"It's true that the worst crimes don't always happen in the biggest cities, but there are more of them, statistically, and after a while it starts to break the man inside of you," he said. "Over time, you become less human. You begin to operate like a machine. Maybe it's a safety catch – I mean, how much shit can one mind take – but in the end it's a false kind of helmet to wear because the crap still gets inside your head and it sits there until it's ready to come out and fuck you up. I've seen it happen to a lot of colleagues over the years and I assumed it might happen to me one day. All it takes is one case, and that one case for me involved a baby girl who was maybe four or five days old, no more than that. Her body was found on a rubbish tip, thrown away in a plastic bag."

Cara gasped. Before she could think of anything to say, Antoni kissed the top of her head and continued.

"I was one of the officers assigned to the case and we were told that the injuries she had sustained might have occurred before or after her death, it was hard to say because of where she was found. But I knew from the moment I saw her that this was one death too many for me. I was haunted by the tiny face of this baby girl and so I asked to be transferred at the earliest opportunity to somewhere quiet. I'd done all the murders, incest cases and gangland attacks that my stomach could cope with. The baby was the last straw. Of course, it wasn't just the death of the child I couldn't accept, it was all the other shit that would come out during the investigation; all the pain, the torment and tears. Babies don't just die and get thrown away. Somewhere there would be a mother battling her own private hell, whatever the truth. And I'm sure the problems Elena had trying to keep a baby also played their part in my decision to leave, but the baby was the catalyst. That was the moment I said I was done with the big city. It was slowly killing me."

As he finished, Cara knew she had no words that might offer some comfort, so instead she stretched her neck and reached for his lips.

The next morning when they woke up, still wrapped in each other's arms, there was a new level of intimacy between them, and though nothing was said openly, the change was apparent when they headed downstairs for breakfast. It was in the casual stroke of an arm and the gentle kiss on the head as plates were put on the table and coffee was poured into mugs. There was a new freedom to their movement and it felt good, to both of them.

Antoni left the kitchen to wait for his vegan breakfast at the dining table, picking up a magazine on the way. As he flicked through the pages, his attention was caught by an image of the Kaliteros Hotel and he smiled, realising this must be the magazine interview that had triggered his romance with Cara. It was strange to think that only a couple of months had passed since that first meeting – their intimacy made it feel like a lifetime ago – and he was intrigued to see what Cara had written about him.

The article was short, only 300 words or so, which surprised him as he'd written longer shopping lists, but there was an accurate quote from him near the top of the piece, which was always a relief when dealing with the media. However, his relief quickly turned to confusion as he read on.

"Police have yet to confirm whether the incident is linked to the death of the dog even though a paw print drawn at the side of the pool might suggest that it is."

Adonis took a deep breath. The statement was accurate enough, but he hadn't actually revealed the paw print detail at that point of the investigation. It was only later, when the Mayor of Dromos went bleating to the media about the message left on his door, that he let the information regarding the other paw print be generally circulated.

Closing the magazine, Antoni looked towards the kitchen where Cara was busy doing something with a frying pan. Perhaps sensing him staring, she turned around and flashed him a kilowatt smile that he couldn't fail to respond to. Shaking his head, he quietly laughed to himself thinking the police force had made him an unduly suspicious man.

Chapter Thirteen

"Would you ever move back home?" Lillian asked as they waited for a car's tail lights to fade in the distance.

"Why? Are you thinking of returning?" Cara replied.

"Not on your life." Lillian laughed before raising a perfectly shaped eyebrow. "I have to say, that looks a little weird from here."

Cara glanced at the effigy, face down on her lap.

"It's better than looking at his boss-eyed face. He's creeping me out." Cara lifted the dummy to show Emilia's uneven needlework. Under a khaki cap, glued onto a pillow case filled with cushion stuffing, Emilia had drawn a bulbous nose and a wide, sneering mouth in black felt tip pen. Large grey buttons represented the eyes, but they were hopelessly askew.

"I was tired," Emilia protested from the front passenger seat of Lillian's car. "Nobody said anything about the dummy having to look like Brad Pitt."

"Nobody said it had to look like Marty Feldman either," Lillian teased, but the joke was lost on Emilia who had never heard of the British actor.

"So, come on. Would either of you move back home? I'm curious because I read a Facebook post today about a couple leaving Cyprus because, and I quote, the sense of animal care is barbaric and Cyprus is, apparently, not a country they want their souls associated with."

"And the UK has such a great record on animal welfare, doesn't it," Cara replied. "Has nobody heard of the RSPCA taking people to court for abusing animals? Or of slaughterhouse workers stubbing cigarettes out on the bodies of terrified pigs? Or dairy farmers urinating on young calves? As for that quaint English sport of fox hunting and government-sanctioned badger culls. Man, give me strength…"

"You think you've got it bad? I'm from Romania," Emilia told her. "We don't give a shit about the Roma, let alone animals."

"So, that will be a 'no', then? That you're both staying put?" Lillian asked with a smile.

"Well, I'd never say never, but I can't see me going back," Cara replied. "Of course, you don't know what might happen in the future, but at the moment I'm happy where I am. Besides, I'm not sure I'd cope with the British weather anymore. I've grown soft."

"Oh, me too," Lillian sympathised. "When we first moved here, I was wearing t-shirts in February, now I'm in two jumpers." She looked across to Emilia. "What about you? Would you go back to Romania?"

Emilia shook her head. "It will never happen," she said with absolute certainty. "I have Adonis now. How could I afford to take him with me? And you know I would never leave him. Even when he dies, I will stay here because my heart will be in the ground with him. No, this is it for me. I will live on this island until I breathe my very last breath."

In the car, there was a second or two of silence.

"Well, this has taken a more sombre turn than anticipated," Lillian confessed. To her relief, Emilia smiled and even laughed a little.

"I'm just tired," she apologised. "And as you both know I can be dark when tired."

"Then let's wake you up and get this show on the road," Cara said cheerfully, nodding at the road ahead of them which was now free of traffic.

"Yes, let's get going," Lillian agreed. "All for one..."

"... and one for dogs!" Cara and Emilia finished.

They left Lillian's car 100 yards or so down a beaten track, next to a discarded tractor tyre, and walked to the edge of a village called Sparmos. Thanks to Janet being unlikely pals with the animal liberation lot, they quickly found what they were looking for;

a green bin on the turning into the village where, some days earlier, a young hunting dog had been tied up and abandoned, half-
starved and slowly dying from a huge gash to its throat. Right now,
the dog was clinging to life, against the odds, because someone
not only took pity on her but also took her to a vet. The rescuers
were quietly hopeful, and their supporters quickly rallied round
to pay for the veterinary costs. But there was little chance that the
psycho responsible would ever be brought to justice, and this was
something a lot of people were very angry about.

"Have you got the rope?" Cara asked Lillian. She nodded and
reached into her bag.

Carefully putting the effigy into place, Cara looped the rope
around its 'neck', which hadn't been completely attached to the
head, as Emilia had only sewn it onto the back of the 'body', pur-
posely leaving the front open, to look like someone had taken a
knife to it.

"Right, he's all yours," Cara told Emilia.

She stepped forward clutching a large bottle of ketchup, the
contents of which she liberally applied to the 'neck' of the effigy
until it dripped down the camouflage clothing Cara had acquired
from an army store during her trip to Limassol. The three women
then stepped back to admire their handiwork.

There were no street lights to bring out the colour of the scene,
so the ketchup resembled sticky tar in the moonlight. In the cold
light of day, however, they hoped it would look like blood which,
if they were lucky, might attract flies and possibly ants to crank up
the horror of the scene.

"What about the sign?" Lillian asked.

"Prop it against the body, perhaps facing the main road?" suggested Emilia and, as everyone agreed that would reach the widest
audience, she took the sign and placed it next to the effigy. The
words were written in Greek and painted red, next to a paw print
in black. They warned, "We will find you."

"Nice one," Cara said smiling.

The three friends briefly hugged before making their way back to the car where Lillian had a flask of coffee and some foil wrapped vegan cheese snacks waiting. It was going to be a long night.

As 2.30 approached, Lillian pulled up at the top of a residential street, killed the engine and turned off the lights. She then coasted down the road before applying the brakes in front of a tired old bungalow.

The property was bordered by chicken wire fencing and a wall of weeds. A little to the right of the building was a badly rusting oil drum, laid on its side with an old dog sleeping inside of it, lying on a blanket that had once belonged to Lillian.

"What if he barks?" Cara whispered.

"Hopefully he won't. He kind of knows me, but just in case I've brought something with me." With a wink, Lillian leaned over Emilia to reach into the glove compartment where she pulled out something wrapped in tin foil.

"You've made him a vegan cheese sandwich?" Cara asked.

"Steak," Lillian replied. "Sorry."

"Fair enough," Cara responded. "I guess he's not in the best position to make an ethical lifestyle choice."

"I'm sure he'll come around to tofu when he's free," said Lillian.

"Do you think?"

"Almost certainly. I mean, who wouldn't?"

"Have you ever tasted tofu?" Emilia asked, and even the vegan among them had to admit that she hadn't. "It's like eating a sponge. Trust me, no dog will ever come around to tofu."

"Dogs have been known to eat sponges," replied Cara. "And if my experience is anything to go by, they're also partial to freshly washed knickers, socks and tea towels."

"This is why I prefer cats," said Lillian. "You don't get cats after your knickers. Actually, at my age you don't get anyone after your knickers."

"Lillian!" whispered Cara.

Emilia shook her head. She then pulled down her balaclava and reached for the door handle. "Let's do this," she said.

With a quick glance up and down the street, the three women crept through the front gate armed with their supplies. As they were in a residential area with street lighting, they also came armed with a plan, allowing them to get the job done with little need for chatter, not that it would matter if the dog went batshit crazy on their approach.

As they tiptoed past the house, Old Boy stirred and Lillian lifted her ski mask to show her face and whisper a greeting. The dog's large tail thumped heavily against the confines of the only home he had ever known and all three women were relieved when that was as loud as he got. Having worked out their roles beforehand they got moving. Lillian took the bolt cutters she had bought from Home Depot and after a little more effort than she had envisaged, she freed the dog from the tree he was chained to. Looking, slightly perplexed, but not unhappy with this development, Old Boy followed Lillian down the driveway, past his owner's Mercedes-Benz, through the gate and onto the backseat of her less ostentatious Pajero. Meanwhile, Emilia emptied the dog's food bowl and tipped out the water. She refilled one bowl with a carton of engine oil and the other with the nuts and bolts Cara had bought from the scrap yard. To her left, Cara took the heavy-duty chain hanging over her shoulder and carefully threaded it under and over the front wheel drive shaft of the Mercedes. She then attached the chain to the tree with a hefty padlock. Next, she filled the keyhole with superglue left over from the job on the mayor's house. Once she was done, she looked over at Emilia who was already walking away. By the time Cara caught up, Emilia was putting the finishing touches to their signature calling card on the pillar by the gate.

"Done," Cara whispered.

"Me too," Emilia whispered back, and they headed for Lillian's car.

As Lillian released the handbrake to freewheel further down the road, Cara glanced at the passenger by her side. His black and white head was as big as a basketball and his neck was hairless and raw. He smelled a little ripe, but his eyes were bright and beautiful.

"He's a big bugger, isn't he?" Cara remarked, and the other two laughed, mainly as a way to release the tension stretching their nerves.

Lillian turned the key in the ignition, switched on the lights and they drove away.

"Well, I don't think anyone saw us," she said.

"Not that I noticed," Emilia replied.

"Me neither," Cara added.

But someone had noticed, and behind the black windows of the house opposite Old Boy's former place of unhappy residence, an elderly woman wiped the tears from her eyes with the hem of her nightdress.

For years, Eirini Panagi had suffered nightmares thinking about the poor dog across the road. She had called the government vet on numerous occasions, with no result, and she had even tried to reason with the owner. But she was a pensioner now and though her children lived nearby, she was mostly on her own and sometimes that made her scared to cause too much of a fuss. Life was hard enough. So instead, she had prayed for help to arrive, and that night, as she battled to find sleep through the fog of loneliness that had descended on her since the death of her husband, she heard a car pull up followed by muffled footsteps. Alarmed by the kind of thoughts that only come at night, she forced herself out of bed to take a look, very nearly screaming at the sight of three masked figures lurking in the street. By the time it took her to find her phone, she returned to the window to see one of the figures leading the old dog away. His tail was wagging and her fears turned first to disbelief and then joy.

"So, angels don't always have wings," she whispered as she made the mark of the cross on her chest.

Parked in a tree-lined street, Emilia considered their options before putting them to the other two women, as well as a rather baf-
fled looking mastiff-cross.

"If the car is locked and alarmed, the game is up," she said.

"So, let's do the restaurant first, followed by the front of the
house, and then we can be ready to run if there is an alarm and it
goes off," Cara suggested.

"Makes sense to me," Lillian agreed.

"And what about him?" Cara asked, looking at the huge head of
their guest who was currently blocking much of her view. Lillian
winked before reaching into the glove box to produce a rather
fine-looking bone wrapped in an orange plastic bag.

"Christ, it's like a mini abattoir in there," observed Cara.

"Well, don't sign a petition about it, that's the last of the dead
animals," Lillian joked, "and it should keep him busy for a while."

Handing the bone over, Lillian smiled as Old Boy settled into
the back seat to eat, quite unfazed by the strange turn his life had
taken.

After checking the coast was clear, the three women grabbed
their bags and pulled down their masks before walking around the
corner towards the Thalassa Taverna. The restaurant was located
in Paphos; a town-sized city popular with tourists who liked their
holidays a little more sedate than the ecstasy-charged clubbers of
Ayia Napa. Situated on the outskirts of the old town, far from the
bright lights of Bar Street, the restaurant was a modern-looking
building set back from the main road. However, an earlier recce by
Lillian had led to a more traditional discovery – the family quarters were behind the premises – which made planning an assault
on the man who liked to cook up endangered songbirds that much
easier.

Despite a thorough internet search, Emilia had been unable to
locate the home of Stelios Loizou, the man arrested by police for
illegal bird trapping, but tonight was not only about retribution,
but about sending a message; a message to Stelios and every other

heartless bastard on the island who considered torture, neglect and abuse against another sentient being an acceptable form of conduct.

"Right," Emilia said as they prepared to go in. "Marigolds on."

With their hands protected by rubber gloves, they took out their paint pots and brushes and got busy. First, Emilia painted the inside door handle of the restaurant, followed by the steps leading to the door. They had chosen 'Grey' for this section as it was the closest colour to concrete. Once a very thick coating had been applied to the entrance of the restaurant, they picked up their tools and moved to the back of the taverna where they wordlessly got to work painting a metre square section of the path immediately in front of the house. This was in 'Brick Red'. Again, they didn't spare the contents of the paint pot. Once done, they all stopped in front of the restaurant owner's car. It was nothing fancy, a Renault Megane, but it was black and that helped.

The three friends looked at each other and with a brief nod to show they were ready, Lillian and Emilia took off their marigolds and deposited them in a bin liner, along with their empty paint pots and dirty brushes. Before returning to the car, Emilia drew their calling card on the Perspex menu display at the front of the restaurant.

Behind the restaurant, Cara stood stock still for a few minutes in order to give her friends time to get back to the car. Although she tried to stay calm, the blood was pounding so hard in her ears she could hardly hear herself think. With a deep breath, and a slow count to three, she reached for the door handle of the Megane. To her utter amazement, the door opened with a small click, and no alarm.

"Oh, my bloody God," she whispered, half in prayer and half in relief. Quickly getting to work, Cara applied what was left of the paint to the underside of the steering wheel and then, after gently pushing the door closed, she applied the last of it to the underside of the driver's door handle. Once finished, she forced herself to walk calmly back to Lillian's car even though every sinew in her body was urging her to run.

Finally reaching the others, Cara took off her gloves and discarded them in the waiting bin liner along with the paint pot and brush she carried, all of which she then threw in the boot of the car. Easing herself into the backseat with Old Boy, she was surprised to find he was still chewing his bone.

"He's savouring that," she said.

"It's almost like he's tormenting you" Emilia replied.

"Typical man."

"Handsome man," Lillian said, smiling. And maybe because she had been the one to ask the others to save him, and beauty was in the eye of the beholder after all, neither Cara or Emilia said a word.

"You know what? I am so proud of us!" Lillian half squealed as she started the car, being careful to respect the speed limit as she drove away. Though they were less high-pitched about their involvement, both Emilia and Cara agreed.

After leaving the old town, Lillian stopped at a small car park by the city's one and only cinema where Cara had left her own vehicle some hours earlier. As she got out, she wished her friends 'good luck'.

"Drive safely and call me when you can," she said.

"*Kalinikta*, comrade," Emilia replied with a salute.

"Goodnight, Cara," Lillian responded as she rolled her eyes at Emilia. She might be a criminal and an animal rights extremist, but she was very far from being a communist.

Chapter Fourteen

A few kilometres past Protaras, at the eastern end of the island, Lillian sat on a small stony beach next to the imposing form of Old Boy. Having changed out of her black clothes, she wore a green t-shirt and brown shorts, and a gentle wind played with her auburn hair. In the past few hours, Old Boy had also undergone something of a transformation; the heavy chain was missing from his neck and Sudocrem had been liberally applied to the calloused skin that told the story of his life-long confinement.

"I'm sorry, Old Boy," Lillian said quietly, gazing ahead, her eyes focussed on a distant point out to sea. "I'm sorry you had to live the life you did. I'm sorry for the pain you suffered. I'm sorry for the loneliness and the isolation and the prison that you had to en-dure. But most of all, I'm sorry I didn't save you sooner."

As a tear rolled down Lillian's cheek, she turned to look at the dog. She didn't expect a reply or any form of absolution, but she hoped he understood. In her mind's eye she imagined his cold, wet nose pressed against her cheek; a sign that he not only understood, but that he also forgave her. And maybe he did, but there was no cold, wet nose to tell her such a thing. Instead, Old Boy yawned, got unsteadily to his feet and wandered away to take a dump on a nearby rock. When business was concluded, he wandered back, sniffed at her feet and lay down beside her. For Lillian, that was enough. How could it not be?

From the car, Emilia watched the scene unfold. She looked in-side Lillian's Tardis-like glove compartment for a bag she might use to clean up the dog's mess once their goodbyes were done. Despite the now sweltering heat, Emilia hadn't joined Lillian on the beach because it didn't seem her place to do so. This was Lil-lian's moment. She had been the one to suggest they free the dog, she had been the one to invest her time, concern and blanket in the boy and Emilia thought the least she deserved was a quiet moment with him before he was handed over to the rescue shelter that had agreed to take him. According to Lillian's contact there, helpfully supplied by Janet, the charity was more than happy to provide Old Boy with a space – no questions asked – but as luck would have it, and within hours of the arrangement being made, a volunteer at the shelter decided to offer the dog a home for the last few years of his life. It would be a proper home, in a loving environment with a soft bed and a roof over his head, and all those days spent in the searing heat, relentless rain and bitter cold would be a thing of the past. It had been a long time coming, and Emilia hated to think how many years the poor dog had needed to wait, but he was about to get the life he deserved. A few hours later, when Inspector Antoni Giagkos was asked to visit Old Boy's former owner, he left feeling much the same way.

Pulling up outside the bungalow, accompanied by Special Constable Michalis Georgiou, the first thing Antoni noticed was a very irate man shouting into his phone. The second thing he noticed was a dog paw drawn on one of the pillars at the front gate. It was something that initially confused him because he had presumed that he was attending a prank involving someone's car. He failed to see how it might be an animal rights issue. When Antoni pointed out the paw print to the irate man, it came as a surprise to him because he hadn't yet seen it, possibly because he was too busy being irate. His temper wasn't eased any when he invited the police officers into his garden to inspect the scene of the crime.

Trying to keep his face a mask of professional gravity, Antoni looked at what was a very nice Mercedes-Benz C-Class attached to a tree. He noted that the chain used was incredibly heavy and would require more than a bolt cutter to get through it. Putting on a pair of gloves, Antoni bent down to pick up a large padlock fixed to the chain. The key had been glued into the lock. Glancing around, he noted the rusting oil drum nearby, laid on its side with an opening so brittle and ragged it looked like a death trap. Inside, there was a worn blanket that might once have been blue. Next to the drum were two bowls, one of which appeared to be filled with nuts and bolts while the other was filled to the brim with some kind of oil.

"Do you have a dog?" Antoni asked the man.

"I did have. It was here when I went to bed last night. Now, it's gone."

"Was it chained to the tree, perhaps?"

"It's a guard dog."

"But now your guard dog is stolen and your car has taken its place. Interesting."

The irate man, pulled at his thick mop of hair in undisguised frustration. "It's not interesting," he railed. "It's criminal! I swear on all that is holy that if my car is damaged in anyway, I'll have the necks of those bastards."

"So, you think there's more than one bastard involved?" Antoni asked calmly.

"How am I supposed to know? You're the policeman. You work it out."

Antoni smiled and pointed at the two bowls by the oil drum. "Well, at least your car was given some supper last night."

"You think this is funny?" The man stopped pacing to stare at Antoni. "You think this is some kind of joke?"

"Well, it's quite funny," Antoni replied and having grown tired of the man's tone, he started to walk away. "Michalis, take some details from this guy."

Without another word, Antoni headed for the front gate. Reaching the road, he looked around to investigate the possibility of potential witnesses and noticed an elderly lady watching him from the house opposite. She was stood in an upstairs window and though he couldn't be sure, given the light and the distance, she appeared to be laughing. Just as he was about to walk over and introduce himself, the two-way radio fixed to his chest crackled into action. The Paphos police were investigating an incident he might be interested in.

"Why? What is it?" he asked.

"The details are still coming in," Maria in Control informed him, "but we're told it involves a restaurant owner who was caught with a dozen dead songbirds in his kitchen. A calling card was left on the premises."

"A dog's paw print?"

"A dog's paw print."

It was an emotional parting for Lillian as she kissed Old Boy good-bye and though the dog didn't say anything, neither did he mark the occasion by taking a dump. Instead, he took all the hugs with good grace, his eyes as bright and wide as a kid at Christmas waiting for the next surprise to be revealed.

Lillian wiped her eyes with the heel of her palm, unsure why she was so tearful, though she suspected it might have something to do with her life in general. Conscious that now was not the time or place to open that Pandora's Box, she took a deep breath, stood tall and shook the emotion from her fingertips so she might fully enjoy the sight of Old Boy padding over a gravel car park to jump into the back of a waiting jeep, helped with a push from a young Cypriot man with dreadlocks and a young Cypriot girl wearing tassels on her boots.

"Gotta love those hippies," Emilia said as she watched them go.

"Oh, I do," Lillian replied.

After expressing their gratitude for the umpteenth time to the shelter's manager, they returned to the car and headed for the A3 to Larnaca. Despite the lack of sleep, having only grabbed an hour or two in the car while waiting for the day to reach an acceptable hour before arriving at the shelter, neither Lillian nor Emilia felt particularly tired. In Lillian's case, it was most likely adrenalin that kept her going. In Emilia's, it might have been the caffeine pills she had been popping since the previous evening.

"Did you ever think, a year ago, that you'd be smuggling dogs across the island?" Emilia asked as they joined the highway, and Lillian laughed long and hard.

"A year ago, I would have thought twice about even touching a dog."

"You're kidding me," Emilia replied, genuinely perplexed before remembering Derek's allergy. "Is your husband that bad?"

"The reactions can be severe," Lillian admitted. "That's why I've never had pets in the house. The cats don't seem to affect him as much, though I take care to wash and change before I go touching everything in the house. But the dogs..."

"So, what changed?" Emilia asked. "How come you're willing to touch dogs now? Did Derek find a cure?"

"He found something, but I'm not sure I'd call it a cure," Lillian replied dryly before laughing away the comment. "Derek's not home as much as he used to be, thanks to the change in his shifts, so there's plenty of time to clean up before he arrives. Anyway, enough about him and his silly allergies, how much further is this place we're going to?"

"About ten kilometres or so," Emilia replied, oblivious to Lillian's abrupt change of topic. "There should be a turning on the left, just after the airport road."

"Well, that doesn't sound too complicated."

"I'm told it's pretty easy to find."

"Even so, we best keep our eyes open and our minds on the job, although I have to say Emilia, I do hope you're wrong about this place."

"Me too."

Despite the increase in criminal activity committed by Antoni's unknown gang of extremists, he had to admit that he hadn't had cause to laugh so much in a long while. Although they had added trespassing and theft to their list of somewhat random misdemeanours, they had done it with humour, right down to the feeding bowls left for the Mercedes they had tied to a tree. However, this latest act of, what he assumed was, vigilante-style justice, had to be his favourite so far.

He looked at Nikos Demetriades who was stood in front of him in stunned silence. The apoplexy of rage that had first taken him had subsided and he was quiet – quiet and sticky.

Stood in a pair of slippers because his shoes were currently stuck in a shallow pool of anti-climb paint left at the threshold of his front door, his fingers were black and getting harder to move and his hair was stood on end after he had accidentally rubbed his head in anger and frustration.

"Are you OK?" Antoni asked.

"Do I look OK to you?" the restaurant owner replied.

Antoni tried not to smile, but the guy wasn't making it easy.

"Tell me," he said, "weren't you recently arrested with several pans of songbirds on the stove?"

"You know I was."

"And do you not think this might be related?"

"You think I'm the victim of twitchers?" Demetriades asked incredulously.

"Perhaps," Antoni replied, casually bending down to look at the underside of the man's car handle that had also been liberally daubed with anti-climb paint. "From what I understand, and my knowledge in this field is not extensive, but from what I understand poachers often use lime sticks to trap these birds, don't they?"

"I believe so, yes."

"And lime sticks basically act as a glue, trapping these birds by the wings?"

"Apparently so, yes."

"And the more they struggle the more stuck they become?"

"Look, what is this…"

"And these birds remain stuck to these sticks until a hunter comes along and rescues them by slitting their throats, no?" Antoni stood up and faced the man squarely. "As I said, I'm not a great authority on the matter, but my initial thought would be that you're the victim of some very angry bird lovers and, it seems to me, you may have got off lightly."

Just as the restaurant owner was about to protest, a desperate voice called for attention from the front of the premises.

"Oh, Mr Nikos! Mr Nikos? Please, come help, Mr Nikos!"

Antoni and Nikos Demetriades ran up the path leading to the restaurant. Turning the corner, they were greeted by the sight of a young Bangladeshi woman who was having difficulty moving as both her feet appeared to be stuck to the floor in front of the main door.

"And she is?" Antoni asked.

"The cleaner," Demetriades informed him.

"In that case, you might want to buy her some new shoes, once my colleague gets his photographic evidence. After that, I'd advise you to find some white spirit and get scrubbing. Anti-climb paint is not so easy to get off."

Parked up on a dry grass verge, out of view of the large racing yard ahead of them, Lillian waited for Emilia to conduct her investigations. 'Death Alley,' she had called the place; a series of paddocks tucked away at the back of the yard where row upon row of retired or injured horses were kept in the most basic conditions as they slowly starved to death.

"Why not find them new homes?" Lillian had asked, genuinely shocked despite her own knowledge and experiences.

"Horses are an expensive hobby," Emilia had replied, "and ex-racehorses need serious retraining. In some cases, it's impossible thanks to owners who only have their eyes on the betting money rather than the welfare of the animal. Lillian, this is a sport that can leave lasting damage on a horse, both physically and psychologically. Pumped up on a diet of protein, stress and all manner of drugs such as anti-inflammatories, pain killers and others that control bleeding in the lungs, these horses have only one purpose in life and that is to race. If they can't do that or they can no longer do that, they are simply an expense. Nothing more. Julia told me that some of them are slaughtered while others are simply left to die in places like this."

"God, what a life."

"Tell me about it. There is rarely any gratitude in this sport for a job well done. Not even for the best ones. It's a horror show. And it's not just here, America is among the worst countries for race-horse abuse. I remember reading an article in one of your British newspapers that said most racehorses are lucky if they see their fifth birthday. Apparently, many of them are shipped off to France and slaughtered there because the French like to eat such meat. Here, well fuck knows what happens to them, but something does."

"It's just heart breaking."

"It's barbaric."

And with that Emilia left the car to see if there was any truth to Julia's nightmare vision of Death Alley.

Although Lillian had offered to go with Emilia, she was told there would be less chance of them getting caught if she went alone, and though her offer was genuine, she was relieved to miss the experience. With nothing to do but wait, Lillian texted Cara.

'At horse place. Old Boy gone and happy!'

Two minutes later, Cara replied. 'Gr8. Wish I was with you!'

'Us too, but Cooper and Peaches need Mum. Em has offered to cook tomorrow night.'

'I'll be there.'

'See you at 7pm.'

'Well done all! xx'

As Lillian returned the phone to the pocket of her shorts, she looked up to see Emilia heading towards her, stumbling through the uneven fields. Even from a distance, Lillian could see things hadn't gone well and when Emilia got into the car, she kept her gaze averted. Her cheeks were pale and wet with tears.

"Let's go," was all she said.

Throughout the morning, Cara kept checking the Facebook page of the Cyprus Animal Rescue Committee. The group's timeline was a fairly depressing catalogue of ills perpetrated against the island's animals, but shortly after midday Cara found something she could actually smile about. Under a collection of six photographs of the effigy they had made, including a close-up of their dummy's 'bloody' neck and the warning sign Emilia had painted, there was a comment from the organisation in both Greek and English.

"Bravo, our heroes!!! One week passed since we posted a photograph of that poor dog left to bleed to death tied to a bin by DISGUSTING BARBARIANS with NO HEART and NO SOUL!!! But today we were told something else was there to see. So we went and how HAPPY our hearts were when we got there. It was THE BEST message and it was THE RIGHT message!!! WARNING TO all animal hunters who think nothing of cutting the throats of unwanted dogs, you are being watched and our friends – whoever they are – WILL FIND YOU!!!"

Although Cara didn't strictly approve of the multiple exclamation marks and the random capitalisations peppering the post, she was moved by the support, and even more so when she noticed another post on the same page two hours later.

"This is a DOG PAW that is the sign of our HEROES!!! The Dromos Mayor knows the sign, the Kaliteros Hotel knows the sign, the hunters know the sign and now the songbird killing THALASSA TAVERNA IN PAPHOS knows the sign. SHOW SOLIDARITY with our heroes. Make the sign YOUR PROFILE!!!! The animals of Cyprus are finally getting JUSTICE!!!!"

After reading the post a couple of times, Cara felt both honoured and a little nervous. Switching pages to the Cyprus Mail, it didn't take long to find a decent-sized article about the Thalassa Taverna being vandalised with "sticky" anti-climb paint. There was also an update to the original article informing readers of an incident at a private residence in Dromos involving the theft of a dog. The newspaper had no photograph of the taverna or the stolen dog, but it did use a graphic of a dog's paw print with a caption that read, "Calling card of culprits". There was also a quote from Antoni.

"These incidents have all involved some form of criminal damage and whatever the motives behind these crimes, they are crimes and they are being treated with the utmost seriousness by the police."

Cara returned to the Facebook page of the Cyprus Animal Rescue Committee and, good as their overly exclamation-marked word, there was a dog's paw print added to their profile photo, which happened to be a sorry-looking hunting dog in a cage. Within minutes, more and more profile pictures of people in various poses and locations began to display a paw print in the bottom righthand corner of their photographs. As she moved from page to page, Cara felt like she was watching a virus spread and, as such, she began to wonder if they were prepared for what they may have unleashed.

Emilia was grateful for Lillian's silence. Although she knew she would eventually reveal what she had seen, she also knew that if she tried to speak at that point in time the words would turn to ash in her throat and choke her.

There must have been thirty or more horses in that hellhole behind the racing yard, and it wasn't so much an alley as an arid wasteland where every last bit of scrub had been torn from the parched earth until the horses could do nothing more but stand dazed and defeated. Many of them were so weak they could hardly move their tails to keep the flies from feeding on the wounds and scratches lacing their emaciated bodies. Their noble heads hung heavy on scrawny necks and hip bones protruded from their frames like coat hangers upon which their skin was draped. It was shocking and cruel and Emilia could think of no way to help them. It wasn't as if she could throw them in the back of Lillian's car and rehome them with a couple of well-meaning hippies. So, she had to walk away – while her legs could still carry her.

"It was terrible," Emilia finally muttered, looking straight ahead at the road in front of them. When Lillian's hand reached out to gently squeeze her arm, the tears fell, and they carried on falling because Emilia had no way of stopping them. Half-blinded by grief, it took her more than ten minutes to realise they had come off the highway to travel, at considerable speed, through the western suburbs of Limassol. As Lillian ran a red light, it dawned on Emilia that they were following a metallic grey Land Cruiser V8.

"Lillian?"

"Not now, Emilia, if you don't mind," replied Lillian, her eyes focussed on the car in front.

She knew she must look crazy – and God knows she felt it – but when Lillian saw Derek's car pulling off the highway, she could think of nothing else to do but follow. At first it was fine; Emilia was too busy crying to notice what was going on and it gave her the space to consider all possibilities. The first possibility was that it was Derek driving his car after coming home unexpectedly from Qatar. Another possibility was that it was the parking people treating Derek's car like their own while he was away, hence the cheap parking. There was also the possibility that the car was stolen. And finally, there was the possibility that it could be something else entirely. Lillian didn't want to think too much about that. But then Derek's car pulled up at a tidy block of flats and Lillian had no choice but to think about it.

Stopping a little behind the V8, Lillian watched a tall, lithe and much younger woman get out of the driving seat of her husband's car. The woman tottered in a pair of high heels to collect two bags of groceries from the boot. The bags were clearly heavy and one of them had a small tear in it, which opened up, spilling most of the contents onto the floor. That was when Lillian spied the tin of Illy ground coffee. It was only a small thing, a silly thing perhaps, but coupled with the car and the pretty young woman driving it, the sight almost finished her. The Italian coffee was Derek's favourite. He wouldn't drink anything else.

Lillian took a deep breath. "I've seen enough."

Emilia looked over at the woman struggling with her shopping, and though she was burning to ask questions, she bit her tongue.

Chapter Fifteen

Lying in bed, watching the clock tick down to a new day, Emilia struggled with the absurdity of being too exhausted to sleep. By rights, if someone was as tired as she was, they should be out for the count the moment they crawled under the duvet. But not Emilia. Though her head ached for sleep, her thoughts refused to lie still. Her mind was like a hyperactive child in the care of a pensioner, and she felt on the verge of a meltdown.

It wasn't only the image of skeletal horses in Death Alley that kept her awake, there was also the personal crap she had yet to deal with, which she'd done a pretty good job of so far ignoring. The money she'd extorted from Savvas was close to gone, and though she'd used it to pay her rent in advance rather than piss it up a wall in some seedy last chance saloon, she'd been unable to secure another job. Part of the problem was her hours and her health. She needed to keep the mornings to do the yard work that paid for her horse's livery, and once the sun went down it was getting harder to function. This was another reason why she felt so cheated when sleep evaded her. However, a part of her was also grateful because there were times when she feared she might go to sleep and never wake up again. As well as the occasions when bits of her body refused to move and she'd have to employ the concentration of a neuroscientist to make them work, there were times when she'd fall sleep only to be rudely awoken by her body jolting into action because she'd stopped breathing. She would then have to consciously think about the process of breathing, all of which was pretty distressing because life was tough enough without having to worry about her heart taking a break whenever her mind shut down for a nap.

"Mother of God!" Emilia half screamed. She threw back the duvet and got up.

By the time, Emilia got to Julia's, having walked because she was scared to use the moped, the sun was breaking over the hills and it cast a technicolour glow over the yard. Naturally, Emilia made straight for Adonis who was stood in his stable looking a little surprised at her early appearance. As he softly snickered and reached for her hand, she wondered whether he had missed her the previous day, and the images of Death Alley came flooding back. Emilia buried her face in her horse's mane, shedding tears onto his soft neck as she embraced the vitality and strength that set him apart from those skeletal horses that hadn't been so lucky in life.

"I love you so much, Adonis," Emilia sobbed, and Adonis took her love without moving an inch.

As it turned out, this was all that Emilia had needed – time with her horse – and the sleep that had evaded her as she lay in bed, finally arrived. An hour later, when Julia turned up to find Emilia sleeping in the hay next to her boy, she tutted, woke her gently, ushered her out of the stable and went ballistic.

"Do you know how stupidly dangerous that is?" she demanded, her blue eyes sharp and livid. "It only takes a second for a horse to crush you. What the hell were you thinking?"

"I couldn't sleep," Emilia replied calmly, knowing there was no use in arguing. Julia was right.

"Sometimes I can't sleep either, but I don't think risking half a ton of horse landing on my head is any kind of solution."

"It might be a solution of sorts."

"This is not a joke, Emilia! So, don't even try to turn it into one."

Taking them both by surprise, Emilia sniffed as tears welled in her eyes. In her defence, she was still tired and there was a lot on her mind, which made it difficult to deal with all the shouting.

"I went to Death Alley yesterday," she half mumbled, knowing it would be enough to stop Julia in her tracks.

'Ah.' Julia bit her tongue because what more was there to say? Death Alley could crush anyone with an ounce of compassion for an animal, let alone someone whose world revolved around their horse. Julia pinched the bridge of her nose, counted to three and put an arm around Emilia's shoulders. "Come on," she said. "Let's do what those Brits do in times of crisis."

"Hold a referendum and make things worse?"

"Well, we could do that, but I was thinking more along the lines of putting the kettle on."

Half an hour later, over coffee and Hobnobs, Julia let Emilia exhaust her anger and rage at the racing community, before calmly bringing her to reason.

"Not every yard is the same," she said quietly. "Not every owner is a monster, and not every crime against horses is committed by the racing community. Listen, I've been to enough competitions on this island to know how appalling some riders treat their horses; beating them to jump fences they have no hope of clearing, forcing their heads down with straps to create an outline, killing their spirit by bullying them into submission, destroying their mouths with harsh bits, tearing their sides with unforgiving spurs and basically annihilating any willingness the horse might have to work with a rider. Training through fear only yields results for so long, and these people sicken me as much as those money-grabbing racehorse owners sicken you. True horsemanship, in whatever form, is not about domination, but respect. What really staggers me is the number of people who willingly hand over the animals they love to brutes masquerading as trainers. This is why I stopped going to shows, both here and abroad – it wasn't solely because Yiannis died. I stopped because I could no longer concentrate on the good of the sport when the bad so often went unchecked."

For a long while, Lillian sat motionless in front of the steering wheel, deaf and blind to the comings and goings of the Alpha Mega car park. Somewhere at the back of her mind, like an echo in a canyon, was a voice reminding her to get going as it was almost 6.45pm, but she found it hard to motivate herself and when she finally stirred from the daze of her thoughts, she actually had no recollection of having entered the supermarket. In fact, if the evidence hadn't been sat on the front passenger seat, she might have gone shopping a second time. But the evidence was there; two bottles of Pinot Grigio that were to be Lillian's contribution to the evening meal at Emilia's. Cara was in charge of dessert.

As per usual, the main subject occupying Lillian's mind was Derek. When she followed his car the previous day it had never occurred to her that he might have been in the flat of the woman she had seen. She was almost certain something was going on between them, but she assumed he was still in Qatar. This might have been due to the Skype call earlier in the week showing him in his office, where he usually took their calls. But last night, as she tried to find sleep, it occurred to her that Derek could be Skyping from anywhere that had a beige wall in the background, including a flat in Limassol – chewing the cud with his wife as he waited for his mistress to bring him his favourite coffee. And with that sudden realisation, Lillian had bolted out of bed to throw up in the bathroom.

After emptying her stomach, Lillian found herself consumed with vengeful thoughts. At one point, she considered reporting Derek's car as stolen; hotwired by a long-legged, blonde-haired floozie who appeared to share the same taste in coffee as her husband. But then common sense prevailed and she thought better of it. Lillian was not an uncharitable person and though her husband had shown himself to be weak and foolish, she had no knowledge of the young woman who allowed him to be both of those things, and as pretty young girls rarely go with tired, old men unless they need to, she could only guess at the horror lurking in the girl's background. Furthermore, she had to think of Dan and Lucy. Whatever she did now, should she choose to do anything at all, it would have a profound impact on their lives and she needed to be sure that her marriage had irretrievably broken down before she agreed to subject her children to that kind of circus. As it stood, she simply wasn't sure how she felt about things. She loved Derek, she hated him, she pitied him, and she was scared. The only positive was that Lillian now knew she wasn't a paranoid old woman. Her husband was having an affair. And she needed to collect her thoughts and work out her own priorities before confronting him.

Perhaps because Emilia had her mind on other things, and she also needed to cook, and Lillian was still in a state of shock and partly mourning the potential death of her marriage, only Cara picked up on the subdued atmosphere of their post-mischief-making celebrations.

She had arrived a little late because Antoni was manning the night desk and as they were still very taken with each other, they had agreed that an afternoon in bed was the most agreeable course of action before his shift began. It also meant that she had been absent from social media for the previous four hours, so with Emilia in the kitchen and Lillian focussed on her wine glass, Cara took out her phone to check Facebook.

"Bloody hell, we've got 1,454 likes so far!" Cara shouted, breaking the strange silence in the flat that would have been deafening if everyone's minds hadn't been so busy with other things.

Emilia poked her head through the kitchen door, spatula in hand, to see what was going on. "What are you talking about?"

"The photo of our hunter dummy – it has 1,454 likes on the CARC Facebook page. We've also got messages of support from people not only in Cyprus and the UK, but Germany, Spain and, weirdly, Papua New Guinea."

"Aren't there cannibals in Papua New Guinea?" Lillian asked. "I'm sure they ate one of the Rockefeller children."

"Okay, that's quite a weird response," Cara replied.

She glanced at Emilia who shrugged before heading back into the kitchen shouting, "Vegan falafels wait for no man."

A minute or so later, Cara looked up from her iPhone. "Michael Rockefeller," she said. "According to Wikipedia, he was travelling in the region of Papua New Guinea in the early 1960s when his boat either sank and he was eaten by sharks or he was abducted by a tribe of cannibals and eaten. His body was never found so nobody really knows."

"Poor soul," Lillian shuddered, making the sign of the cross on her chest.

"Poor soul, indeed. This is the cursed family, isn't it?" asked Cara, vaguely remembering something from the Daily Mail. When Lillian looked at her blankly, she added. "Wasn't there a grandson kidnapped by the mafia or something and because the grandfather refused to pay the ransom, they cut off his ear?"

"Oh right, I'm with you now," Lillian replied, half laughing as she rolled her eyes and patted the back of her auburn hair as if to check it was still there. "No, you're thinking of the Getty family."

"Oh yes, the Gettys. That's the one. The kidnapped boy went on to have a stroke, I think, leaving him blind and crippled. As for the grandfather who had refused to pay his ransom, I'm sure I read that none of his family visited him when he was dying. Only his mistresses."

"Hardly surprising. I mean what kind of heartless old git wouldn't pay his grandson's ran..."

Before Lillian could finish the sentence, an anguished scream rang out from the kitchen. Cara dropped her phone and sprinted to help, with Lillian marginally ahead of her.

"For god's sake, Emilia!" Lillian screamed, reaching for a towel to take away the pan of boiling oil that was spilling over her friend's arms and hands. Hurriedly placing the pan on the worktop, she forcefully pulled the younger woman to the sink. Emilia's face was white with pain and her pupils were dilated. Turning on the tap, Lillian plunged Emilia's oil-burned hands into the cold running water.

"I'm sorry. I'm sorry," Emilia muttered, wincing as the first wave of shock subsided to reveal the full pain of her injures.

"Shouldn't we take her to hospital?" Cara asked anxiously.

"No!" Emilia shouted, even as the tears fell from her eyes. "It's OK. I'm alright."

"You're not alright, Emilia."

"Please no, Cara. Just no."

Cara shook her head and held up her palms in bewildered frustration. "Well, do you at least have some kind of medical box?"

Emilia kicked the cupboard to the right of her. "In there. You'll also find aloe vera gel."

"Good. Grab the gel, Cara. It should help," ordered Lillian, still firmly holding Emilia's hands under the running water. "We'll also need some form of ice pack."

"There are peas in the freezer," Emilia told them.

"Good, good," Lillian replied and then, as the immediate panic of the situation eased, she lifted Emilia's face using her forehead against her chin, to look into her eyes. "What on earth happened, Emilia? Why didn't you just let go?"

"I couldn't," she confessed, trying to avoid the full power of Lillian's gaze. "My hand spasmed. I couldn't hold the pan and I couldn't think and then my other hand came up and I couldn't let go. It's my fault. I only have myself to blame."

"Don't be silly. It was an accident," Lillian said softly. But Emilia shook her head violently, and her tears turned into body-racking sobs.

"No, it's not just an accident. It is my fault. But the medication. It's so expensive. And I thought, well, I thought I could cope. I thought I would be okay. God help me, I thought it might go away."

Emilia sank to the floor, the full weight of her despair making it impossible for Lillian to keep her up and on her feet. In the doorway, holding a bag of frozen garden peas, Cara looked on, bewildered.

It took a little over an hour before Emilia was able to convince
Lillian there was no need for a trip to the local hospital. With aloe
vera liberally applied to her burns, and with both arms carefully
bandaged, she finally started to talk in a way that made some kind
of sense. Sitting next to Lillian on the sofa, she smiled sheepishly
at Cara who remained on her feet in the doorway of the kitchen
ready to alternate the frozen bags of peas and assorted vegetables
needed to keep Emilia's wounds cool and the pain more bearable.

"I have MS," Emilia said, revealing her condition almost matter-of-factly. "I have Multiple Sclerosis."

Both Lillian and Cara responded with a shake of their heads and
muttered condolences, but though they had heard of the disease,
neither of them knew much about it. As it wasn't so long ago that
Emilia had also been blissfully ignorant of her condition, she helpfully explained, saving her friends the embarrassment of having to
ask her to.

"It's a neurological disease; your nerves get paralysed and they
slowly die. It's usually genetic, but nobody really understands it.
They say it can be brought on by stress, exercise, heat, you name it.
But nobody really knows how it starts and, unfortunately, there's
no cure. One day I will end up in a wheelchair. That's the bottom
line. That's what the doctors have told me."

"Oh Emilia..." Lillian moved closer for a hug, but Emilia gently
pushed her away.

"Don't," she begged softly. "If you are too kind, I won't be able
to finish."

Lillian tried to smile as she backed off, not offended in the
slightest, but feeling utterly powerless to help a young woman she
had grown to love.

"So, as you have seen," Emilia continued. "I get these episodes,
these attacks, call it what you will, and they tend to happen without warning. They just hit you. The first one was by far the worst.
I was with Adonis and I suddenly fell against the wall of his stable,
unable to move. It was Julia who found me and she took me to

a neurologist she knew at the hospital who put me in some kind of skull cap spewing cables that were connected to a device on a computer. For 40 minutes or more this went on as various medical people sat at a computer observing things, like I was some kind of steam punk guinea pig. 'Just relax,' they kept saying, which is one of the most stupid orders you can get from a doctor who's trying to work out why you can't move one side of your body.

"Anyway, I had to wait a week for the results. No brain tumour, apparently, which was a relief. The doctors then conducted an MRI scan for MS. At that stage, I didn't know what MS was exactly, but I'd heard of it and assumed it was an old person's disease. But no, MS usually hits between 20 and 40 and it most commonly affects women. Apparently, it's the only disease that doctors have no idea what causes it. As I said, they think it's maybe genetic or linked to a deficiency in Vitamin D or stress related, but they don't know. It's all guesswork. All they can truly tell you is that you have it or you don't have it and my scan clearly revealed many white spots on my brain, showing MS lesions. It was then explained that my nerve cells were dying slowly, which can cause muscle atrophy meaning my muscles will eventually weaken to the point where I can no longer stand. Needless to say, I was shitting myself and my fears weren't helped in anyway by that first attack of paralysis, which lasted for days before it eventually subsided and I regained control of the left side of my body. Anyway, thankfully, I've not had a repeat attack of that severity, although it's always the left side of my body that's affected. Most of the time though, I'm just extremely tired. Fatigue has become my biggest enemy in leading a normal life and there are days I can feel my legs trembling with the exertion of having to keep going. I usually feel it in my limbs, but I can also forget things or find myself saying things that don't make much sense."

As Emilia paused to swap frozen packets of peas, Cara asked about the medication she had mentioned, and her friend responded with a humourless laugh.

"There are pills. I am on Dimethyl fumarate, and it costs €2,500 a month."

"You're kidding!" Cara said, genuinely shocked. "How the hell can you afford that?"

"I can't," Emilia admitted. "I don't have a medical card and I didn't have insurance so Julia had to give me the money for my medication. She insisted on it. But I feel shit about it so I've been trying to cut down to make her money last longer. Rather than every day, I've been taking my pills every other day, thinking it might be okay. But then I crashed my moped and I lost my job because I kept dropping plates and, now, I don't even know where I will get the money for my rent, and all this stress, it's frying my brain because I really don't think I deserve this. I'm not such a bad person. I may swear a bit and I've been selfish, but no more than the next person. So why am I being punished?"

While Lillian and Cara didn't believe for a minute that Emilia deserved the brutal hand fate had dealt her, they were both lost for words. What could they say that would make her feel even remotely better? There were no words. All they had to give was their support and friendship.

"Don't worry about your rent, Emilia," Lillian eventually said. "You're moving in with me."

Chapter 16

Lillian handed Emilia a cup of coffee, while carefully avoiding her gaze because she wasn't sure she could hide her concern. She hadn't been snooping, she had been making a hot drink, but Emilia's cupboards were practically bare. It broke Lillian's heart to think of her friend living hand to mouth, no doubt wondering where her next meal was coming from let alone the medication she needed that cost thousands of euros a month.

Faced with the extent of her financial hardship, Lillian struggled to understand why Emilia hadn't said anything. They might have been poles apart in many ways, but she thought they were better friends than that, and she was momentarily hurt to think that they weren't. But then Lillian reviewed her own circumstances, and the fact that she was currently wrestling with the possibility that her husband was leading a double life. She hadn't mentioned anything about that either. It didn't mean she didn't feel close enough to confide in her friends, it was simply a matter of keeping the personal private until she was ready to put it out there. Why should Emilia be any different? Maybe she too had been waiting for a time when she was ready to face up to things a little more publicly. However, as they had all so recently found out, not everyone has the luxury of time.

Because Emilia had point-blank refused to have her burns treated in hospital, and Cara had to go home to her dogs, Lillian was the one who stayed overnight to make sure that frozen peas were administered when needed, and anything else for that matter. Once Emilia's pain reached the point of bearable, sometime around 4am, they both crawled into her double bed because the only alternative for Lillian was the floor or the sofa. As the floor was tiled and the sofa was wicker, the bed was in fact the only option. Unprepared for a sleepover, Lillian was given a long t-shirt to sleep in, on the front of which was a picture of the grim reaper playing a bass guitar.

"I'm guessing it's not your usual bedtime wear," Emilia said.

"You'd be right. I'm more winceyette than death metal."

Emilia smiled at the joke, but found herself unable to tease Lillian more because she was utterly exhausted and a little overwhelmed by the kindness and compassion shown by her friends.

As they lay side by side under a bedsheet, with only a small breeze blowing in over the balcony to offer relief from the suffocating heat, they chatted for a while about Emilia's condition and her fear that one day she would end up in a wheelchair.

"Is it inevitable?" Lillian had asked.

"Not one hundred percent, but the doctors aren't hopeful."

"And is there a way you can delay the process? How much time do you have?"

"I've no idea and what's worse is the doctors have no idea either. I get so much conflicting advice. Some say I shouldn't exercise, others say I should and all the while my body grinds to a halt for reasons I don't understand. There's no pattern to it or trigger I can put my finger on. It just happens. I guess one day something will happen that I won't get up from and I won't walk again."

"Oh Emilia, that must be so frightening."

"It is, but I try not to think about it. Of course, there are also times that I can't help but think about it." Emilia paused for a moment before quietly confiding, "I've started looking at saddles for para-equestrians. You can probably guess how much they cost."

Because it was dark rather than pitch black, Lillian clearly saw the tears sliding down the contours of Emilia's face. Her throat tightened in response and her arms ached to hold the girl, but she wasn't sure how much of an embrace Emilia could tolerate, being the least tactile of their group and horribly injured, so Lillian reached for her hand, being careful not to touch her bandages. To her relief, Emilia reciprocated the gesture with a soft squeeze of her fingers and then, much to Lillian's amazement, she fell asleep.

Realising just how exhausted and terrified she must have been, Lillian watched Emilia for a while, feeling concerned and afraid for her. It was perhaps the first time she had properly looked at her friend and she soaked up all the small details that made up the whole. Though Emilia was in her late 30s, she looked like a teenager in the moonlight that streamed through the open windows. She had such a pretty face; long lashes, a perfectly straight nose and dainty, rosebud lips. Lillian was surprised she hadn't noticed her beauty before, though Emilia's face was usually obscured by a shock of black hair and a scowl. Asleep, the picture was very different. Emilia looked peaceful, so much so it was hard to believe her body was betraying her in such a cruel fashion.

As Lillian's eyes drifted from Emilia's face to her arms, she inspected the tattoos she had once found so unsightly, finally understanding how they painted their own story of a life she barely knew – none more so than the tattoo on the upper arm nearest her. Under a red rose, and framed by angel wings, was the word *mami*. It took Lillian a long while to get to sleep after making the connection.

"How's your coffee?"

"Great," Emilia replied, trying not to show her embarrassment because she knew the state her cupboards were in. "Actually, I'm surprised you found any. I've been meaning to go to the supermarket, but what with one thing and another."

"God, don't I know that feeling," Lillian laughed, but it sounded theatrical even to her ears and she moved to the balcony to hide her face and watch the tourists below playing sunbed chess around the communal pool. Turning to speak to Emilia, who remained inside in the shade, she asked, "When is your rent due?"

"Not until mid-July," Emilia replied. "Don't worry, I've still got time to sort something."

"I'm not worried at all," Lillian replied honestly. "I'm just wondering how much time I have to prepare your quarters."

"It's okay Lillian, you don't have to."

"I know I don't have to, Emilia. I want to."

Emilia lowered her head. She was so touched by Lillian's kindness she had to stop speaking.

Sometime after 9am, once Lillian had taken Emilia to the stables so she could get her fix of Adonis, and explain to Julia why she might not be pushing many wheelbarrows that morning, Lillian went shopping for groceries. She didn't want Emilia to feel like a complete charity case, but neither would she allow her to go hungry for the sake of silly pride, so she bought a few basics; potatoes, carrots, broccoli, pita, chickpeas, tomatoes, onions, chicken, coffee and a family-sized pack of Dairy Milk chocolate. It wasn't much, a mere gesture, and it was one of two she made that morning.

After returning her trolley to the small bay in front of the supermarket, she spotted a Rav 4 parking up. Shrinking into the shadows, she watched as a squat, dough-faced man got out. She then watched him waddle into the store, her blood pressure rising as he passed a matter of metres from her. To Lillian's surprise, the man was much shorter than she had imagined, and she could only assume this was due to the angle she usually viewed him from; on her bum as he drove away shouting expletives in her direction.

As the automatic doors closed behind him, like a toad swallowing a fly, a kind of madness took over Lillian. Without giving her brain time to catch up with her thoughts, she returned to her car, took two potatoes from Emilia's grocery bag, walked over to the Rav 4 and stuffed them up the exhaust pipe. Job done, she calmly walked back to her own vehicle and drove off.

Returning from their walk in the hills, Cara treated Cooper and Peaches to a dental stick, partly because it was good for their teeth, but mainly because Cooper had been eating human shit. Cara was livid that, once again, someone had used the beautiful outdoors as their personal toilet. She could only assume it was the handiwork of someone suffering from a bowel disease that rendered them incapable of holding their shit together for the five-minute drive back to town.

"You dirty bastards!" she had screamed at the top of her lungs, hearing her anger echo around the valley as she covered the offending crap with loose rocks. If there was one thing guaranteed to set her teeth on edge it was the thought of her dogs eating someone's shit. Goat shit, sheep shit, horse shit, even their own shit, was just about bearable. But human shit was one level of shit too much for Cara to take.

By the time she got home and took off her bum bag – loaded with recall treats, a hypodermic needle and anti-venom capsules – Cara was calm enough to remember there were greater problems in life than dealing with human faeces in the hills. She texted Lillian and received a reply almost immediately.

'Emilia is fine. Sore but fine.'

'Good. Shocking night. Speak later xx'

After putting on the kettle, Cara sat down to begin her morning ritual of harvesting the local papers for work. She always started with the Cyprus Mail followed by a handful of other, less reliable, English-speaking news sites to see if there were any stories worth developing for the UK Press. It was roughly two seconds into this process that she discovered that she and her friends were making front page news.

'Dog Paw Gang's Night of Fury' screamed one headline, sitting above a graphic of a paw print. As she read on, Cara didn't know whether to laugh or cry.

Unknown culprits went on the rampage in the Paphos region last night, targeting individuals, businesses and communities suspected of animal rights abuses.

In an early-hours crime spree, the gang – who always leave a dog paw signature wherever they strike – tied an effigy of a hunter with its throat cut to a village dustbin; stole a dog from a private residence; chained a car to a tree; and daubed glue-like anti-climb paint on the premises of a restaurateur arrested last month for cooking songbirds in his kitchen.

Inspector Antoni Giakgos told reporters:"It's still early days in the investigation, but it would seem that the underlying motive behind these crimes is animal cruelty, or perceived animal cruelty."

Cara couldn't help but smile as she imagined Antoni having to hide his frustration at being required to state the obvious. Then, after scrolling down, further into the story, passed the continuing outrage of the Mayor of Dromos and the carefully worded support of the Animal Party, she laughed out loud at the collage of photographs showing their misdeeds. They included the dummy tied to the communal bin, an irate former dog owner standing next to his chained-up Mercedes and, to her absolute delight, a pair of women's shoes stuck to the floor of the Thalassa Taverna entrance.

"Bingo," Cara chuckled before bending down to kiss Cooper who had wandered over to see what the joke was. Cara then wiped her mouth after remembering he had been eating human shit less than an hour ago.

Julia was furious, but more than that she was upset and bemused to hear Emilia confess to skimping on her medication in order to make it last longer and cost less. Not trusting herself to speak at first, she had insisted on checking Emilia's wounds for any sign of infection. As she gently unwrapped the bandages, her stomach churned, not at the sight of the huge, fluid-filled blisters that covered her arms, but because she knew the kind of pain they represented.

After accepting the wounds were clean, Julia rebandaged Emilia with quiet efficiency before heading to the bathroom where she grabbed the nearest towel and held it to her mouth to muffle the anguish erupting inside of her. When she was done, she moved to the bedroom, checked herself in the mirror, applied eyedrops and powdered her face. Only once she felt composed did she return to the picnic bench overlooking the arena to speak to Emilia.

"Right, young lady, let me tell you something. I am alone here on this island. I have no children, I have no husband, I have horses and a few cats that I feed. That's it. My financial situation is more than comfortable and when I die the state will no doubt benefit handsomely from what I leave behind. So, spare me the martyrdom. I am paying for your medication because I have the money, you need it and, more importantly, because I care, Emilia. You have brought a rare ray of sunshine back to this yard and I am more grateful to you and Adonis than you can possibly know. So, do me a favour and damn well take your tablets. Every day. Okay?"

Emilia mutely accepted Julia's kindness with a nod, too scared and exhausted to defy her, but also knowing she couldn't go on without the medication she needed.

"Good," Julia said. "And another thing. You will receive a weekly wage from me, cash in hand, for the work you do here."

"But the livery..." Emilia protested.

"Relax. It won't be an executive salary; you're shovelling shit not negotiating a takeover. But it will be enough to cover your food and spends as long as your tastes remain pedestrian."

Emilia smiled at Julia's brusque manner. If it wasn't for the accent, she could easily pass for a Brit.

"And if there is anything – anything – more I can do, please do me the courtesy of telling me."

"I will, I promise," Emilia replied.

Half-tempted to get up and hug Julia, she was distracted by the sight of Cara descending the stone steps to the yard. Julia looked at Emilia who shrugged sheepishly.

"She offered to groom Adonis."

"The boy won't die because you didn't condition his mane for 24 hours," Julia moaned.

"I know, but she offered to do it and she's my friend."

"So am I, Emilia. So am I."

With that said, Julia went inside to put the kettle on.

In the week that followed their night of animal-rights rampaging, all hell appeared to break loose on the island, and there was little that Cara, Emilia or Lillian could do about it except sit back and watch.

First came the newspaper reports, followed by more messages of support written on various Facebook sites and the proliferation of profile pictures bearing paw prints. Via texts and phone calls, all three of them agreed this was "fine". But then it all began to get oddly heated the more the story gained traction.

It started with a phone-in on an English-speaking radio station in which lots of angry Brits described their disgust at the appalling way Cypriots treated their animals. This triggered lots of English-speaking Cypriots to voice their own anger and disgust at sweeping generalisations that did nothing to solve the problem, and if the British didn't like it maybe they should bugger off back to their own country. Next came the articles in the Greek-speaking Press and mentions on the TV news. There was even a skit on a satirical Friday night comedy show in which actors dressed in dog costumes pretended to drive pick-ups with hunters loaded into metal cages in the back. Though it wasn't especially funny, Cara, Lillian and Emilia thought this was just about "fine" too. After all, any publicity had to be good publicity. But too much publicity also had the potential to embarrass certain authorities, and the bigger the story got, the more the authorities got involved.

Because the attack on the Thalassa Taverna was in Paphos old town rather than Dromos, the district police chief found himself rolled out in front of the Press to speak on the subject, confidently declaring the culprits would soon be caught while admitting the force knew next to nothing about them. Meanwhile, in the capital, a number of politicians began to see the mileage to be gained from wading in on the action, and representatives from all parties were now talking with the Animal Party to find a solution to the growing clamour for better animal welfare laws and, more importantly, the implementation of them. As the politicians talked the talk, the public, as ever, walked the walk. Where once there were slogans daubed on the country's walls in support of resistance fighters battling the British, now there were paw prints. There were also random acts of sabotage involving dogs freed from cages and in one rather bizarre incident on a Thursday afternoon, a litter of pigs enjoying a leisurely stroll in a Limassol village after being liberated by a group of schoolchildren.

Then, on Friday morning, the police arrived at Lillian's house.

Chapter 17

Derek had been home for less than 30 minutes when Special Constable Michalis Georgiou knocked on the door.

"I am here for Mrs Lillian Chambers," Michalis said bluntly.

Derek's eyes narrowed and he stood a little taller, almost filling
the doorframe. "What do you mean 'for'?"

"Sorry?"

"What do you mean when you say you're here *for* my wife?"

"Oh, she your wife?"

"Yes."

"Very good. And your wife, she is here?"

"Yes."

"Good because I come for her."

"Look, I won't ask you again. What do you mean by…"

"It's okay, Derek." Lillian came to stand by her husband's side.
She gently pressed his upper arm, vaguely surprised at how soft it
had become, and moved to stand in front of him. Though her heart
was beating nineteen to the dozen, her mind was strangely calm.
It was a shock to get a visit from the police, but there was also an
air of inevitability about the intrusion. Lillian had half-expected
the moment to come and she had occasionally imagined how it
might happen. Now that it had happened for real, she was mildly
disappointed that they had sent the guy who manned the school
crossing to arrest her.

Lillian held out her hands. "I'm ready when you are, Officer."

"Lillian, what the hell is going on? What have you done?" Derek
stepped forward and Lillian felt the heat from his chest warm her
back. Once upon a time, she might have found it reassuring and
protective, now it felt like background noise.

Lillian looked at Special Constable Georgiou, also apparently
puzzled to be confronted by her outstretched arms

"No," he finally said, shaking his head. "I come for talk to you, Mrs Lillian Chambers. Here in Cyprus, we no arrest ladies for potatoes."

"Potatoes?" Lillian dropped her arms, unable to fathom what the man meant, wondering if something had been lost in translation or whether it was some quaint colloquial phrase she had yet to come across, but then the penny dropped and she almost laughed with relief.

"Please Officer, come inside. Is there anything I can get you? Coffee or a cup of tea perhaps?" Ushering Special Constable Georgiou into the house and past the bulk of her husband who was still taking up space in the doorway, she rolled her eyes. "Come on Derek, don't just stand there. You're not a bouncer."

Once inside, it didn't take long to discover Special Constable Georgiou's weakness for coffee and cake, and Lillian exploited it to the full as she slowly cut through the fog of his pidgin English to understand that she had been correctly identified as the person responsible for stuffing a potato or two up the exhaust pipe of a Rav 4 in the local supermarket car park, all of which was caught on CCTV. Apparently, it wasn't immediately clear to the Rav 4's Russian owner that spuds were responsible for the repetitive stalling of his vehicle's engine. It wasn't immediately clear to the guy who came with the tow truck either. Only when they got the car to a garage did the reason reveal itself, and the Russian was livid.

"Very rude man," Michalis admitted to Lillian and also to Derek who was sat on the edge of his seat watching his wife in a way that could only be described as wary as she freely admitted to the crime.

"I really don't know what came over me," she explained to the officer. "I saw the car and because I was sick and tired of this awful man trying to run me over, I decided to punish him."

"He try to run you over?"

"Yes."

"With car?"

"Yes."

"But why? And why you not come tell us?"

"The Russian doesn't like me feeding the cats and I was waiting to get more evidence before coming to see you. This is why I wear a GoPro."

"You wear GoPro?"

"Yes, on my head."

Now it was Michalis' turn to stare warily at Lillian. Taking another bite of orange cake, which was delicious, he shook his head. The British were great time keepers, but they could be crazy at times.

"*Endaxi*, Mrs Lillian Chambers."

"Please, call me Lillian."

Michalis paused in confusion. With a slight shrug, he continued. "Okay, Mrs *Lillian* Chambers. You are lucky for three reasons. One, you make good cake. Two, we don't like Russians coming to station shouting like Putin. Three, there was no big damage to car. And..." Michalis paused, realising he actually had four reasons, and wondering whether anyone else in the room would notice an extra one. "And finally, the supermarket owner is good friend of mine and he not show CCTV to angry Russian guy, only me."

"Meaning?"

"Meaning, I must give you the warning and if you do again, maybe I arrest you. I don't know. You see, it could have been a big damage to car. So, stop with the potatoes, yes?"

"You have my word," Lillian promised.

Michalis nodded and waited. As the silence bordered on awkward, he finally had to ask. "Is the word 'yes'?"

"Yes, it's yes," Lillian laughed, and Michalis got to his feet grinning, feeling wholly satisfied from all the cake, not to mention the good conclusion to their meeting.

Once he had gone, and the door had closed behind him, Derek turned to his wife. She could tell by his face he was in one of his 'moods'.

"What were you thinking?" he demanded through clenched teeth.

Lillian got to her feet and began clearing the plates. "I thought the potatoes would shoot out of the exhaust pipe, you know, like a bullet from a gun. I had no idea it would simply stall the engine. Anyway, not to worry, it worked to some degree."

"What do you mean it worked to some degree?"

"Oh Derek, calm down, no one got killed."

"No, Lillian. I will not calm down," Derek shouted, and Lillian felt so cross with his tone, in a way she had never felt before, that she tutted at him, sternly.

Emilia stared at the scars decorating her lower arms, a series of perfectly formed circles, paler than her natural skin that were once blisters. Two weeks had passed since the accident yet it felt like a lifetime ago because so much had changed. In many ways it was like the end of a chapter and the beginning of a new one, with less pain. For so long, her every move had felt like a lie. She had given the impression she was in good health and coping financially; she had told no one she had lost her job, she had quietly stopped taking her meds and, most tragically of all, she had pretended to be happy. She had pretended to be "fine".

But Emilia hadn't been fine, she had been very far from fine, and now everyone knew that, life became easier. For the first time in a long while, Emilia didn't feel buried by everything. More than that, she knew that should the walls ever close in again she only had to reach out to someone to help push them back. She had friends, real friends, and it was a realisation that sometimes moved her to tears. For much of her life she had surrounded herself with people who paid only lip service to the ties of friendship, and she was as guilty of this as any of them. She used to think of herself as invincible, like most people with youth on their side. In her mind, the people around her were secondary characters in the film that was her life. All of which was bullshit, of course, but she had to find that out the hard way

Despite there being another six weeks before she needed to leave her flat, Emilia had started collecting boxes here and there to get what little stuff she possessed packed and ready for the change of address. Though she had always travelled light, she had been in her flat for more than two years and it was surprising how much she had accumulated in a relatively short time and how much she had forgotten, or rather, allowed to rest.

Emilia gazed at the photograph in her hands, taken of her mother on her wedding day. Her long dark hair shone like silk under a white veil and her eyes sparkled with excitement, love and huge possibility. Ten years later she was dead, her beautiful face ravaged by cancer, her hair destroyed by what were meant to be life-saving drugs, her lithe young body wasted by pain and disease. She was 29 years old when she died, and she passed away in the midst of another cold winter. Emilia was barely nine years old when she watched men she didn't know, lower her mother's body into the frozen ground. Her father was devastated and, in the end, the only way he could continue living was to fill the hole left by his wife by getting a new one. Emilia's love hadn't been enough for him, and yet it was too much for the new wife. And so, Emilia grieved a second time. Not that her feelings seemed to matter much; she understood she was merely a secondary character in the film of their lives. So, when she had the means, she left to take centre stage in her own new world.

Emilia tenderly stroked the photograph in her hands and gazed at it until her mother's face blurred and disappeared beneath her tears.

Cara set the phone on the counter, looked at Cooper and Peaches, who were both watching her expectantly because she was stood in the kitchen, and asked, "What to do?"

It was the second call from a national newspaper in the space of an hour and they pretty much wanted the same thing; a feature about the recent incidents involving the Dog Paw Gang pinned to profiles of British rescuers living on the island. Clearly, this was a fairly easy task and a quick call to Lillian to ask her friend Janet to find some likely candidates yielded quick results. The next call she made was to her boyfriend.

"I need to speak to you," she said.

"Sounds serious. Are you pregnant?"

"What? No!"

"Shame," he said. Cara was so flustered she didn't know how to respond. "So, come, *agapi mou,* what is it? What do you need from me?"

Cara shook her head, trying not to read too much into the fact that he'd mentioned children and had just called her *my love.*

"I need more quotes from you."

"For the British magazine?"

"No, it's for the newspapers this time."

"About the animal crimes?"

"Yes."

Antoni groaned a little before answering. "Okay, it's no problem for me to speak to you, but if you want to use my name, I have to get clearance. Other police districts are involved now, and the politicians, of course. Let me get back to you."

"Sure, no problem." Cara was trying hard to sound calm, but her heart was racing like a driver who suddenly discovers the brakes no longer work while travelling downhill.

Ten minutes later, Antoni called her back. "Sorry Cara, I've been told to refer you to our Press Office in Nicosia."

"Don't worry. It's no big deal. I don't want to get you in trouble."

"Pity. I was hoping you would."

Cara laughed, but even to her ears it sounded borderline hysterical. "You're in a frisky mood today."

"Frisky?"

"Yes. Naughty, sexy, that sort of thing."

"Always," Antoni laughed, revealing none of the tension that had been evident in Cara's laughter. "Anyway, do you want to have dinner tonight? I'm sure I can tell you things for your article, but not with my name. Okay?"

"Sounds great."

"So, I pick you up at eight."

"That's a date at eight, then," she confirmed before rolling her eyes at her own cheesiness. "Every time," she muttered when the line went dead.

Getting flustered wasn't an entirely new phenomenon for Cara, so she understood the cause; she was starting to care about what Antoni thought of her.

It was actually ten past eight when Antoni picked her up, which was as good as "English time" in a country like Cyprus where the locals usually scheduled their events two hours later than their verbal commitments.

It was a typically warm summer evening with only a light breeze to ease the humidity. As it was too hot for jeans, Cara had opted for a light blue shift dress with matching ankle chain, which naturally caused an internal debate as to whether she was too old for such jewellery. In fact, she came close to taking it off before rightly dismissing her concerns as "ridiculous". This was another downside of her being interested in someone; she suddenly became self-conscious, in a way that she wasn't when she charted the world alone. Cara found it an annoying flaw in her character, a weakness that was compounded by the fact that she hadn't ever heard Antoni be critical of anyone. Even when he moaned about Michalis, there was a hint of tenderness in his exasperation.

"Nobody knows anyone completely," he once said during one of their late-night chats, which were still a regular occurrence as they hadn't yet reached the stage in which post-coital discussions started and ended with the checking of the alarm clock.

"I'm not sure that's wholly correct," Cara had replied. "Friends, lovers, family members; they might know each other better than most."

"Better than most, yes, but better is not everything. Happy marriages can end in bad divorces with both sides no longer recognising the person they once loved."

"True," Cara conceded.

"Although I was actually speaking more generally, about people you see on the street who may dress a bit different to you, or women who upset other women by being too pretty, or others who make fun of people simply because they do something strange. People are quick to judge, and they usually judge wrong. For this reason, I always think it's better to be kind than not. No one knows the shit happening in someone's life. No one knows what kind of day they've had so why be the asshole to make it worse for them? What do you get out of it?"

"Knocked down a realm if you're a Buddhist who believes in reincarnation."

"Not much of a deterrent in Dromos," Antoni replied. "We're mainly Greek Orthodox, in case you hadn't noticed."

Cara had laughed at that, which only reinforced her belief that she actually liked Antoni a lot. So, coupled with the pregnancy joke and the *agapi mou* endearment, it brought an element of pressure to date night that she hadn't anticipated. Thankfully, the wine was quick to flow when they got to the restaurant and by the end of her mushroom puri starter, Cara had relaxed enough to forget that she might be getting a little ahead of herself. Once her nerves subsided, the tension she had brought to the meal disappeared and she started to feel all starry-eyed again. That's possibly why the hammer blow, when it came, left her completely and utterly winded.

It was midway through Cara's Tarka Dal that the subject of children came up. In between bites of Makhani Butter Chicken, Antoni asked whether it had been a conscious decision not to have children and Cara tutted good-naturedly and shook her head.

"It was a conscious decision by Tom, not necessarily by me. I was relaxed about it either way. If it happened, it happened. If it didn't, well, it didn't. And it didn't."

"Do you regret that it didn't?"

"Regret is perhaps too strong a word. It just didn't happen and, as things turned out, it was probably best that it didn't."

"Maybe you're right, but still, it's a shame. You'd be a good mum and, I like to think, I'd be a good dad."

"So, you're still keen on having children?" Cara asked, not thinking ahead quick enough to disengage her mouth.

"Yes, of course. I definitely want a family. The larger the better, but don't be scared," he teased.

"Okay, I won't be," Cara replied, and she laughed, right up to the point when Antoni told her he wasn't joking.

And there it was, with her guard down, the bomb was dropped. It was one of the most bittersweet moments Cara had experienced in a long time. On the one hand, she was having dinner with a beautiful man who was suggesting he may want to start a family with her. On the other hand, the days when Cara used to think about having kids had long gone.

Refilling her wine glass, she looked into Antoni's handsome face and tried to be brave. Brave and honest. "I might be a bit old for all that now."

Antoni smirked in response. "Oh, come on. These days, it's not unusual for women to have children in their 30s."

Cara almost choked on her dal.

"How old do you think I am?" she asked.

Antoni shrugged, looking puzzled. "I don't know. Maybe 37 or 38?"

"Maybe you should try adding another decade onto that," Cara said carefully. She then tried hard to mask her disappointment as she watched his eyes widen, so much so she could almost see his thought process as he tried to work out the implications of dating a woman hurtling towards 50.

Chapter Eighteen

Cara and Emilia arrived at Lillian's house bang on 7pm. As it was still daylight and hot as hell, Lillian pulled down the blinds and cranked up the air con in the sitting room where she had placed three of her best corduroy bean bags in front of a widescreen TV, all within reaching distance of a long, but low coffee table offering refreshments and an assortment of intentionally, and accidentally, vegan snacks.

"How can something be accidentally vegan?" Emilia asked.

"The product just happens to be vegan. The manufacturer didn't specifically create a vegan product," Cara explained.

"Like lettuce?"

"If you like."

"Or beetroot?"

"Yes."

"What about potatoes?"

"Don't even mention potatoes," Lillian quipped as she entered the sitting room from the kitchen holding a tray of drinks. "Did you know that beef and tomato Pot Noodle is accidentally vegan?"

"I knew that," Cara admitted. "You tend to learn these things over time. Smokey bacon Pringles are also accidentally vegan, though why a vegan would want to be reminded of the taste of burnt pig is anyone's guess."

Lillian's eyes darted to the Pringles she had emptied into a bowl on the coffee table. After distracting her guests with a Skinny Hurricane made from rum, orange and cranberry juice, she casually picked up the bowl and pushed it under the seat of Derek's favourite armchair; a battered, old Chesterfield the colour of ox blood. To her relief, no one appeared to notice.

"No Derek tonight?" Cara asked.

"I packed him off to the pub," Lillian replied. "He thinks we're having an Ann Summers party."

"No wonder he didn't hang around," Cara laughed before explaining to the Romanian among them why a British man might find a group of drunk middle-aged women shopping for lingerie and sex toys a terrifying prospect.

"Skittles anyone?" Lillian asked as she lowered herself onto the last free bean bag clutching a party pack of sweets and the remote control.

"Don't mind if I do," Emilia replied. "Accidentally vegan?"

"But of course," she said as she settled in front of the TV.

Although the current affairs programme that they had gathered to watch wasn't starting for another 45 minutes, Lillian turned on the telly, keeping the volume low as they chatted, because there was always the possibility that once they began drinking and dissecting various events in their lives, the reason behind that night's essential viewing might be forgotten. And it was essential viewing, which is why Lillian had directed Emilia to the middle beanbag because it would be easier to hear her translation of the show, which was in Greek.

As it was, there was no reason for Lillian to fear the show might pass by unnoticed because Cara was like a coiled spring that evening, unable to concentrate on anything other than the TV screen in front of them. Emilia was also in a subdued mood, but this had always been her default setting, even before the MS diagnosis.

At 7.45 in a flurry of eye-catching stills depicting car crashes, prisoners in handcuffs, football riots and protesters marching to the beat of thumping music, the show started. As soon as the lights came on in the studio, the camera zoomed in on the face of a stern looking anchor woman sat behind a desk. Her name was Maria Panaretou and she was dressed in a high-necked blouse. Her black hair shone like polished jet, the strong make up she wore accentuated her almond-shaped eyes and she spoke rapidly, throwing out words from her painted mouth like bullets from a gun. Emilia nodded before waving her hands impatiently at the screen.

"Private school fees .... management of future gas revenues .... stalemate in Ankara ... and .... here we go ... first on the agenda is animal welfare vigilantes."

"Vigilantes?" Lillian asked, balking at the term as it always reminded her of lynch mobs in Wild West movies. She glanced at the other two to see if they shared her concern, but Emilia was deep in concentration and Cara was also glued to the screen, which seemed reasonable enough – her boyfriend was on the show.

The camera panned out from the sternly beautiful face of Maria Panaretou to offer viewers a glimpse of the waiting panel. Tonight, Maria would be joined by a member of the Animal Party, a representative of the Hunting Federation and Police Inspector Antoni Giagkos.

"Oh, he's good looking, Cara," Lillian said. "Like a Greek Tom Hardy."

Cara raised her eyebrows and squinted at the screen. "I suppose he does have something of the Hardy about him. I'd never noticed before."

"It's the lips." Lillian told her.

"Ladies please, I'm trying to concentrate," Emilia hissed just as a map of Cyprus appeared on the screen. To no one's surprise, Dromos was clearly marked on the west coast along with five red dots depicting "crime scenes", but there were other red dots scattered about the country, illustrating crimes that had taken place in Limassol, Pyla, Tochni, Trimiklini and Nicosia.

"Have you lot been moonlighting behind my back?" Lillian joked, before shutting up for the rest of the programme because Emilia told her to 'hush' and it was clear that Cara was unusually tense.

Finding her stride, Emilia kept up extremely well with the dialogue as she relayed the voice over revelations detailing the activity in and around Dromos as well as a number of "copycat crimes" elsewhere in the country. Apparently, the latter crimes included

slashed tyres, broken windows and released farm animals as well as
other acts of vandalism carried out on premises housing animals,
alive or dead as a butcher's shop was also targeted.

Maria Panaretou turned to Antoni and asked him why the police were so sure these were copycat incidents.

"In the Paphos region, the perpetrators of these crimes have
left a signature of sorts – a drawing of a dog's paw print – and
while some of the incidents elsewhere on the island have seen a
similar signature left at the scene, there is enough variation in the
drawings to suggest they have not been drawn by the same hand.
Furthermore, there is a distinct difference between the crimes that
have taken place in Dromos and elsewhere. The incidents we are
looking at have all had, I guess we can say, 'some humour' about
them. Don't misunderstand me, the police take these crimes as
seriously as any other, but there is an element of thought behind
the Paphos incidents, in as much as the type of crime committed
is often tailored to whatever alleged outrage these criminals feel
has taken place."

"For example?" asked Maria Panaretou, sternly.

"For example, a restaurateur in Paphos who was arrested earlier this year for cooking songbirds woke up to find large parts of
his premises, as well as the handle and steering wheel of his car,
covered in anti-climb paint – mimicking the glue-like lime sticks
used to illegally trap songbirds on the island. In another incident, a
Dromos resident who used to keep his dog chained to a tree, woke
up to find the dog gone and his car chained to the tree instead."

A small snigger escaped from the audience and even Maria
Panaretou let slip a smile before reiterating Antoni's earlier statement that these were serious crimes.

"And do you have any idea who the perpetrators are?" she asked.

"Not so far, but it's highly likely, due to the timing and scale of
some of these incidents, that there is a team at work here rather
than one individual."

Maria nodded and the camera panned away from Antoni, signalling his role in the show had come to an end. The spotlight then turned on the other two panellists. When asked for their views, the Animal Party representative gave cautious justification for the crimes, while stopping short of offering support, declaring that "right-thinking members of this country are sick of the abuse taking place, day in and day out, against animals on the island and these crimes are a symptom of the helplessness many feel." Meanwhile, the hunting guy made it clear that his members would never be deterred by "vigilante-style intimidation" and that the law of the land gave them every right to fire bullets at the wildlife whenever the seasons allowed for it.

"There speaks a true arsehole," Emilia said, before clarifying that she was referring to the hunter and not Cara's boyfriend.

"If he's still my boyfriend," Cara replied, and all eyes turned to her.

Despite muttering the line matter-of-factly, Cara couldn't have created more interest if she'd set off a flare gun in Lillian's living room. It was Lillian who was first to respond by getting up to refresh their glasses and tear open a box of accidentally-vegan Ritz crackers. Although Cara didn't especially feel like speaking, she had rather stupidly backed herself into a corner with no easy escape, so she flatly relived the meal she'd shared with Antoni and how it had all been going well until he discovered how old she was.

"He didn't know?" Emilia asked.

"Apparently not."

"Well, I'm sure he didn't take it that badly," Lillian assured her, but Cara shook her head.

"Lillian, he couldn't have looked more upset if I'd told him I used to be called Darren."

Two days after his TV appearance, Antoni got in touch with Cara, texting her to say he would be staying in Nicosia for a while as there were family issues to sort out, "and family is important, no?"

Now, Cara was an intelligent woman, and even if she wasn't,

she couldn't have failed to get the message, and it floored her. Expecting a time-out period of reflection, she never dreamed Antoni would cast her aside so easily, like soiled goods that had passed their expiry date. It was humiliating. Naturally, she told herself she was better off without him, and she was, but she couldn't escape the dirty, itchy feeling that now rested in her gut, telling her she was less of a woman than she had supposed herself to be. In the ping of a text message, she had become a washed-out, dried-up has-been, no longer within the age bracket of desirability. To think otherwise was delusional.

"Are you sure you're not being a little hasty? After all, he doesn't say it's over."

Cara shrugged, Lillian had a point, but after the meal there had been complete radio silence until this one brief message. More than that, she couldn't forget the look of horror on Antoni's face when he discovered her age. Even if it wasn't over for him, and she was pretty sure it was, it was certainly over for her. No man had the right to make her feel of diminished value. No matter her age.

"It's over, Lillian. I know him well enough to read between the, admittedly brief, lines."

"Well, in that case, it's disgusting, if you don't mind me saying." Lillian's top lip curled as she spoke, unable to fathom how any man could finish a relationship with a message on a phone. "Cowardly too. Men are such shits."

Cara took her eyes off Emilia, who was attempting some fancy footwork with her horse, and looked at Lillian. She couldn't put her finger on it, but there was something different about her these days, and it wasn't just the mild expletives. The hair was less perfect, the clothes a little edgier, and there was a different manner about her. She hadn't grown hard as such, but she was definitely fiercer than she used to be.

"What's she doing again?" Lillian asked, staring at Emilia in some confusion, unaware she was being scrutinised by Cara. "Is it a half passage?"

"A half pass, I think she said."

"And is she doing it correctly?"

"I've no idea. But whatever she's doing it looks kind of pretty."

"And she's smiling."

"Yes, she is. It's almost worth all the flies just to see that."

"I wouldn't go that far." Lillian slapped at her bare legs. "These buggers bite."

"I know! I had no idea flies bit people. Defecating and puking on their food, yes, but biting?"

"I can't recall ever being bitten by one in England."

"Did you hang around horse yards in those days?"

"No, not really. I usually hung around Debenhams."

Later that morning – once Emilia had stopped riding in order to baffle her friends with the technical details of what she was trying to achieve, what she had failed to achieve and what she would now work on in order to achieve it – they shared a late lunch at Cara's house. The spread included a huge bowl of tabbouleh and a platter of vegan cheese, grapes and nuts with toasted pita bread. To quench their thirst, there was fresh watermelon juice and a bottle of sauvignon blanc. Everyone took a glass of each, and once they had eaten, they got to work.

Despite the condemnation of the police and most politicians, their efforts to help Cyprus's animals had garnered the growing support of the public. Though they had never set out to raise awareness as such, it was gratifying to see that they had triggered a very real, and sometimes heated, debate about animal welfare on the island. The copycat incidents still taking place were as much a hindrance as a help because while they kept the fire burning, it was occasionally a little too fiercely for those with more conservative values who went to bed at night worrying about anarchists. However, there was increasingly vocal support from the animal rescue community, of which there was a staggering number of interconnecting, and sometimes warring, factions along with well-meaning individuals fighting their own battles for the animals of the country. So, after taking all of this into consideration, it was decided that after a period of rest in order to let the dust lie, they might as well continue what they had started.

"The thing is, if we really want to make a difference, we may need to up our game," Cara told them, ready to come out fighting now she was single.

"What do you mean by 'up our game'?" asked Lillian cautiously.

"Well, we could go on with our funny little escapades, raising the odd smile as we save one animal at a time, or we could send out a very clear, and very loud message, that this abuse has to stop." Cara paused to reach over to the sideboard where there was a folder holding copies of a news article and a number of Facebook posts detailing a farm-cum-shelter-cum-morgue in Kivotos on the outskirts of Paphos. Lillian and Emilia took their sheets of paper. As they read, they shook their heads, though Emilia recognised the place from her own research.

The farm in Kivotos had been in the Press some time ago, having been the subject of a police investigation and court action, and yet like a psycho phoenix rising from the ashes, it had opened again to repeat the same atrocities. In recent days, a couple of tourists had stumbled upon the place only to find sick and starving dogs lying in their own faeces without food or water. Some were feeding off the flesh of other dogs that had died in the same cages. According to the news articles, a local man was paid by the council to take dogs off the street. When he was arrested for neglect a couple of years ago, he had claimed that the farm had fallen into disrepair after his wife had fallen ill and he needed to care for her. However, after the tourists posted new photos of the current state of the place, and the dire living conditions of up to 20 dogs there, a couple of rescuers managed to release at least four from their cages, only to be told by the police to give them back or face arrest. The man wanted his dogs, perhaps to sell to hunters when the next season came around, perhaps because he was mentally ill, but the farm had reverted back to the hell it was known for and, once again, dogs were dying in their own filth and disease.

When everyone had finished reading, there was a moment of silence as they individually digested the horrific reality facing the dogs in Kivotos.

"I have no words," Lillian eventually said.

"And I have no plan yet," Cara replied. "But I wanted you to read about this farm, what it was and what it is again, and then tell me whether you might want to do something about it, permanently."

"It's a no-brainer for me," Emilia told her. "I was already aware of the place and I absolutely want to shut the fucker down."

"Me too," Lillian said sombrely.

"In that case, let's give it some thought. Clearly, we'll need to check it out, if only to see where it is exactly and what we might do to help those poor dogs."

"You know me, I'm no kind of extremist," said Lillian. "But I would happily cut off this man's testicles if it meant I could stop this abuse once and for all."

"Sounds a little extreme to me," Emilia teased. "Though I would willingly hold him down while you perform the surgery. And while we're looking at the bigger picture, I also have an impossible request I'd like to put out there. For the life of me, I don't know what we can do about this situation, but Death Alley has been playing on my mind since I checked it out, so I'd be grateful if we could at least give it some thought."

"Yes, of course," both Lillian and Cara agreed.

"Thank you," said Emilia. "Then, I formally announce that the Dromos Animal Liberation Front is once again operational."

The three friends raised their glasses.

"All for one…"

"… and one for dogs!"

"And horses," added Emilia.

Chapter Nineteen

To the surprise of at least three residents of Dromos, the interest in the 'Dog Paw Gang' didn't die down as quickly as the Dromos Animal Liberation Front had envisaged it might, and after some cryptic texting, because it paid to be careful, a meeting of the three founding members, who were in fact the only members, brought unanimous agreement that they should "keep the fuck out of the way" for a little while longer. Emilia was chairing that particular meeting.

While everyone agreed that the publicity was gratifying, they also found it exasperating because while everyone appeared to be talking about animal welfare and the need for steeper fines and harsher punishments for abusers, as well as the implementation of more stringent laws, nothing appeared to be getting done. Meanwhile, not a day went by that didn't see more stray dogs posted on Facebook in various states of distress and injury, as well as warnings about poison being laid in public areas and the usual roll call of abuse including dogs hung by the neck, cats being shot, a Rottweiler dragged to its death, puppies thrown out of cars onto the highway, and an act of bestiality caught on CCTV by a suspicious sheep farmer. Despite Cara, Lillian and Emilia's efforts, as well as those of the wider community, the catalogue of crimes carried out against animals showed no sign of abating, and this was in a climate of public outrage.

"It's great that more people are finally speaking up for animals, but the trouble is, when people talk too much, the authorities look to silence them," Emilia said, which seemed a little dark, but no one could fault the logic in staying under the radar while the police faced increasing pressure to bring in results.

"Well, I've got a feature to write on a former nun working as a tour rep in Ayia Napa," Cara said. "I guess I could get on with that and pay some bills. My electricity bill is off the scale this month."

"Well, this is the reality of a monopoly; they can charge pretty much what they like," Emilia remarked. "I'm no capitalist, but there are companies on this island that could do with competition."

"The taxi service for one," said Lillian. "It's going to cost me a small fortune to get to Paphos and back when my car goes in for a service this week. I also need to get on and finish your room, Emilia."

"Oh man, don't go to too much trouble. I only need a bed and a wash basin."

Lillian rolled her eyes. "I'm not a Mormon, darling. I'm sure we can go one better than a wash basin."

"Wash basin and jug?" Cara suggested.

"I may even throw in a flannel," Lillian replied.

"Well, now you're just spoiling me," Emilia laughed, playing along though she felt a little uncomfortable about it.

"And how will you spend this free time?" Lillian asked Emilia.

"Yes, do tell us, we haven't the faintest idea," Cara said.

"Who knows," Emilia replied. "But maybe I'll look in on Adonis."

"Good idea, that half pass could do with some work," Lillian teased.

"You don't have enough bend," Cara agreed.

"So, everyone's a critic now," Emilia moaned, though she couldn't fault their accuracy; the half pass did need work and there wasn't enough bend.

Despite everything that had recently happened, Emilia was happier than she could remember being for a long while. The weight she had unwittingly carried on her shoulders as she tried to pretend, even to herself, that she was fine, lifted as soon as she was forced to admit she wasn't. And though in some ways it felt like she had regressed 30 years, with her friends stepping in to play mother, Emilia was glad of their care. She was tired of fending for herself. She was tired of being strong. And, much of the time, she was just plain tired. But now she had minimal hours to work, daily medication to keep her steadier on her feet and as much time as she needed to spend with her horse. Overnight, life had become easier, nicer, kinder. And maybe because she was more relaxed, her riding had improved and she felt herself beginning to mould into Adonis, becoming a part of him as their minds connected through the balanced harmony of their bodies. When she rode her horse, it felt like their spirits were melting into one. Though Emilia had tried on a number of occasions to explain to Cara and Lillian how it felt riding Adonis, she knew they didn't get it. Not really. It was a feeling that was almost impossible to understand without experiencing it, which was one of the many reasons she revelled in the company of Julia. Emilia had always been a keen student of subjects she had a passion for and she soaked up the knowledge of those who possessed it. Whenever she experienced a lightbulb moment during her riding, she loved the fact that she could simply glance in Julia's direction and Julia would get it. Her friends no doubt thought she was obsessed, and they were right. Horses had a magic to them and when they allowed you in, nothing else mattered. Nothing at all. Not until the moment you stepped away and trudged back to reality. And then, of course, the same old worries were there and the usual insecurities, but Emilia wasn't alone in feeling vulnerable, which she found selfishly comforting.

"My greatest fear about getting old is not watching my looks disappear or my body slow down or my hair and teeth falling out or even peeing myself when I laugh," Julia told Emilia, who looked suitably horrified by all that was to come. "No, the thing that concerns me most is that one day I'll have to stop all this. There will be no more animals – not a horse or a dog or even a cat. At that point, I know I will be truly alone. All my life I have had animals, but if I died, who would look after them? Who would love them the way

I love them and care for them the way I care for them? And that is my greatest fear in life."

Emilia nodded, but said nothing immediately. She was aching to tell Julia that she needn't worry, that she would always step in, that she wouldn't allow her horses to perish or go unloved, but the chances of her being around much longer than Julia weren't great. So, she tried to lighten the mood. "Have you thought about getting a Tamagotchi?"

Cara never meant to lose her temper. In fact, she thought it would be the last thing she'd do. The situation was bad enough without causing a scene, but she had imagined that Antoni might come looking for her at some point, and when he did, she had imagined she would be polite, impeccably dressed, and open to talk about things; in order to coldly shut him down once he'd finished. You see, Cara knew from experience that in situations like this, the very worst thing she could do was go looking for answers. So, the very worst thing she could do was exactly the very worst thing she did.

At first, there was nothing to indicate the day would go so spectacularly awry, in fact the start of it was pretty standard, with Cooper clawing at her face as soon as the sun came up. This was kind of annoying in the summer when dawn arrived at 5.50am, but she duly got out of bed and let both dogs outside to pee. Then, once Cooper and Peaches had finished their breakfast, they all clambered into the car and headed for the hills before the goats were released to roam the area. After returning home, Cara gave her dogs time to cool off before going to pick up a package waiting for her at the Post Office. As it wasn't even close to her birthday or Christmas, she assumed the package was a book she had ordered some weeks earlier, The Song for Achilles by Madeline Miller. It had received great reviews and she hoped it would distract her for a while, so off she went in her trusty Ford Puma, the music on and the windows down because the air con no longer worked, and everything was pretty much as it should be, until she saw his car.

Antoni's BMW was pretty distinctive as far as cars went because it had two racing stripes running down the centre of the
paintwork. Cara was no seasoned detective, but when she saw the
BMW sat in the police station car park, she could only conclude
that Antoni had returned from Nicosia and returned to work. Or-
dinarily, she might have known this because he would have texted
to say this was the case. So, to find out like this, on the way to the
Post Office to pick up a book she hoped would take her mind off
him, was simply unbearable, and because she still retained some of
the hot-headedness that had been the hallmark of her youth, she
pulled into the police station car park with a screech of tyres and
went looking for answers.

Storming through the station's gated entrance, the wind was
momentarily knocked out of her sails by the sight of an empty
reception desk and a middle-aged Cypriot guy sat on a chair weep-
ing. Cara looked around, feeling her cheeks burn as she belatedly
realised that she was acting like a deranged stalker. But just as she
was about to try and save face by spinning on her heels, she heard
a voice she vaguely recognised.

"*Yiassou* Cara *mou*, I'll tell him you are here."

Before Cara had chance to tell Special Constable Michalis
Georgiou that there was really no need and it had all been a terrible mistake, he was gone. Feeling the walls creeping in as her
embarrassment grew, she vaguely pondered the idea of making a
run for it, but then the crying man looked at her and all hope of
escape vanished.

"I'm sorry," he said.

"Sorry?"

"It's… my dog," the man gasped, lifting the dog lead he held in
his hands like it was some form of explanation. "I'm sorry."

"Please, don't apologise."

Wiping roughly at his eyes, the man straightened his back,
sniffed hard and Cara gave him a moment to compose himself.

"This is maybe stupid to you, I don't know," he said, finally finding enough control over his emotions to speak. "But to me, this is the end. I see no tomorrow."

"Why? What has happened to your dog?"

"He killed him. He killed my boy, my beautiful Milo – the happiest, friendliest, most good souled dog a man ever had. And he poisoned him. Milo died a terrible way, shaking and vomiting, and he looked at me to help him, but what could I do? There was no time. I could do nothing. I had to watch him suffer. I felt his heart stop and I pushed his body and I tried to keep him alive, but he was gone and so I carried him home in my arms. I walked two miles to my house, then I dig and make hole to bury him. I covered my beautiful boy with the dirt of this country. This country that breeds monsters who murder."

Cara shook her head, her heart instinctively going out to this wreck of a man who had lost his best friend. "Are you sure you know who laid the poison that killed your dog?"

"One hundred percent," he said fiercely. "That bastard who spends his life drinking and smoking and living in the shadows, he put a bowl of poisoned food on the ground, in the reach of every living animal passing by. So, now I am here and I want justice. I want him in prison. He is a murderer, nothing less. I pray to God no other person goes through what I go through today. He must be stopped. It is not the first time he has killed, and it won't be the last, but nothing is ever done. But this time I will make sure he pays for what he has done, even if I kill him myself."

"So, who did this?"

"Nicos Andreou, the murdering bastard at the old Astraea Taverna."

Cara had never heard of the Astraea Taverna, but just as she was about to ask where it might be, Michalis returned to the front desk.

"Sorry, Miss Cara. Antoni in meeting and not speak now."

Caught off guard, having momentarily forgotten her reason for being there, Cara's cheeks went nuclear as she tried to deal with the embarrassment of not only being in the police station, but of being fobbed off in the police station. Michalis looked at her and she could see the pity in his eyes. It was mortifying.

"Thank you, Michalis," she said, before tipping her head towards the Cypriot guy who was crying again. "That poor man. Still, at least you know who killed his dog."

"Do we?" Michalis replied laughing, which struck Cara as fairly callous under the circumstances. "He say who kills dog, but where is proof? Dog eat the proof and dog now buried. Sad, but what can we do?"

"You mean, the poisoner will get away with it?"

"Meh," was all Special Constable Michalis replied before shrugging his shoulders for added indifference. Cara was furious.

As she turned to leave, Michalis shouted at her, asking if she wanted to leave a message for Antoni.

"Yes," Cara said, calmly looking over her shoulder. "Please tell him to go fuck himself."

Chapter Twenty

Once they were agreed that something needed to be done, which didn't take long, the three members of the Dromos Animal Liberation Front put a plan together. This took a little while longer. First on the agenda was pinpointing exactly where the Astraea Taverna was. Lillian got on the phone to Janet.

"Oh, the Ashtray Taverna, as I call it," Janet said. "Yes, I know where it is; up in the hills on the road to Polis towards the back of Dromos. Why do you ask?"

"No reason," Lillian replied breezily, but Janet was a seasoned veteran of village intrigue and as she already had an inkling that Lillian was up to stuff she wholeheartedly agreed with, she knew there had to be a valid reason for her asking. Still, better to be in the dark than in the heat of the sun, and so she asked no more questions. Instead, and without invitation, she divulged everything she knew about the taverna, just in case the details might be helpful to someone asking for no reason.

"The Astraea is now called Nicos Taverna and it's owned and managed, if that's what you can call it, by a swivel-eyed little weasel called Nicos Andreou. His father is a big noise in the district council who's currently throwing up apartments all along the coastline in the hope that the fabled marina will finally get the go ahead. His son is just as greedy, but not as clever about it. My Alfred, who's always been short of backbone, but big on cards, used to attend the gambling nights up at the taverna, until I got wind of it. Every Wednesday they happen. Just Nicos and a few old drunks easily parted from their money. From what I recall, they usually meet at nine and are skint by twelve. It's dark up there. No street lights. And occasionally, once the others have gone, Nicos sleeps where he drops because one floor is as good as another since his wife kicked him out."

"I have to say, that's all very helpful," Lillian told Janet, now certain beyond doubt that 'Old Peg Leg' knew she was involved in some way with the Dromos Animal Liberation Front.

"You'd be surprised by what I know," Janet replied. "If there's anything else you need, just shout."

And because there seemed no point in being coy, Lillian confided that she did in fact need something else. "You don't own a gun, do you?"

For a moment, the line went quiet. Just as Lillian was about to laugh away the comment as a joke, Janet quietly confessed that she did in fact know someone selling firearms.

"It depends what you want them for," she said. "These guns might not be suitable because they've been decommissioned".

"Decommissioned?"

"They no longer fire bullets, though they look like they do, a bit like my Alfred."

Lillian paused, wondering how far she ought to involve Janet. It wasn't that she didn't trust her, but if things went wrong, trust often fell by the wayside among acquaintances. However, if their plan was to work, they badly needed a weapon, or at least something that looked like a weapon. Lillian had already scoured the nearest toy shops and even the most convincing replica would have seen them laughed out of the playground let alone the bar of a hard-drinking swivel-eyed weasel. So, guns that were actually guns sounded ideal.

"I'm interested," she told Janet quietly.

"Then I'll get the address."

Later that day, Cara took a deep breath before knocking on the door in front of her, not knowing what to expect, but imagining she might be about to meet her first survivalist. Instead, she came face-to-face with a woman who was barely 5ft tall called Doris.

"You must be here about the guns," she said.

"That obvious?"

"It is when you've had only one inquiry, from a woman with a British accent," replied Doris who appeared to possess a lot of firearms and no sense of humour.

The tiny woman, who must have been pushing seventy, invited Cara into her home, a very nice, detached bungalow on the coastal road next to a banana plantation. The rooms were light and airy and, for the most part, painted magnolia. Cara noticed the paint was fresh. She took another look around, seeing the house was furnished, but not overly so. In fact, it looked like a show house rather than a home.

"Have you been here long?" Cara asked.

"Nearly 27 years," Doris revealed. "But I'm done now. My husband died last year and I thought I might be able to cope, but after forty years of marriage you get used to company. I'm lonely. It's time to move back to the UK and spend how many years I have left with my children and grandchildren."

Cara smiled in sympathy. Doris's story wasn't unique. A lot of pensioners retired here for the sun only to return home for their own setting of it.

"I'm sorry to hear about your husband," she said.

"Thank you. The guns you want were his. He had a thing for them, but didn't trust them too much, that's why they're all deactivated. Well, for that reason and postal regulations. Anyway, I never liked them much when he was alive and I sure as hell don't like them any more now that he's dead. If I can sell them, I will, if not the collection goes on the scrap heap."

"How many are there?" Cara asked, taken aback by talk of a collection.

"Perhaps 20 or more. I'm not sure. But they all have to go."

And that's why, when Cara drove to Doris's house to buy herself a convincing firearm, she left with a small arsenal of handguns in the boot of her car that included a Glock, a Browning, a Ruger, a Dan Wesson, a Bersa Firestorm and a locally-bought, and working, air rifle.

"Why on earth did you buy them all?" Lillian asked, her face quite incredulous as Cara upended the haul onto her carpet.

"She wouldn't sell them piecemeal. It was all or nothing."

"Oh, this is freaking awesome!" shrieked Emilia, picking up a gun and glancing at the label the dear-departed husband of Doris had attached to it. "The Glock is definitely mine."

"They all look the same to me," Cara admitted before rummaging around and opting for the Dan Wesson. "Lillian?"

Lillian shook her head, hardly believing what she was doing. Then, with a smile, she picked up two handguns. "The Browning for the belt," she said, tucking the barrel into her shorts, "and the Ruger for the shooting."

"They've been decommissioned," Cara reminded her.

"That's OK," Lillian replied. "I'm good at sound effects. I'm like that guy from Police Academy." Taking the Browning from her belt she waved both guns above her head. "Po-pow-pow-pow."

Gathering everything they needed didn't take as long as envisaged, possibly because the guns were expected to be the main sticking point. Now they had more guns than they could handle, and Cara had already thought of a use for the air rifle. So, when the next Wednesday came around, the three members of the Dromos Animal Liberation Front decided they were ready to return to the frontline.

At 10pm, Cara drove to Lillian's house, leaving Peaches and Cooper tucked up in their beds, sleeping to the soothing sounds of Sol Seppy. As she pulled up, her phone vibrated with a text message. Her first thought was that the plan had been aborted.

"Busy week! Sorry! Dinner tomorrow?"

Above the message, the phone's display showed the text was from ANTONI.

Naturally, Cara's heart raced at the contact, as pathetic and flimsy as it was, but whereas a few years earlier she might have hurled herself at such a lifeline in order to salvage the romance, today she wasn't so keen. She understood she deserved better.

"No, can do. Busy too!" she replied.

Twenty seconds later, there was another text.

"Busy all week?"

"All year, I suspect."

There was a couple of minutes silence before the phone pinged a reply. "OK. I get it. I'm sorry. Let's talk."

Cara hesitated, not sure how to respond, before deciding that ignoring the text was probably the best response she could give. Anything more would have looked like encouragement or weakness and she was in no mood for either. Cara had been played and mollified enough in the past. She was no longer that woman. She would never be that woman again. And with that decided, she put the phone in her pocket and got out of the car, dressed head to toe in black and clutching a balaclava.

Letting herself in through the back door, Cara found Lillian and Emilia in the kitchen. The lights were on, the curtains were drawn and they were gathering their tools on the kitchen table; three decommissioned handguns, an old skipping rope (without handles and cut in two); and a box of chocolate truffles.

"Nervous?" Lillian asked in greeting.

"A bit," Cara admitted.

"I know I am," said Emilia. "In fact, I could really do with a poo."

"You better go then," Lillian advised, and she pointed her towards the toilet under the stairs.

"I think I might go, too," Cara said, and Lillian rolled her eyes before ushering her down the hallway towards the en suite bathroom in the spare bedroom.

As Emilia and Cara did what they needed to do, Lillian rechecked everything on the table before putting the rope and chocolates in the Louis Vuitton that Derek had bought her for their 20th wedding anniversary. It seemed a lifetime ago and not a little ironic to think that her marriage had dated more badly than the bag.

"That's better," Cara said as she returned to the kitchen.

"That was quick," Lillian remarked.

"False alarm. Wind."

"Perils of being a vegan, I imagine."

"OK, I'm ready," Emilia said as she also returned to the kitchen, a little slower than Cara suggesting her predicament had less to do with the hazards of a plant-based diet.

With only the guns left on the kitchen table, the three friends took hold of their weapon of choice and looked at each other.

"All for one…" Cara said.

"… and all for dogs."

After a group high five, they turned out the lights and got going because the hour was getting late and they had work to do.

Picking a vantage point some way above the Nicos Taverna, they sat in the dark with the windows down, thankful for the hilltop breeze because it was another hot night and they were all dressed like the man from Milk Tray. As far as they could tell, there were two other vehicles parked outside the taverna, which meant the card game must be on. From various drive-pasts earlier in the week, they had ascertained that Nicos owned a battered old Land Rover which he usually parked at the back of the premises.

Incredibly, it was the first time that Lillian, Cara and Emilia had experienced the island's nocturnal life, rather than its nightlife, and they found themselves amazed by how loud it was, with none of them able to identify, with any certainty, the various calls of nature beyond the hoot of an owl. They fared little better when their attention turned to the bright canopy of constellations above their heads.

"Americans call the Plough the Big Dipper," Cara mentioned.

"I thought the Big Dipper was a roller coaster," replied Emilia.

"It was," confirmed Lillian. "At one stage it was a huge attraction in London – until it killed five passengers."

"I can see why that might put people off," said Cara.

"People are weak," muttered Emilia, who was only half joking.

Cara edged forward from the back seat of Lillian's car. "Hold up, is that movement?"

Ahead of them, a crack of light appeared at the entrance to the taverna, allowing them to see the indistinct form of a man bouncing off the doorframe and stumbling onto the broken pathway before making a sharp right to face a prickly hedge.

"Is he peeing?" Lillian asked, slightly aghast.

"Looks like it," Cara said.

"Doesn't the place have toilets?"

"Some men prefer to piss in the open," replied Emilia.

"They also like to shit there, in my experience," Cara said.

"Then, you may have been dating the wrong guys."

"Ain't that the truth."

In the driver's seat, Lillian tutted, not at Cara or Emilia for once, but rather at the man peeing in the hedge. She didn't stop shaking her head until he bounced back indoors and the taverna once again descended into near darkness.

As the clock steadily ticked towards midnight, the three friends kept themselves entertained by throwing out random questions requiring some effort of thought. Would you sleep with someone for €1million? (Yes, yes, no). If you could kill someone and get away with it, who would it be? (Donald Trump, Joseph Kony, the person who invented CAPTCHAs). The best music to have sex to? (Adagio for Strings, anything by Ennio Morricone, Motorhead). And if you could give your 16-year-old self one piece of advice, what would it be?

"Get health insurance," quipped Emilia.

Despite the seriousness of her situation, both Lillian and Cara laughed. It was an answer they couldn't beat, but before they could even try, they were silenced by light escaping from the front door of the taverna. On this occasion, there was no random man pee-ing in the bushes, but rather a group of random men who heaved themselves into the two vehicles parked at the front of the prem-ises with varying degrees of agility. Lights switched on, engines started, tyres crunched on the crumbling surface and slowly they drove away, heading towards Dromos.

Neither Lillian, Cara or Emilia said a word as they watched the vehicles' tail lights fade and disappear. They then got out of Lillian's car and walked on foot to the taverna. Having gone over the plan, time and again, paying meticulous attention to the detail, the three of them operated as one, without needing direction. Reaching the restaurant, they made their way to the back of the premises and waited by the door. As hoped, within ten minutes of their arrival, the lights went out, the back door opened and a wiry, middle-aged man, who was clearly inebriated, emerged. As he turned to lock the door, Emilia stepped forward and with a calmness that sur-prised even her, she placed the barrel of her gun against the man's neck and spoke to him in Greek.

"Hello Nicos. We'd like a word, if you please."

Even in the dark, the white of the man's eyes was clear to see. He rummaged in his pockets and pulled out a wad of rolled up Euros.

"Here, take it, take it! Take it all!" he shouted and Emilia re-sponded by pressing the gun harder into his neck.

"Keep your voice down and go back inside," she ordered.

Nicos duly opened the door, stumbling over the back step as he re-entered the taverna. As he slipped, Emilia somehow managed to keep hold of one arm and returned the barrel of the gun to the base of his neck. However, once inside the kitchen, Nicos hit the light switch and span around quickly, no doubt hoping to catch his attacker off guard. Unfortunately for him, his attacker was sober and she also had back up – back up that now had their guns trained on his face.

"Please, what is it you want?" Nicos begged, feeling tears sting his eyes because it had been a tough year thanks to his wife kicking him out and the last thing he needed was to be robbed at gunpoint in his own taverna.

Emilia looked to her side and nodded at Cara who stepped forward, grabbed a chair and placed it in the middle of the room. Lillian then joined her and together they pressed on Nicos' shoulders, encouraging him to take a seat. Cara next took his arms, placed them behind his back and bound his hands using cable ties while Lillian tied his feet to the chair legs using the skipping rope from her bag. Once it was clear Nicos was going nowhere fast, Cara and Lillian retreated to their positions behind Emilia as she placed a chair in front of their victim and sat down to face him.

"Well, I guess you may be wondering why we are here," she began. "We're here, Nicos because of a dog named Milo; a beloved pet that died in agony because you left poisoned meat outside your taverna and he ate it. Now, I feel I must warn you that we are very big animal lovers. In fact, you may have heard of us because we have been in the news rather a lot lately, administering justice for those without the means to do so for themselves. And because it is only right and holy that an eye should be given for an eye, we have prepared a fitting punishment for you. Yes, you are about to get a taste of your own medicine in a handy bite-sized chocolate. Isn't that exciting?"

As Nicos rocked in his chair, trying to get away now he knew what was coming, he opened his mouth to scream only to be silenced by the firearm Emilia rammed into his crotch. Under the ski mask she wore, she smiled.

"We are not inhuman," she continued, speaking softly, as though to a baby. "And we are fair. So, we are going to give you the chance to decide your fate. You see, we have gone to a lot of trouble to create some special chocolates for you. They won't taste great, thanks to the poison in them, and they might burn your throat on their way down to attack your vital organs. The chances are you will also shit your pants almost immediately, but – and this is where the choice comes in – you have a 30% survival rate if you are found within 24 hours. Of course, maybe you don't like the idea of eating these chocolates and maybe you'll decide you don't want to eat them. That's fine. We live in a democracy; you have a choice. But I think I must tell you that if you don't eat your chocolates, I will shoot your testicles. This may also burn a little and I'd be surprised if you didn't soil your pants, but there is a 40% chance that you will survive the loss of blood. Of course, you'll never be able to pee like a man again or make sweet, sweet love to that estranged wife of yours, but, as I said, the choice is yours. Testicles or chocolates."

Emilia nodded at Lillian, who stepped forward holding a box of chocolates. Taking one out with gloved fingers she placed it near their victim's mouth. At first, he turned his head away, but after Emilia reminded him of the other option by pressing the barrel of the gun more firmly into his privates, he opened his mouth, whimpering as he did so. As the first chocolate went in, the tears began to fall and Lillian had to force his mouth shut. At the initial heat burning his mouth, his eyes bulged and he gasped for air. As he did so, Lillian took the opportunity to pop another chocolate in. Meanwhile, and to help Nicos better understand what he was experiencing, Cara talked him through it.

"You'll probably feel nauseous soon, to the point where you might vomit. There will be pain, of course, which is pretty understandable because of the internal bleeding you'll suffer as the poison hits your stomach. Then your breathing will become increasingly difficult, you'll probably begin to convulse and your organs will slowly start to shut down, which is about the point where you'll shit yourself. Anyway, enjoy. It's free chocolate and who doesn't enjoy free chocolate?"

Emilia nodded again at Lillian who continued to force feed Nicos until the man peed his pants in panic and passed out. Emilia immediately moved her chair away from the mess he had become, and Cara and Lillian placed two more chairs either side of her.

"Dostoevsky?" Lillian asked, using the code word they had arranged earlier.

Cara raised a finger and shook her head. After waiting another ten minutes, she finally said in English, "Well, that was easier than I thought it would be."

Chapter Twenty-One

Inspector Antoni Giagkos didn't know what to do for the best. He had been utterly stupid, selfish and insensitive, but he also felt entitled to a certain amount of idiocy. It had been a shock to discover he was dating a woman who was eight years older than him. Rightly or wrongly, he had a lot to think about. Having buried his dreams of becoming a father once, he wasn't sure he could do it again. And even if, by some miracle, he could convince Cara to start a family, should they ever get to that stage, by the time their kid reached 15 she would be entitled to a pension. It was a sobering thought. And for a few days, Antoni dealt with it by getting drunk. Then, once the shock of the facts began to wear off, and the hangover kicked in, he started to remember how funny and clever and hot she was, and the idea of Cara being close to retirement seemed somehow farcical. More than that, he missed her.

Having come to this realisation before Cara pitched up at his place of work, her timing had been unfortunate and her parting comment gave room for doubt that they'd be laughing about this episode anytime soon. At first, Antoni had been confused as to why Cara should leave such a message with Michalis, but then events tripped into place. He had been remote while in Nicosia, too busy naval-gazing to appreciate how his silence might be affecting her. Then he was called into work earlier than he might have wished because the district police chief insisted on meeting him. In fact, it was Superintendent Constantinos Parpis he was speaking to when Cara turned up at the station. If he had been in her shoes, he too might have believed that the only reason he couldn't speak with her was because he didn't want to. Cara was angry and she had every right to be, which triggered a whole new cycle of naval-gazing, this time wondering whether he was the right man for her, rather than her being the right woman for him. It took Antoni a few days to consider he might be over analysing things. He then decided to rectify the situation that Wednesday. As fate would have it, he was on the evening shift and couldn't do much about it until 10pm, when he was free to go home. Thankfully, he'd had the foresight to buy wine and flowers earlier in the day. So, equipped with all the relevant accessories, he drove to Cara's house, only to find the dogs alone listening to some weirdness on the stereo.

Antoni's first thought was to call Cara's phone, but as her car wasn't in the drive, he rightfully guessed she was with friends and it probably wasn't the most opportune moment to try and make amends. Even so, having made up his mind to make up, he couldn't let another evening pass without some effort on his part. So, he texted. To his surprise Cara answered quickly, which was slightly reassuring until he read the message. After that he wasn't sure what to do, other than turn the car around, go home and try again in the morning. However, the gods appeared to be working against him because the sun had barely risen before he received a call from the office. There had been an attempted murder, and as this was unusual territory for Dromos, no one was quite sure what to do about it.

By the time Antoni got to the station, the Chief Inspector was pacing the office waiting for him. There was a glint in his eye that could have been excitement, nerves or borderline hysteria.

"I need you to go to the old Astraea Taverna with forensics," he said abruptly. "Last night the proprietor Nicos Andreou was tied to a chair and force-fed poison. Unfortunately, the place has been partially compromised by his father who received an anonymous tip-off about his son. You'll need to speak to him at some point. Michalis will give you the details."

"Michalis?"

"Yes, take him with you. It's good experience. There's also a protest at the Akamas today. The Greens are up in arms about building work along the coastline, so we're short on manpower."

"And where is the victim?"

"In the hospital being seen to, having tests, still alive. We'll know more later."

With little choice in the matter, Antoni grabbed a coffee and spoke with the forensics team from Paphos who were already en route. He then picked up Michalis from the local coffee shop and together they made their way to the old Astraea Taverna.

"Shouldn't we have the siren on?" Michalis asked, while rubbing at a food stain on his shirt.

"Does it look like we're being hindered by traffic?"

"But this is serious police work."

"All police work is serious."

"Oh, come on, let's put on the siren."

"No."

"Please."

"For the love of God, how old are you?"

Antoni's exasperation with Michalis was compounded by a nagging feeling that he was missing something. There was a thread of a memory he couldn't catch hold of. He was almost certain he had heard the victim's name before, and quite recently. He simply couldn't figure out where and why.

Ten minutes later, sirens blaring, Antoni and Michalis arrived at the taverna. Forensics had turned up some moments earlier and the team leader feigned surprise as they got out of the car.

"Look at you guys sneaking up on us."

As the other men smiled Antoni died a little inside.

After telling Michalis to stay in the patrol car, Antoni looked around the place. He had passed the taverna once or twice before and had assumed it was derelict. Apparently not. Despite its ramshackle appearance and the devastation of the grounds surrounding it, inside there was a fully functioning bar, despite half the room being used as a skip. The place also smelled of recently smoked cigarettes. In the kitchen, the odour was mainly that of bodily functions.

"I think he pissed himself," Michalis said, appearing at the back door and pointing at the puddle that had formed under a chair.

"I thought I told you to stay in the car."

Michalis turned his head, pretending not to hear. As there was a police photographer from the district office present in the room, Antoni let the moment go. Besides, Michalis wasn't wrong in his observation; it did look like the guy had pissed himself. A small stream of urine had clearly been making its way to the three other chairs in the room, positioned in a row like theatre seats facing a spectacle. He also noticed a small knife abandoned on the floor.

"Interesting," Antoni muttered, stepping away while indicating to the photographer that he might want to take a picture of the knife. And that's when he remembered where he had heard Nicos Andreou's name before — the dog, Milo. Spinning on his heels, he began to look for the evidence to back up his suspicions.

"Lost something?" Michalis asked from the doorway.

"Not lost, looking," Antoni replied cryptically. Less than a second later he found what he was searching for on the Formica table; a dog's paw print, drawn by a hand that now seemed familiar. Less familiar was the solitary chocolate left at the side of it. He beckoned to the photographer, who duly took more pictures. After marking the spot, the forensic team then bagged the chocolate and it was immediately sent for tests so the hospital might know what poison they were dealing with.

On their return to Dromos, Antoni went to visit Marios Andreou, the father of the victim.

A large man in an expensive suit, Marios was short on small talk and big on self-promotion and as a consequence he was well known in the community. As Antoni was from out of town, he knew him only by reputation. It wasn't great.

"It was an anonymous call, no number," Marios told Antoni.

"What time?"

"About 4.15am."

"And what did they say?"

"It was a woman's voice, she spoke in Greek, but with an accent, like one of those Romanians or Russians, and she said I should go and check on my son at his taverna."

"And you took the call seriously?"

"Well, yes. You know what it's like here. I'm a big man, with a big business and it's about to get a whole lot bigger when the marina is built. It's this kind of success which breeds jealousy and some of my rivals, well, as I said, you know what it's like here."

Antoni nodded because he did know what it was like, and arson attacks on rival restaurants and nightclubs were far from unusual. Though there were fewer guns and home-made bombs on the island than in the past, they hadn't died out completely. However, in this case, Antoni was pretty sure no one had poisoned the son to punish the father. Interesting that it had been a woman caller, though.

"When you got to the taverna, was your son conscious?"

"Barely," said Marios. Shaking his head, he pinched the base of his nose as tears softened his eyes. "Nicos is not a son to be overly proud of, I know this, but he is my son. And when I saw him there, tied to a chair, his pants soiled and stinking, it broke my heart. I ran to him and kissed his face, even though it was a mess of vomit and chocolate. Then by some miracle of God he opened his eyes. 'I need a hospital,' he said. 'They've poisoned me.' Immediately, I untied his arms and legs, well, I had to cut the cable ties around his hands with a knife, and then I put him in the back seat of the car – I didn't care about the mess – and I took him to the hospital."

"Did he say anything on the way, give any clue as to who might have attacked him?"

"No, he was delirious. He was crying about having to piss like a girl and wanting to make love to Maria; the wife who loves him so much she's currently divorcing him."

Approximately two hours later, after first checking with the med-

ics, Antoni and Michalis arrived at the hospital where the hapless
Nicos was pale, but still hanging onto life. The doctors were baf-
fled because they could find no obvious signs of the bleeding dis-
orders commonly associated with rat poison, which was the most
misused poison on the island. So, like the police, they were also
awaiting the results of tests on the chocolate that had been helpfully left at the scene. That in itself gave Antoni cause to wonder.
Clearly, the intent was not to kill, otherwise why call the father
and why leave the chocolate. If anything, it smacked of extreme
intimidation.

"Or terrorism," added Michalis because Antoni had made the
mistake of thinking out loud, but to his surprise, and for the second time that day, he had to admit that Michalis wasn't wrong. This
latest incident, that appeared to be the handiwork of the animal
rights gang, could rightly be construed as an act of terror.

"Did you see your attacker or attackers?" Antoni asked Nicos,
who had found the strength to sit up in his hospital bed.

"There were three of them," he said in a hoarse whisper because
he was still sore from the poison and, more recently, the pipe that
had been inserted down his throat to pump his stomach. "And they
all had guns."

"Guns?" Antoni asked in surprise.

"Yes, proper ones, like the military."

"Interesting. Anything else, any physical description you can
give us?"

"I couldn't see their faces because they were wearing masks.
Only one of them spoke and she spoke Greek with an accent. I also
heard some Russian, I think."

"She?" asked Antoni.

"You were attacked by women?" Michalis interrupted, which
wasn't helpful, not least because he started laughing.

Antoni could barely contain the sigh in his throat as he saw
the panic flicker in Nicos' eyes, heralding an immediate change in
story.

"I meant 'he'," he insisted. "Look man, I'm traumatised. Give me a break. Five Russian guys broke into my taverna and threatened to blow my balls off unless I ate their chocolates."

Antoni stared at Nicos, wondering whether he was in any way conscious of the fact that he was painting himself as the victim of a particularly aggressive marketing campaign by chocolatiers.

"Okay, what exactly did he or she say?" Antoni asked.

"He," Nicos repeated firmly, "he said I had to eat the chocolates or he would blow off my testicles so I would never pee like a man again. There was rat poison in the chocolates."

"So, you ate the chocolates."

"Yes."

"And would you have any idea why someone might want to poison you and leave a dog's paw print on your table."

"A dog's paw print?"

As the information registered in Nicos' brain there was a flicker of recognition in his eyes, shortly before they rolled to the back of his head as he fainted.

By the early afternoon, all hell broke loose at the station as journalists turned up demanding to know more about the attempted murder committed by the Dog Paw Gang. In a small place like Dromos, bad news travels fast, especially when it comes from the mouth of a special constable hoping to impress pretty reporters.

"Great," the chief inspector muttered as he entered Antoni's office. "The Super is on his way and he wants to hold a press conference. Have we got the toxicology report yet?"

"They said tomorrow morning," Antoni replied.

"Tell them they have an hour. The press conference is scheduled for 4.30pm and the order has come in from the top that they want an end to this animal rights stuff and fast."

"But…"

"No more buts, we have to be seen to be close to solving this case. Preferably before someone gets killed."

Shaking his head in despair, Antoni phoned forensics. He then texted Cara because, as exasperated as he was, he also recognised an opportunity when he saw one.

"Press conf at station 4.30pm about animal rights gang you have been writing about. In Greek, but I can translate for you."

Within two minutes, Cara replied: "I'll bring my own translator."

It didn't take long for the seats to fill in the conference room because there weren't that many to start with. Even so, there must have been fifteen reporters in the room along with photographers and cameramen. Towards the back, and facing the bank of chairs, was a trestle table covered with a white cloth upon which was a jug of water, three glasses and a number of microphones and tape recorders. Back stage, also known as the hallway, Antoni was making a last-minute call to forensics while the Chief Inspector listened anxiously and the visiting Super Intendant had the final touches administered to his make up by his personal press officer.

"It's on its way, or so they say," Antoni revealed, handing his mobile to Michalis.

"Then we get on with things and someone can bring in the results when they arrive," Superintendent Constantinos Parpis replied, pulling the paper towel away from his neck as he did so. "How do I look?"

"Bronzed," replied Antoni.

"Is that good?" he asked, turning to the press officer.

"Ideal for the cameras," she replied. She then straightened his tie, in a way that raised eyebrows between Antoni and his immediate boss.

"Right, let's get this show on the road," the Super said, and Antoni stepped back to let him lead the way.

As they filed into the room, which was unusually hot thanks to the number of TV lights present, Antoni glanced around looking for Cara. He found her on the third row, next to a dark-haired tattooed woman, and for a brief moment their eyes met. She then turned away to focus on the Super, unlike her translator who stared at him longer than was probably polite.

After everyone had taken their seats, the Press Officer gave a brief rundown of the events of the previous night, being careful to leave out any details that were case sensitive. She said a "local man" had been "subjected to a terrifying attack" in the early hours of Thursday morning. A number of, so far, unknown assailants held him at gun point and force-fed him poisoned chocolates. The man was later found by his father and he is currently being treated in hospital.

"Although we can't be too specific with the details, we can confirm that a dog's paw print was left at the scene."

The press officer then invited Antoni to say a few words about the previous incidents that had taken place and why the police believed this latest attack was the work of the same gang. After a brief look at the background, Antoni gave the floor to the Super who calmly reassured the public that "the perpetrators will be caught and there's no need for alarm." As he revealed a "number of leads" they were apparently working on, Michalis appeared at the doorway waving a piece of paper. The Super was the first to notice.

"Is that the toxicology report?" he shouted towards the back of the room, and all heads turned towards Michalis.

"Yes!" he shouted back.

"Let's have it then," said the Super, gesturing he should bring the report over. Unfortunately, like a car crash occurring in slow motion, Antoni saw the misunderstanding about to take place and though he heard himself say 'no', it was too late. Michalis was reading the results to the Press.

"The chocolates had traces of a sedative known as temazepam as well as an extraordinary amount of chilli powder and Dulcolax, which I guess is the rat poison," Michalis said, lowering the paper in triumph.

At first there were a few blank stares among the press pack, who turned to each other looking for clarification. They then started sniggering.

Superintendent Constantinos Parpis turned in confusion to his press officer who quietly tried to answer his question, while momentarily forgetting the bank of microphones amplifying and recording their every word.

"Dulcolax is an oral laxative, Sir."

Chapter Twenty-Two

Naturally, the Press had a field day with the latest exploits of the 'Dog Paw Gang'. There was continued speculation as to who they were, what sex they were and how many they were – something that kept a number of TV panels and radio phone-ins busy for a while – but for the most part everyone, to a man, woman or gender indifferent, seemed rather amused by the affair. Although the motive in the case of Nicos Andreou wasn't immediately clear, it didn't take long for reporters to discover there was a link to a poisoned dog named Milo. A day later, his tearful owner got the chance to tell the world about his wonderful dog and how cruel and unnecessary his death was.

"Ruff Justice!" screamed the headline in the main English-speaking paper, with plenty of variations on the theme throughout the rest of the Press. One Greek-language newspaper even went so far as to publish a photo of Nicos under the headline 'Shit Scared'.

Elsewhere, radio and TV news bulletins led with the story for most of the day, and the incident was the main topic of discussion on talk shows, current affairs programmes and comedy skits for days after. Of course, not everyone was in favour of a group of extremists taking the law into their own hands, but these voices usually belonged to previous victims, relatives of victims or friends of the families of victims. Some argued that the potential risk of inducing a heart attack by tying a man to a chair and force-feeding him laxatives was "no laughing matter". Others were concerned that Nicos could have choked on his own vomit after eating so much chocolate.

"Fair comment," Emilia remarked as she relayed that particular TV debate to the others. When the programme's host pointed out that the 'Dog Paw Gang' had called the victim's father, suggesting they wanted him to find his son "before he choked on his own vomit," the audience applauded. More interestingly, however, when someone brought up the subject of firearms, the female presenter raised an eyebrow. "If there *were* guns involved," she said. "So far, the police have no proof that weapons were used at the scene of the crime, they only have the victim's word for it. Let's not forget this is the same victim that had trouble recollecting whether he was accosted by three women or five, burly Russian men."

"Great comeback," Emilia laughed, after translating it for the others, and they all applauded this woman who was clearly no slave to the tenet of journalistic impartiality.

As it was, the three of them hadn't actually planned on watching TV that afternoon because they were finding the circus somewhat exhausting. But Emilia had brought a number of boxes to Lillian's and the TV happened to be on because Lillian liked the background noise. It made the house feel less empty without Derek.

"Have you told him I'm moving in yet?" asked Emilia.

"Not yet."

"And what if he says no?"

"No is not an option," replied Lillian, and Cara and Emilia looked at each other. It wasn't the first time they had noticed a steely determination in their friend's voice, but it was the first time they suspected it had something to do with Derek.

A few hours later, after emptying the content of her boxes into cupboards, Emilia called it a day as she was feeling "utterly exhausted".

"Moving home is supposed to be one of the most stressful things you can do," Lillian sympathised, but they all knew the real reason for their friend's exhaustion. Although Emilia looked relatively normal, she was actually very sick and because she looked so well it was sometimes easy to forget that fact.

Closing the door on her new room, which was in fact the downstairs bedroom, Cara could see Emilia was happy with the arrangement. She was a woman of few words, but her eyes were an open book.

"I'll give you a lift back if you like," Cara said, glancing at her watch knowing she too would have to run. The dogs would be wondering where she was, or more to the point, where their dinner was, and she had cooking to do.

"You don't have to do that," Emilia told her.

"I know I don't have to," she replied. "I need the money. I'm charging you ten euros."

"I'm not sure I feel comfortable feeding your broccoli habit."

"It's okay. I've moved on to kale. Now come on, get in the car. I've got silken tofu to fry."

Actually, Cara didn't have tofu to fry, she couldn't stand the stuff, she also didn't want to cook anything too exotic, partly because she couldn't be bothered, but mainly because she didn't want it to look like she was making an effort. She was cooking for two.

After sitting on Antoni's text for two days, Cara had decided it was probably best to talk, if only to draw a line under the relationship. As this was the mood she was in, and she needed a clear head, she didn't buy wine either. There were a couple of beers in the fridge. They would do.

In contrast, when Antoni arrived at her home, bang on 8.30pm, he came armed with a huge bouquet of flowers and a very decent bottle of white. Cara had no idea what kind of flowers they were, other than yellow, white, lilac and blue, but the colours reminded her of spring, the season of new beginnings. Antoni also brought vegan chocolates. Not that it did him much good.

Following a clumsy attempt to kiss her on the doorstep, before she disappeared into the kitchen muttering something about dinner burning, Antoni braced himself for the night that was to come.

"I should have bought two bottles," he mumbled to himself.

Following Cara inside, he was pleased to receive a warm welcome from the dogs at least, or at least once they'd finished eating. He then sat himself at the dining table and waited.

"Did you get any stories published from the news conference?"

he asked, once Cara emerged from the kitchen holding two bowls of lentil curry. Though he didn't mention anything, he noted the lack of starter. There was no naan bread either, which wasn't a crime in itself, but it was most certainly a message. If there was no dessert at the end of the meal, he was a dead man walking.

"A couple of the nationals ran small pieces and I got a larger piece in a magazine. So, thanks for the tip off."

"Well, it wasn't quite a tip off," Antoni said, flashing his most winning smile.

"You know what I mean," Cara replied tersely.

Looking up from her bowl, she almost faltered in her determination to remain ice-cold because she could see how hard Antoni was trying. In fact, she almost reached out to touch him. But then she recalled a time, not so long ago, when she too must have looked just as crestfallen, and no hand had reached out to comfort her. Instead, Antoni had made her feel tarnished by age, in a way she had never felt before. It was the oddest and most uncomfortable feeling because she had never previously considered her age to be anything other than something she was. It certainly wasn't anything she had ever felt the need to hide or lie about. It had never been an issue.

"Who was your translator?" Antoni asked out of nowhere, and it took her a moment to understand he was still referring to the press conference.

"A friend of mine called Emilia."

"Don't think I've heard you speak about her before."

"Then perhaps you can add that to your list of things I forgot to tell you about," she replied. Antoni flinched. Putting down his fork he took a sip of wine, which tasted more bitter than he remembered, and decided to address the elephant in the room.

"Look, I'm sorry," he said simply. "I know I hurt you and I don't know how to fix it, but believe me, I want to fix it."

Cara paused. It was exactly what she wanted to hear yet also what she had dreaded hearing because it put her firmly in the driver's seat of a car with no steering wheel. Throughout the day she had imagined how the evening might play out, and though it swayed between a tearful goodbye and a night of reckless abandon, she had remained calm and collected at all times. The reality, of course, was very much different. Cara was paralysed by hurt and embarrassment. In some respects, the situation reminded her of her time with Tom, only with better weather. In fact, when she looked at both men objectively, she saw that Antoni and Tom were actually similar in character, in as much as they possessed a rare ability to make her feel like shit as well as make her feel like she was the bad one. Cara wasn't sure she was prepared to jump on that merry-go-round again.

"I need some time to think things through," she finally admitted.

Antoni raised his thick eyebrows, a sad smile playing on his lips. "I understand. I was a selfish pig," he told her. "Shall we finish eating or should I leave so you can start this thinking?"

He gave a half-hearted laugh that did little to ease the tension between them.

"It's probably better if you go," Cara admitted. "I'm sorry."

Antoni nodded and got up from his seat. "No, Cara. I am the one who is sorry."

He took his half-finished meal to the kitchen, even though she said he didn't have to. As he placed his bowl on the worktop, he was saddened but not surprised to see no sign of a dessert. He then had another, more work related, thought. As he headed to the front door, he asked, "Your friend the translator, is she Greek?"

"No, Romanian. Why do you ask?"

"No reason."

Antoni leaned forward and kissed Cara on both cheeks before taking her face in his hands to stare intently into her eyes. "Try and forgive me," he said.

Without waiting for an answer, he lowered his hands and left. As he got into his car, he thought again of Cara's translator friend.

It triggered a suspicion so insane he almost laughed. Shaking his head, he drove away.

A couple of weeks after revenging the death of Milo the dog, Nicos went into hiding after discovering the hard way that the vast majority of people appeared to be more against animal cruelty than attempted murder by laxative. Meanwhile, the politicians continued to debate potential new laws to deal with animal abusers, even as they called for the swift arrest of those who abuse animal abusers. As a result, the police were knocking on the doors of anyone even remotely connected with the rescue community, leading to a flurry of online indignation, in both Greek and English. Thankfully, the Dromos Animal Liberation Front managed to escape the same scrutiny, having had the foresight to not set up a Facebook page about their exploits. So, it was pretty much business as usual for the group's founding members with Lillian preparing for the arrival of her husband once again, and Cara enticing Emilia into more mischief.

"What time do you need me?" Emilia asked.

"Before sun up, about 5am?"

"This is crazy. You're crazy. But it's my kind of crazy. I'm in."

And so it was, on a typically humid August morning, that Cara and Emilia drove into the hills that formed the backdrop to Dromos. After parking down a track that was well shielded from the main road, they walked to a rocky outcrop using torches to light their way as they scaled huge boulders and loose rock to get to one of the small caves that nature had gouged into the hillside. Cara took a blanket from the bag she carried and laid it on the floor. She next retrieved the air rifle she had bought earlier in the month and handed it to Emilia. Once they had checked for tarantulas and snakes, they took up position, lying on their stomachs to survey the land below them.

"What time do they come?" Emilia asked.

"No idea," Cara replied honestly. "They might not come at all."

"That would be disappointing."

"Tell me about it. I've been dreaming of this moment."

As the two friends waited, they did their best to stay awake by righting the wrongs of the world. By the time they had exhausted Syria, the scourge of plastic, the Battle for Mosul and white extremism, they turned to the Russian invasion of Cyprus. Where once it was the Brits that had kept the tourism industry afloat, it was now the Russians, and like most European countries it wasn't only travellers' cheques being pumped into the national economy.

"Do you think Putin might be the reincarnation of Rasputin?" Emilia asked.

"What? And he just dropped the 'Ras' to stop anyone finding out?"

"It might be a double bluff type thing – make it so obvious that nobody would believe it."

"Nobody does believe it."

"Some people do. Of course, some people believe his castrated penis has magical powers?"

"Putin was castrated?"

"No, Rasputin. Apparently, it was huge. At least 12 inches. It was cut off when he was murdered and it eventually found its way to Paris where it was used as a fertility charm. "

"No way. That's unbelievable."

"I know. And it was unbelievable. Tests later revealed the penis was actually a sea cucumber."

"Oh, come on, you're making this up?" Cara laughed.

"No, it's true. I read it in a magazine."

"Then it must be true."

"That's not the end of it…"

"Said the actress to the mad monk."

Emilia rolled on to her side to better look at Cara. "What actress?"

"Forget it. It's a British thing. So, what happened to Rasputin's penis? I'm intrigued."

"It's in an erotica museum in St Petersburg and men can be cured of impotence just by looking at it."

"Ah, Viagra for lunatics. What a way to be remembered," Cara joked. She then looked below and immediately ducked her head. "Oh God, he's here."

"No way?" Emilia half-ducked and half-tried-to-look, curious to see what kind of man it was that they had been waiting for. By now the sun was up, the flies were out, the birds were singing and about 150 yards away a hunter dressed in camouflage was wandering towards a ledge clutching a handful of tissues.

Cara nudged Emilia, urging her to lift the air rifle. According to Emilia, she was quite the hotshot after spending two years living with an Austrian. "They're all gun nuts to varying degrees," she explained. "Gun nuts in lederhosen."

Emilia smiled as she took hold of the air rifle. Snapping it open, she checked there was a pellet in place, and snapped it closed again before placing the butt against her shoulder and lifting the iron sight. Emilia then trained the tip of the barrel on the hunter.

"You cool?" Cara asked, noticing Emilia's arm was trembling.

"Pins and needles," Emilia assured her. "Nothing to worry about."

Cara stared at the hunter who was busy unbuckling his belt. She didn't recognise him, but that was no surprise, she tended to shy away from men who killed animals for sport. Given the timing of his deposits, she had assumed he was a hunter, meaning the summer hunting season would be her best chance to catch him because hunters were forbidden to use dogs during the annual massacre of woodpigeons and turtle doves. Dogs would have been problematic.

As the hunter lowered his light brown ass to hover two inches above the ground, Emilia moved the tip of the barrel half a metre to the right of him. Next to her, she could hear Cara's heart beating and her finger tensed on the trigger. Unfortunately, it didn't stop tensing. The gun went off with a deafening bang followed, almost immediately, by a scream. Cara and Emilia looked towards the hunter who was now off the ledge and writhing on the stony ground, clutching his ass, which was a mess of blood and faeces.

"Holy crap, you were only meant to scare him!" Cara hissed.

"I slipped!" Emilia protested, though she was finding it hard not to laugh.

"Christ, come on we need to get out of here."

Emilia handed her the gun. "You're going to have to help me up. I'm having a twerk moment."

"What? Right now?"

"I don't plan them to piss you off, Cara."

Cara shook her head and apologised before helping her friend get to her feet. "Can you walk?"

"Yes, as long as you help me over some of the bigger rocks."

"I've got you," she promised before grabbing the blanket, the gun and Emilia, dragging them all out of the cave and back down the hillside.

Once they made it back to the track, they half ran, half hobbled towards a battered red jeep.

"That must be his car," Emilia said, stopping to catch her breath. "Shall I draw a paw?"

Cara shook her head. "No, this wasn't business, it was personal."

"Roger that," Emilia replied.

While Cara and Emilia were busy shooting hunters in the ass, Lillian drove to Limassol to meet Derek who had flown into Larnaca airport that morning. There had been some fuss about her plans because Derek didn't like surprises, but Lillian was adamant.

"I've booked us a night in a five-star hotel, so you'll meet me there," she said. When he continued to protest, she added, "Humour me, Derek. I think you know as well as I do that we need this."

Maybe it was the tone of her voice or the truth of her words, either way, Derek shut up whinging and took down the details. An hour or so later he pulled into the Amathus Hotel car park to find his wife suitably relaxed having arrived four hours earlier to fit in a lavender massage.

In his battered old jeans and checked shirt, Derek looked tired and jaded. Lillian was sympathetic to a degree, but it was hardly a long flight from Qatar and his lack of enthusiasm for her surprise was doing him few favours. Even so, she found his bolshiness helpful.

After a stroll along the beach, which was sweet enough, they had dinner at the hotel's Limanaki Fish Restaurant. Situated on the water's edge, the location was breathtaking and for the first time in a long while they relaxed enough to enjoy the other's company. Over two bottles of wine, they talked about the kids and the many foolish things they did when they too were kids. Derek recalled their wedding night, when Lillian was so racked with nerves by what was to come that she passed out in the bathroom, knocking her head against something, perhaps the sink, perhaps the toilet, and had to be taken to hospital with concussion. She was kept in overnight for observation.

"That was a tough one to explain to your parents," Derek said, and as he laughed Lillian was struck by how good his teeth were.

Derek had always possessed lovely straight teeth, and a lifetime of non-smoking and moderate drinking had treated them kindly. In fact, under the moonlight and in the soft glow of the vanilla candles burning between them, he reminded her of the boy she once married. Derek was the man she had loved all her adult life and, as she gazed at him across the table, she felt her heart could collapse under the weight of that love. Like a rush of beautiful pictures, she remembered the first time he held her hand as they walked home from the cinema; the time he chased away her tears after she accidentally ran over a cat; the day he guided her down the slopes of Serre Chevalier even though he had no idea what he was doing either; the time he cried tears of happiness when he held his newborn children; and the time he somehow kept her standing as they buried both her parents.

"I love you, Derek," she said as they finished their Calypso Coffees. Derek's eyes looked surprised for a second before softening.

"I love you too, Lil."

That night, when they went to bed, they didn't make love, it had been a busy day and they were both exhausted and a little drunk, but they slept in each other's arms and, when they awoke, they had a smile for each other.

After checking out, Derek headed for his car, intending to put his suitcase in the boot before Lillian stopped him.

"I've something to show you," she said, urging him to come to her own vehicle. "If you leave the case in yours, it might get stolen."

Though Cyprus was hardly a hotbed of criminal activity, it wasn't Disneyland either, so Derek shrugged in agreement. When he strapped himself into the passenger seat, he playfully promised to resist commenting on her driving. In fairness to Derek, Lillian understood his backseat driving was borne of a fear of not being in control, especially in matters of life and death, which used to be a regular feature of his wife's driving.

As they pulled out of the hotel, Lillian took them deeper into the city before turning westwards into the suburbs. At first, a sense of amusement emanated from Derek as he tried to second guess Lillian, but once they passed the Petrolina garage on the right and the Donut House on the left, she heard his breathing grow shallower. Lillian finally pulled up outside a block of flats where she turned off the engine.

When she turned in her seat to face him, he couldn't lift his head to meet her eyes.

"I know, Derek."

"Lillian, I..."

"I know," she persisted gently. "I've known for a while now and that has given me time to consider all the options, not to mention the potential repercussions of those options."

"Oh God, Lil. I do love you..."

"I know, Derek. I know you do. But please, let me finish. Don't make this any harder than it has to be."

Derek swallowed the bile rising in his throat and because Lillian saw he was on the verge of tears, she felt her own eyes sting in response. Where she got the strength from, she didn't know, but she gave a small cough, straightened her back and began speaking.

"I want you to stay with your mistress," she told him. "You need to live this relationship as a reality if you are to make a qualified decision about where you want to spend the rest of your life and who with. A week stolen here and there is not the same as living with someone. This is what you need to experience for a while. Who knows, maybe you will decide to live this new life forever. All I know right now is that there is no place for you in my home."

"But I don't want…"

"This isn't about what you want anymore," Lillian responded quickly, hearing the anger enter her voice because there was no room for debate in this matter. She had taken control and for once Derek would surrender to her will. "Please, take your bag from the boot of my car. From now on, you take your leave here until I feel ready to discuss things with you again. I don't especially blame you, Derek, but I can't live with you either."

As Lillian made it clear there was nothing more to be said, Derek got out of the car and shuffled to the boot to retrieve his case. As he pressed the backdoor shut, Lillian could feel the weight of sadness in his touch. Even so, she looked in the rear-view mirror, indicated right and pulled away without another backwards glance. After taking the next left, she followed the main road towards the highway before turning right onto an open area of wasteland being used as a car park. With some urgency, Lillian kicked open the door, leaned out of the car and threw up. When she was done, she flung herself back into the driving seat as her mouth struggled to find breath through the anguish that contorted her face and flooded her eyes.

Chapter Twenty-Three

It wasn't the easiest of nights, but when Lillian woke the next morning, she was surprised by how light she felt. 'Light' was the best way she could describe it. It wasn't a feeling of happiness or relief, but a strange kind of weightlessness, as though the previous day's trauma that had ended in vomit and tears had been an emotional detox, cleansing her soul of the fear, trepidation, disappointment and rage that had dogged her for months. She didn't know if the feeling would last, and she fully expected to be stung by regret, embarrassment and grief at some point, but right now, the day after the possible end of her old life or the start of a new one, she felt something close to airy.

"Good grief, that took some nerve," Cara said with a whistle as she drove them to the outskirts of Paphos.

"I wasn't sure I'd be brave enough to go through with it," Lillian admitted. "And even if I was, I wasn't sure I could stop myself from saying something before the time was right or demanding answers over dinner. But the thing was, I didn't want an argument or an angry confrontation. I wanted Derek to see me as a woman again so he might fully understand what he was about to lose. And do you want to know the really weird part?"

"Go on."

"I really enjoyed Derek's company that evening, something I haven't done for years."

"Do you regret it now, cutting him loose to be with another woman?"

"Perhaps. I don't know. It's a gamble. He might love his new life and I might end up pining for my old one, or it could be that he hates his new life and I love my freedom. Only time will tell."

"But why didn't you mention something before? I had no idea your marriage was in such trouble."

"I really don't know. Maybe I wasn't ready to face the truth. If I voiced my suspicions there would be no more pretending. I simply wasn't ready until the moment came."

"Well, all I can say is, well done you." Cara draped an arm over her friend's shoulders. She would have hugged her, but that would have meant stopping the car. "It sounds like you handled the situation with amazing dignity and respect. I don't think I could have done the same if I'd been in your shoes. I can hardly look at Antoni I feel so humiliated."

"Dinner didn't go well then?" Lillian inquired gently.

"That would be an understatement. He left before we got to the dessert that I hadn't made."

"Ouch. So, you two are done then?"

"I don't know. I really don't know."

"Do you have feelings for him."

"I thought I did, until he made me feel like a shrivelled, old hag."

Lillian laughed. "That would be enough to dampen anyone's ardour. Hey, eyes on the road, isn't the next turning ours?"

Cara glanced at the directions she had scribbled onto a piece of paper now sitting on the dashboard.

"Yep, this is the one," she confirmed.

Cara pulled over, stopping at the side of the road where no yellow lines were painted to say that she shouldn't. Not that it would make any difference if there were; yellow lines were merely tarmac decoration in Cyprus. After taking a few pictures on her iPhone, they started walking. Because they hadn't formulated a plan as yet, and because Emilia couldn't join them as she had a riding lesson with Julia, Cara had thought it best to keep a record of the recce just in case it triggered ideas when they met up later in the day. So far, the scene was par for the course, away from the tourist hotspots; a crumbling tarmac road skirting an industrial estate of concrete blocks and workshops cooking under corrugated iron roofs. Old cars and lorries littered the landscape along with a few buses, all in varying degrees of road worthiness and rust. Around

the industrial estate there was nothing but parched wasteland in-
termittingly broken by dry green scrub.

Having parked by a huge, seemingly random and presumably
abandoned, storm drain pipe, they took the right turning opposite. After walking for ten minutes or more, the tarmac finally gave
up any pretence of being a road and turned into a rubble track.
Another right turning just before a dead end eventually brought
them to a large gravelled area that was presumably a car park.
Some 70 metres away were a series of cages about 6ft tall and 3ft
wide, inside of which were a number of dogs, many of them too
exhausted, hungry and sick to even bark at the strangers in front of
them. As Cara and Lillian neared, they could see that all the pens
without exception were covered in faeces. What buckets were in
the pens were dry, all the food bowels were empty, and every dog
they saw had eyes that were distant and defeated.

"Oh God," Lillian said, bringing a hand to her mouth. Blinking
away hot tears, she looked around for water, eventually finding a
hose pipe attached to a tap near an old wooden building behind the
cages. She quickly got to work, filling all the buckets and concrete
troughs with water, poking the hose through the pens that were
padlocked, all the while cursing herself for not bringing any food.
Cara took a look about to see if she could find any, but it was a
fruitless search and she returned shaking her head.

"It's like death row without the humanity of a lethal injection at
the end," she said. She then took a few more pictures before telling
Lillian she had seen enough.

As they walked away, it felt like an act of betrayal.

"It makes me sick, really," Emilia said as she looked at Cara's photos. "I know exactly how you must have felt leaving them behind. It
was the same when I turned my back on the horses in Death Alley."

Cara went to the fridge and took out three beers. On the way
she passed Cooper and Peaches, flat out on the cool tiles and her
heart ached for those dogs who might never know the comfort of

a safe, loving home. Returning to the main room, she handed out the beers before opening the folder waiting on the table in front of them.

"Okay," she said, before shaking her shoulders and coughing in an effort to expel the taste of hopelessness in her mouth. "Let's look at the facts as we know them. Kivotos Dog Farm is the work of one man, apparently employed by the council, who takes strays off the street. He was arrested once before for cruelty yet pleaded not guilty on the grounds that his wife's health problems had kept him away from the dogs, an excuse the court seemed to buy. He received no fine and he wasn't banned from keeping dogs, even though police officers found several dogs dead in their cages and 12 others in an horrific state of malnutrition and disease. Then, a few months ago, when animal welfare groups acted on a tip off from a member of the public that the place was again operational, and a number of dogs were again starving and dying, they went in and managed to release five of them only to be later arrested for trespassing and theft. They were also ordered to return the dogs."

"So basically, we have to find a way to get out, how many dogs?" asked Emilia.

"I counted 21, but I couldn't see inside all the cages," Lillian replied.

"In that case we are dealing with at least 21 dogs that we need to find a safe place for, and somehow transport them to this safe place we find, while making sure this hellhole never becomes operational again?"

"That's about it, yes," Cara agreed.

"Well, I can't see that being a problem," Emilia laughed, though there was no humour in the sound. She was then distracted by her mobile phone ringing. As it was Julia calling, she wandered outside, through Cara's patio doors, and into the small courtyard.

Cara looked again at the photos on her phone, racking her brains to think of something they could possibly do to stop this cruel and unnecessary story repeating itself time and again.

"Have you got any ideas?" she asked turning to Lillian, but before she could answer, Emilia returned to the room. Adonis had
colic and she needed a lift to the stables.

It was Cara who dropped Emilia off at the entrance to Julia's yard.
Though she offered to stay, Emilia said there was no point because
the bouts of colic that Adonis was prone to often lasted an hour or
more and there was little anyone could do other than walk him,
watch him, walk him again and watch a little more until he managed to expel the blockage or trapped wind that was agonising his
gut.

"Well, you know where I am," Cara said. "Call when you need
a lift back. I need to go food shopping at some point today so it's
no biggie."

Emilia promised she would be in touch later. Armed with a bottle of water, she went to check on her boy.

When she got to his stable, she found Julia trying to force
Adonis to his feet in an effort to get him walking, something that
usually eased the pain and got the bowels moving.

"Don't worry, I'll do it," Emilia offered and Julia stepped back,
looking concerned, but not overly worried.

"Right, you get him walking while I get the injection ready," she
said. "I'll be back in a minute."

"Okay," Emilia replied, already picturing Julia rifling through
a medical box that was loaded with all manner of antibiotics and
painkillers from Flunixin to Phenylbutazone. She had no idea what
any of them did or what medicine was good for what, but as long
as Julia did and it worked on her boy, Emilia was thankful. In fact,
there were times when Julia could have pumped Adonis with crack
cocaine and she wouldn't have cared as long as it eased his pain. As
Julia left the stable, Emilia went in to embrace her boy. "Oh Boo,"
she whispered, feeling hot tears burning the back of her eyes as
she looked at his handsome face, already grazed and bloody from
scrapes along the floor or the wall as he battled the pain eating

his insides. Emilia gently placed a head collar over his ears. Then, taking the lead rope, she coaxed him out of the stable and into the sand arena where she sang to him as they walked.

"So, shine bright tonight, you and I, we're beautiful, like diamonds in the sky..."

After two circuits of the arena, Julia wandered over, holding a needle.

"Keep him still," she said. Emilia gripped the lead rope tighter under Adonis's jaw while Julia searched for a vein. After tapping his neck a few times, Julia slipped the needle in, pushed and withdrew. Emilia watched the blood ooze out and, after wiping the area clean, they started walking again. Some fifteen minutes later, she took Adonis back to his stable to let him lie down.

Although some think horses with colic should never lie down, this wasn't the case with Adonis. He didn't thrash about, which was the danger. Instead, he stretched his tortured body, something that eventually helped whatever it was obstructing his internal passageways to relax enough or move enough to release whatever it was causing the pain. Usually this was enough. Only today it wasn't.

An hour or so after she arrived, Emilia dragged Adonis to the shower area to aim the hose at his forehead. It was the quickest way to cool a sick horse especially in the height of summer. They then walked again, lay down for a while and walked again until, three hours later, Julia injected Adonis with a second painkiller.

"If we were in any other country, we might get him to a vet to perform surgery," she said. "But here, what can we do but manage his pain the best we can?"

"But he'll be fine, yeah?" Emilia asked.

"I hope so," was the best Julia could manage.

Two hours later, as the sun set, Adonis was close to exhaustion and Emilia began to feel a creeping cold set deep in her heart. His colic had never taken this long to ease before. She had never had to scream at him to stop him dropping to the ground or have to physically drag him to his feet in order to make him walk. Whatever she did, nothing seemed to work. The soft stroking of his distended stomach, that sometimes offered some relief, failed to bring results, and the showers were no longer helping, only wetting his skin for the dirt to cling to as his body became more bruised and bloodied from time spent on the floor.

"Come on, baby," Emilia urged. "You can do this. Please, you have to do this, Adonis." She dragged him to his feet and walked him around the arena again, only vaguely aware that the floodlights had been switched on. When he eventually fell for the third time, she became aware of Julia's hand on her arm.

"Let him rest a bit. He can lie here for a while," she said.

So, Emilia let Adonis rest and as he lay in the sand, she sat by his beautiful head, thankful at least that she no longer had to chase the flies from his face because they had gone with the sun. Now her only job was to keep the light alive in his eyes. But nothing was working and after forty minutes on the ground they were on the move again because if Adonis lay in the one position too long there was a danger that the weight of his body would eventually crush his organs. After walking for only a few minutes Adonis made it clear that he wanted to leave the arena so Emilia took him to the nearest stable where he rested for a while on the fresh straw that waited for him. That's when Cara turned up.

It was Julia she found first, and it was Julia who told her that things weren't looking good; that Adonis had been battling colic for more than nine hours and it would be rare for a horse to recover from such a trauma. There were no more painkillers she could give. The next step would be a strong sedative.

"It won't do much to help, but it will ease him on his journey," she explained.

"His journey?" Cara asked, and Julia looked away. "I better ring Lillian. Is it all right if she…?"

"Yes, of course," said Julia.

So, Cara called Lillian before going to see Emilia and Adonis.

Even though Cara had been prepared by Julia, she was shocked by what she saw; the poor horse's belly was swollen and tight as a drum, his eyes were clouded by pain and exhaustion and Emilia, she could tell, was fighting the battle of her life, trying desperately not to give up hope.

"He'll be fine, he'll be fine," she muttered, but the tears rolling down her face told a different story. "Come on, baby boy. We can do this. We can do this. Shine bright, we're like diamonds in the sky."

Shortly after Lillian arrived, Julia made a flask of coffee and they all came to sit outside Adonis's stable, where they watched Emilia gently stroke her horse's neck. As the hours dragged by, Cara and Lillian asked Julia all the questions Emilia had asked over the years. What's colic? Is there nothing that can be done? How long will it last? Why can't he just lie there? Though Julia was also exhausted, she answered all their questions as though hearing them for the very first time, helping to explain various aspects of the condition by talking about her own experiences over the years and how colic was simply a very general term to describe a huge variety of internal problems that quite often had only one commonality – pain.

Then, as the clock ticked towards midnight, Julia quietly told the others it was probably time to give Emilia and Adonis "a little space". Before they all retired to the house, Julia gave Adonis a strong sedative and came to stand by Emilia, who was sat on a chair in the stable, her dazed eyes simply watching over her boy.

"It may come to the point, Emilia, when Adonis will want to leave the stable. If this happens, let him and try to lead him to the arena, if you can."

"Why the arena?"

Julia blinked back tears as she forced the words out of her mouth. "Your horse will eventually look for somewhere to die."

Though Emilia recognised the truth of what was to come it was probably the hardest thing she had ever had to hear. Almost instantly, her throat constricted as it tried to keep the contents of her stomach from her mouth. However, when the time came, Emilia was grateful for the knowledge.

Shortly after one in the morning, Adonis began to grow restless, turning in his stable as he looked for a way out. When Emilia opened the gate, he followed her to the arena and for a few minutes they walked together under the beam of the main floodlight. In every way, it felt like their last dance together and when he was done, Adonis walked straight for Emilia. Resting his head against her stomach, she held him tightly, allowing the full force of her love to envelop him.

For five minutes or more the two of them stood together, two souls locked in an embrace under a spotlight surrounded by darkness. It was farewell, they both knew it and when all was said that couldn't be said with words, Adonis walked away. As Emilia followed, Adonis barely took three steps before he stumbled. Fighting to regain his footing, he fell again. As he struggled to get up, he tripped over his legs a third time and onto his head before landing heavily on the sand.

Only then did Emilia scream.

Chapter Twenty-Four

When dawn broke, there was a blissful moment when Cara had no recollection of the night before, but then it came back to her and she dragged the covers over her head to try and escape the memory for a few seconds more. Emilia's scream was the closest thing she had ever heard to a heart breaking. She knew the sound of it would stay with her for a lifetime. In fact, when her friend's anguish tore through the night sky, Cara was so unprepared she dropped the glass she held. Looking to Lillian, she found her with her eyes closed and a prayer passing over her lips. As for Julia, well, she was part way out of the door by the time her guests had even begun to understand what had happened.

"Stay here. I'll see to her."

Unable to stop herself, Cara had moved to the kitchen window overlooking the arena. She didn't know what she had expected to see, but the scene that met her was close to surreal. Like a theatre production taking place in front of her, the stage lights were trained on the tragic image of a woman on the ground, clinging to the neck of her dead horse. From the wings, Julia arrived carrying some kind of blanket. She placed it over the horse's body up to his neck. She then sat in the sand next to Emilia. From what Cara could see, there were no words spoken and Emilia didn't register Julia's appearance at first, but after some time she sat up and took the ends of the blanket to pull it up and over her horse's face. By that point, Emilia was no longer crying, and even from a distance, Cara could see that a part of her had shut down.

Wiping tears from her eyes, Cara glanced at the clock by her bed. It was a little after eight, which was surprising because her dogs normally insisted that she get up long before that. She hadn't realised how long she'd been lying there thinking. Reaching for the phone on the bedside table, she texted Lillian.

"Morning. What should we do re Em? x"

The reply was almost immediate because Lillian had been up since six, fighting the urge to contact her husband because she felt sad and alone.

"Text later perhaps. But I think she will contact us when ready. x"

"OK. I'll text around lunch. Sound OK? x"

"Yes, should be fine. x"

Lillian set her phone down on the table, her fingers itching to dial Derek. Rightly or wrongly, it was just so normal to look for him in times of trouble, but the fact was he might be someone else's crutch by now, and maybe he liked it that way. Maybe she did too. There was no way of knowing. What she did know, was that interfering in the process she had started would render the whole exercise futile. Derek had to find out whether the grass was indeed greener where he was, and the mistress had to find out whether she wanted to share that grass fulltime. As for Lillian, she needed to know whether she was happier grazing alone. Besides, there was Emilia to think about, all but ready to move in but carrying a lot more baggage than she had been the day before.

"Poor baby girl," Lillian whispered and she shed another tear for her because she could almost taste Emilia's sorrow despite not knowing the best way to deal with it. From bitter experience, she understood grief was rarely the same demon for everyone.

Inspector Antoni Giagkos looked at the paperwork he had spread over his desk, documenting all the activities of the Dog Paw Gang. He had a nagging suspicion, yet it seemed absurd to even think about it. Even so, all the clues laid out in front of him suggested it was not beyond the realms of possibility.

Despite Nicos Andreou's insistence that he had been mugged by five burly Russian guys carrying enough weapons to form their own militia, forensics had turned up some interesting and con-tradictory facts – such as five pairs of shoe prints, two of which belonged to Nicos and his father while the other three appeared to be smaller in size, narrower and comparatively dainty, suggesting that Nicos' earlier statement that he had been the victim of three women was more likely the correct version of events.

As he mulled this thought over, Special Constable Michalis Georgiou poked his head around the door muttering something about the Akamas protests and a meeting with the Super scheduled for 4pm.

"Oh Michalis," Antoni called as his head disappeared quicker than the rest of his body.

"Yes?"

"Do you recall what day it was that the owner of the poisoned dog came to the station?"

"The one that wouldn't stop crying?"

"Well, yes, unless there were more distraught owners of poisoned dogs visiting us this past week or so."

Michalis nodded. "Well, I'd had haloumi and eggs for breakfast at the Sea View and I always do that on a Thursday, and I know I had eggs that day because some of it was on my shirt and I was trying to rub it off when the guy came in, so yes, I do recall. It was Thursday."

"Thank you," Antoni replied, feeling oddly torn because the information added yet more fuel to his suspicions. It was Thursday that Cara had come to the station, before leaving in a whirl of choice insults.

Cara managed to wait until 1pm before texting Emilia. As she wasn't sure what to say, she kept it simple.

"How are you doing? Shall I come by? x"

The answer when it came was a comfort of sorts. "Don't worry. With Julia. Just sorting things. Thanks for thinking of me. x"

Cara then called Lillian, who had texted 20 minutes earlier and received an almost identical reply.

"Well, at least she's with Julia," Lillian said.

But Emilia wasn't with Julia. She was alone and she wanted it that way. Although she had returned to the yard earlier that morning it was only to find out where Adonis was buried and to clean his tack.

"If you don't mind, I'll leave his stuff here for now," Emilia had said, and Julia replied that she could keep it there for as long as she wanted.

"Take your time. Grieve. See how you cope and when you need me, I'll be here. This was always your safe place, Emilia, and that hasn't changed."

Emilia smiled gratefully. She then walked over to Julia and kissed her lightly on the cheek, which was a fairly tactile moment for the both of them. Before she left, Emilia passed over the wind-sucking collar she held.

"Do me a favour and burn this, will you? I don't care if I never see it again."

Julia nodded, while noticing some of the other items Emilia carried – the white numnah she had first bought for Adonis, the headcollar that was still covered in sand from the night before, and a lock of his mane that had been cut from the bridle path behind his ears some years earlier. Emilia had kept it taped to the inside of her locker.

"If there's anything you need," Julia said gently, but she had been there enough times to know there was nothing she could do that would ease the girl's pain, other than resurrect that which was gone.

"I'll be in touch," Emilia replied, before turning down an offer of a lift home because she preferred to walk. The wind might have been as comforting as a hairdryer blowing in her face, but she needed the air and she didn't want an audience when she visited her horse's grave.

After stopping at the florists, Emilia returned the way she had come until she arrived at the field next door to Julia's yard. It wasn't hard to find Adonis and when she crouched by the side of his grave, she tried to tell him how much he had meant to her, but the words sounded inadequate and staged and, in the end, she walked onto the patch of freshly dug earth and lay on top of him, crying until she could cry no more. When she left, the indent of her body remained on the soil alongside a single red rose.

Once she got back to her flat, Emilia drew the curtains and cried again. When she stopped crying, she lay still. Occasionally, she drifted off to sleep only to wake and cry with fresh grief because for a few seconds everything was fine, until she remembered it wasn't.

Later that night, after answering the tentative enquires of her good friends, Emilia managed to pull herself together long enough to get to work. First, she wrote three emails – one to the leading English-language newspaper in the country, one to the leading Greek-language newspaper and the last to the leading Russian-language newspaper. Emilia didn't actually know enough Russian for the email so she wrote in English, believing someone on the paper would be able to translate it. Before she hit send, she wrote a copy of the emails by hand, three times, because she had no printer. She put each of these copies in three envelopes along with a letter. That done, she hit 'send'. A little after 1am, she packed her things and left, almost 24 hours to the minute that Adonis died.

After a long walk to three separate locations to deliver three almost identical letters, Emilia headed for the nearest taxi rank. She carried a rucksack and a look of grim determination on her face that immediately concerned the one taxi driver still waiting for custom. After she showed him the colour of her money, he nodded his head and opened the back-passenger door, telling her to get in.

"Larnaca," she said.

"The airport?"

"Close to it."

Later that morning, Cara was woken up at a more customary hour by her apparently solar-powered companions, Cooper and Peaches.

"Okay, okay, I'm coming," she ordered before heading to the front door to release them into the garden so they might do whatever it was they needed to do. Disappearing back into the kitchen, she put on the kettle, fixed her breakfast and filled the dogs' bowls. She then trawled through the online papers, like she did every day, vaguely aware of a cooler edge to the breeze.

A little after ten – and having read all that she needed to read to know it would be another quiet work day – Cara looked out of the window, mildly irritated to find she couldn't see the sea thanks to the high level of humidity. Her eye was then caught by the open lid of the post box. It struck her as strange because the postman usually did his rounds later in the day. Cara wandered over, stuck her hand in and retrieved an envelope with her name written on it, alongside a dog's paw print. Her heart started hammering and she opened the envelope gingerly, as though it was attached to an explosive device.

"Dear Cara,

Forgive this note and forgive me for not having had the courage to speak to you directly. I would hate for you to feel this makes you in any way less of a friend in my eyes. That couldn't be further from the truth because you and Lillian have brought me more joy and companionship than you'll ever know.

Unfortunately, life has changed for me now.

As you know, and after a fight lasting close to 14 hours, I lost Adonis. The end when it came was cruel and ugly, but mercifully fast. As you heard, I screamed and then I cried. I cried my tears upon his face, onto his neck, onto his withers. I stroked his neck and I stretched my arms over the stomach that killed him. I wanted to be him. I wanted to melt into him. I wanted to find a way to reach for his soul and scream, 'Please God, wait for me! Wait for me!'

You may remember that an hour or more passed before I could find my feet again, but I had to go before his body lost its warmth. I guess, Julia must have turned off the lights. I don't know. I walked out of the yard without looking back. I don't even remember the drive home. I don't know if it was in your car or Lillian's car. I don't remember if I cried. All I remember is getting into bed and realising that was it.

As dawn broke, I woke up before the birds, and the grieving began. It felt like I couldn't see and, in truth, I really couldn't see a way out of this nightmare. Then, when I dressed and left the house to do the things I had to do, I looked at the path in front of me realising I was staring only one metre ahead, unaware of anything approaching, and I wondered whether this would be it from now on — living a life in which I could only look one metre ahead.

Once Julia texted to say Adonis was at rest, I walked to the florist. I asked for a single red rose. This took some minutes because I couldn't breathe through my tears. The florists were concerned, I was embarrassed and yet a part of me wanted to throw my pain in their face and say 'See how much I loved my horse?' Outside, I let my shoulders shake, I let the wave pass over me, I didn't care who saw and I went to say goodbye to my boy.

I think it was at his grave, that I finally made up my mind as to what I needed to do as I imagined all the shit Adonis must have gone through in his life before I found him. Before he saved me. I imagined him being torn from his mother, being pumped with steroids and God knows what else just to turn him into a money-making racing machine, and I imagined the fear and the stress he must have lived through, that fucked up his system to the extent that he lost his life before his eighth birthday. That's when I knew that to honour his death, I would have to honour the death of every horse that had ever been abused and trashed by the racing industry, that I had to honour the memory of all those who never stood a chance because they were too old or lame or just too slow. I have to do something to make people sit up and think about the real price these beautiful creatures pay for human entertainment and greed. I have to do something about Death Alley.

So, forgive me, my beautiful friend, for not including you in this last mission, but as we discussed before, it is an almost impossible task to help these horses. Almost but not quite. Enclosed in the envelope accompanying *this letter is the Press Release I have sent to the newspapers under my own name, not the Dromos Animal Liberation Front because I hope you will continue the good fight when I no longer can.*

Thank you for everything. Thank you for your friendship.

All my love,

Emilia.

PS All for one...

As Cara reread the letter, she noticed her hands were shaking. She next reached for the envelope that had come with it, but her mobile phone rang and a shiver ran up her spine. Almost too frightened to look, she glanced at the display, almost relieved when she saw Antoni's name. But then she looked at the time, it was only 10.20am, and Cara was taken by an overwhelming sense of foreboding. As she took the call, she felt physically sick.

"Hello?"

"Cara, it's me Antoni."

"I know."

"Yes, of course. Look, I'm sorry to call early, but I have to tell you, the police in Larnaca have found a body. It appears to be a friend of yours. The translator you brought to the press conference a few days ago."

Cara felt her heart catch in her throat. "How did she...?"

"She hanged herself. They found her hanging from the gates of a horse racing yard."

Chapter Twenty-Five

Emilia had planned her death down to the last detail. As well as putting a noose around her neck, there was a placard and a small bag. The placard read 'They starve horses here'. The bag contained her passport, inside of which she had named Julia as her next of kin. Larnaca police dutifully contacted Julia and they also contacted Dromos police station because the records showed their suicide victim came from the village.

When Inspector Antoni Giagkos arrived in Larnaca some two hours later, he recognised the young woman whose body had been transferred to the morgue and he felt a familiar weight land on his chest. He wasn't a robot; he was still affected by another's pain, he was still affected by sadness, he was still affected by death and, on a more professional level, he was still affected by deceit. It didn't take much in the way of detective work to suspect there was something rotten in the state of Larnaca.

After being shown the sign, that pretty much served as suicide note and charge sheet, Antoni was informed by an officer assigned to the case that the police had found nothing to back up the dead woman's claims.

"And when did the yard call you?" Antoni asked the officer in charge.

"Just before eight," he was told.

"And you think a racing yard starts work at eight?" he asked, and the younger officer shifted uncomfortably in his shoes. "Look, even if they *were* starving horses, they would still have to feed the ones making money. My cousin worked at a yard in Nicosia. In the summer they're feeding the horses by 6am, which also means there's someone on the yard well before then. Yet no one thought to call us for an hour or more?"

"Maybe they were in shock," replied the officer, who at least had the good grace to avoid Antoni's eyes.

"Or maybe they needed time," he replied tersely. "Do you mind if I take a look around the place."

"Be my guest," replied the officer. "But you'll find nothing we didn't."

And, of course, Antoni knew his colleague from Larnaca district was right; there would be nothing to see at the yard, least of all a herd of slowly dying horses. However, he also suspected that the woman he now knew to be Emilia Branza was also right, which was why the yard didn't inform the police straightaway.

When Antoni arrived at the racing stables, he found the place oddly quiet and manned by a solitary Syrian teenager. The boy spoke no Greek, he spoke no English either, which made him a useful employee to have for anyone with secrets to keep. Smiling good-naturedly, Antoni took a look around the place, shadowed by the boy whose eyes kept darting back and forth to a small building to the left of the entrance. No doubt this was where his boss was hiding. Not that it mattered to Antoni. The case was all but closed as far as Larnaca was concerned, and he was merely satisfying his own curiosity.

After admiring a number of horses stood in their stables, Antoni wandered to the back of the yard where he found what he was looking for, a row of very orderly paddocks, so pristine they could have been cleaned that very same morning.

"Okay, I'm done," he told the boy who looked at him blankly.

As Antoni walked back to the main entrance, nervously followed by the hired help, he received a call from a female colleague telling him the Press had been on after receiving an email from a woman named Emilia Branza regarding the horses at 'Death Alley'. They wondered whether there might be any connection to the 'Dog Paw Gang'.

"What did you tell them?" he asked.

"I told them they should speak to the Press Office," she replied.

"When in doubt…" he said.

After telling his colleague he would deal with any inquiries once he got back to the station, he had next contacted Cara. It wasn't the easiest call Antoni had ever made and being the one to reveal her friend had committed suicide was unlikely to ease the current tensions in their own relationship. Still, she had a right to know, and a right to hear the news from someone who cared.

As he suspected, Cara took the news quietly. Whereas some people might have wailed or gone crazy or even denied the facts, he knew her well enough to second guess how she might react. She was also English and the English tended to keep their grief contained, rather like their lovemaking. But more than that, Cara was a clever woman. If his suspicions were right, she would do well to stay silent.

Although it was only a hunch, and he had no concrete evidence to back it up, the more Antoni thought about the events of the past year and the more incidents he dragged up from his personal memory bank, the more he thought Cara was somehow involved in the Dog Paw Gang. Though he didn't believe, or rather couldn't believe, she was a key figure, all the signs pointed to some kind of complicity. Firstly, there was the magazine article he had read at her home detailing the Pool of Blood incident at the Kaliteros Hotel, right down to the paw print left at the scene, which was a detail that was never divulged until much later. Then there were the incidents themselves, all of them too delicately executed to be the work of thugs or even men, they had too much finesse about them. There was also the coincidental timing of Cara at the police station along with the poisoned dog guy, not to mention the fact that the night Nicos was attacked was also the night Antoni had driven to Cara's house to try and make amends, only to find her dogs home alone. And finally, there was the hunter who recently turned up at the station with a pellet-sized hole in his ass. Though there was no paw print left at the scene, and therefore no immediate suspicion that the Dog Paw Gang was involved, Antoni understood from the hunter's account of his ordeal that he had been shot somewhere along Cara's dog-walking route, roughly in the area where people liked to take a dump. And knowing all this, and suspecting what he did, he was almost relieved when Cara cut dead his call with an apology that she "couldn't speak right now".

Placing the phone in his pocket, Antoni took one last look around the racing yard. By now he was stood in the small car park directly in front of the main gate where Cara's friend had not so long ago hanged herself. It didn't take much imagination to see how the tragedy might have unfolded. An on-site kid, probably the Syrian boy, would have woken up to feed the horses only to discover a body swinging from the gates. No doubt, he would have phoned his boss who would have raced to the yard, read the sign attached to the dead woman, and loaded the evidence at the back of his premises onto a truck before informing the police. Although Antoni didn't know the owner or the guys on the local force, he was pretty sure they would be known to each other and, at the end of the day, they were dealing with the death of a few dumb horses and a Romanian woman. There was no need to rock the boat or create more work than there needed to be.

Antoni shook his head, spat on the ground and got back in his car.

Because of the nature of Emilia's death, the coroner didn't release her body immediately, which at least allowed her friends some time to arrange her funeral. According to her wishes, detailed in a letter to Julia, Emilia was to be cremated in a non-religious service with her ashes scattered over Adonis's grave. So, this is what they arranged, even as the establishment circled the wagons.

They had all seen the press release Emilia had sent to the newspapers because she had helpfully written out copies for them. She also broke the news to Julia, via her letter, that she had been "harbouring the horse of a wanted criminal".

"Even at the end she was joking," Julia told Cara and Lillian, who had come to her home to make arrangements for Emilia's send off. "And now the bastards in power are painting her as some kind of demented halfwit."

She threw the newspaper she held onto the wooden table they were sat around. As it landed nearest to Cara, she looked again at the article. 'Suicide at Stables' was all the headline disclosed followed by eight short paragraphs in which readers learned that a Romanian woman in her thirties took her own life after being diagnosed with multiple sclerosis. Having contacted the media about horses starving to death at a Larnaca racing yard, the woman hanged herself at the location. Police confirmed they had since searched the premises and found the allegation to be unfounded. A police officer leading the inquiry went on to say, "Clearly, this was a very troubled young woman struggling to come to terms with her illness." There was no further mention of the horses Emilia had sacrificed her life to try and save, only the insinuation that as she was physically ill, she was mentally unhinged.

"I don't understand. How would they even know she had MS?" Lillian asked.

Cara shrugged. "The police had her passport and therefore her name and I assume that because she had been in and out of hospital her details were logged on some kind of national computer system."

"But to concentrate on her illness…" Lillian tailed off, unable to speak she was that angry.

"It's the more intriguing line," Cara said, trying to assess the tragedy with her reporter's head rather than with her heart. "The newspapers had their emails and if Emilia had mentioned her role in the Dromos Animal Liberation Front you can bet that they would have gone with that line and it would have made front-page news. Instead, they had a random email, an apparent motive and then this disclosure from the authorities."

"So, her death was in vain," Lillian said bleakly, only for Julia to half-grunt and half-scream her exasperation through gritted teeth.

"Emilia died because she couldn't live without her horse," she said, leaving no room for debate. "During her early diagnosis, it was only Adonis that kept her going. I should know. I was there. I was there every painful step of the way. I saw the fear in her eyes when she thought she was paralysed. I saw that same fear when the doctors told her this was more or less the future she could look forward to. Yes, I did my best to keep her looking for positives, but it wasn't me that kept her fighting. It was Adonis." Julia banged a fist on the table as she struggled to hold back her tears. "Dear God, I hate myself. I knew how she felt about that horse and yet even when we lost Adonis it never occurred to me that I'd lose her too."

"There's nothing you could have done," Lillian assured Julia. "None of us saw this coming. I thought she was too strong a person to even consider such a thing."

Julia shook her head. "Don't believe everything the Church tells you, Lillian. It's not a sign of weakness to look for a way out. It's a sign of hopelessness. Face facts; what did Emilia have to live for? Truly? She had no kids, no job, no financial security, only an uncertain future ahead of her and some friends who would have preferred her to keep plugging away at life no matter what."

Lillian took a deep breath. She could have taken offence, but she didn't. They were all grieving in their different ways and they all had their views on the reasons for that grief. For most of what she said, Julia was right; Emilia's world did revolve around her horse. "Not so long ago, Emilia told me she was looking at special saddles for the disabled," she admitted. "It damn near broke my heart to hear her speaking like that. But suicide?"

"Or a last hurrah," Cara interrupted, trying to turn the focus back to what they were all forgetting. "Emilia didn't just kill herself. She tried to force people to sit up and take notice of the cruelty happening on their doorstep."

Julia pinched the bridge of her petite nose and reached for the newspaper. "Shame she wasn't successful then," she half whispered before shaking her head. "If the truth be known, I wasn't overly surprised when I heard she was dead. I was shocked, but I didn't find it shocking, if that makes any sense. In the same way, I'm not especially surprised that the various authorities have conspired to ignore the message she tried to send. And I think it's that which upsets me most, that no one will ever know just how huge her heart was. She will only be remembered as a victim of an illness she couldn't cope with."

As Julia finished, her bright blue eyes shone with fresh tears and absolute fury, and neither Cara nor Lillian immediately responded. However, her words hit them like a much-needed wake-up call and they looked at each other, both reading the other's mind. They next looked at Julia.

Approximately 36 hours after Emilia took her life, Antoni turned up on Cara's doorstep. As it was hot, the front door was open and Cooper and Peaches practically launched themselves at him as he walked into the courtyard. When Cara went to see what was going on, she had to admit she was just as glad to see him. In fact, she was so glad, and so utterly heartbroken by what had come to pass, that she fell into his arms. She was grateful when he then closed those arms around her to stop her falling out again.

It took many minutes for Cara's sobs to subside and there were lots of apologies, on both sides, not to mention two confused looking dogs. But ultimately it was the pop of a cork that got the two of them talking, once they retired to the kitchen and opened a bottle of wine. For more than an hour, Antoni gave Cara the floor so she might remember Emilia. He listened quietly as she spoke about her friend's condition and how she had dealt with it not as a victim, but as a hero. She also revealed that Emilia had been mourning the death of her own horse shortly before she took her life, while insisting that there was more to her suicide than grief.

"The newspapers say that Emilia believed horses were starving to death at the place where she hung herself," Cara said carefully, and Antoni confirmed the fact with a nod, fully aware of what had made the newspapers and what hadn't. He was also grateful, in a strange way, that Cara no longer had the means to translate the contents of the Greek language newspapers, some of which had given a platform to a handful of politicians offering soundbites about insanity and immigration laws.

"Did anyone investigate the yard where she hanged herself?" Cara asked.

"By 'anyone' you mean the police?" Antoni replied with a gentle smile, relieved to find it quickly reciprocated.

"Yes, why haven't the police looked into it?"

"We did, but by the time my colleagues at Larnaca were contacted, there were only fit, healthy and well-fed horses on site."

"By the time the police were called? So, you think it's a cover up?"

"I didn't say that."

"No, you didn't, but what do you think?"

Antoni smoothed his brow with his left hand, while reaching for his glass with the other, conscious of feeling like a competitor in a chess match where only one player actually knows the game is on. He chose his words carefully.

"You ask me what I think and I'll say this; I think the point has been made and it is maybe time to stop making points."

"What do you mean?" Cara asked, feeling her heart quicken.

"I think you know what I mean," Antoni replied.

For a second or two, Cara stared at him, afraid to say anything more in case it turned into a full-blown confession. Though she might have been wrong, she thought she saw something in his eyes imploring her to keep quiet. A second later, she simply noticed his eyes and how beautiful they were.

"Would you like to stay tonight?" she asked.

"Yes, I would," he replied. "I would like that very much."

Two days after Emilia died, the coroner released her body after delivering the unsurprising verdict of suicide. By then, Julia had

arranged everything, as requested by the deceased. Two years earlier, this would have been impossible as cremation was illegal, but
people had lobbied for a change in the law and the government
had obliged. As Emilia had expressed, there was no religious service, no prayers or eulogies, only a brief business-like cremation
attended by Julia, Cara and Lillian. The music was Neil Young's
Dead Man Theme.

"Was it meant as a joke?" Cara asked as they later discussed the
choice of funeral song while standing in a barren field next door
to Julia's stables.

"I wouldn't be surprised," Lillian replied. "She had some funny
ideas at times."

"Ain't that the truth," Julia agreed. "For the first six months
I knew her, she thought I was a lesbian dressed as a Frappuccino
coffee."

Cara laughed at the memory. "Yes, she told me about that. She
often assumed there was more to people than met the eye. She
recently told me she thought Putin might be the reincarnation of
Rasputin."

"The Mad Monk?" Lillian asked in surprise, and Cara nodded.
"Did you know he was supposed to have the most enormous ding-
dong?"

"Ding-dong?" Julia laughed. "Is that a British-ism?"

"A Lillian-ism," Cara confirmed, and the three women laughed
a little before it lost its way and they stood, once again, in silence.

"You know, her death still hasn't sunk in," Julia eventually said.
"Emilia had become such a part of my life. I'm not sure what I'll
do now she has gone."

As Julia let the tears fall, Cara looked at Lillian, who nodded.
Cara moved closer to the American and put an arm around her.

"I think we may have something you could do," she said gently.
Julia raised her head, the question evident in her eyes. "First, let's
reunite our girl with her boy. Then we can talk."

Julia glanced over at Lillian who gave a reassuring smile.

"Okay," she said quietly, actually too drained to give the matter anymore thought. She opened the wooden casket she held and after checking which way the breeze was blowing, she gently scattered Emilia over her horse's grave.

Chapter Twenty-Six

A day after Emilia was laid to rest, the surviving founding members of the Dromos Animal Liberation Front held an extraordinary meeting at Lillian's home, attended by two honorary guests – Julia and Janet.

After revealing their undercover roles, which wasn't too big a surprise as both honorary guests had either guessed what they were up to or had been informed the previous day, Cara and Lillian filled in the finer details of their exploits, which brought some much-needed laughter to proceedings. They then outlined their latest plan and the roles they had assigned for both Julia and Janet, should they wish to accept them.

"Of course, you know how this will end, don't you?" Janet asked, and Lillian and Cara nodded. The two of them had thought of nothing else over the past few days. Lillian had even tried to talk Cara out of the plan, but Cara was adamant.

"It's the only way, Lillian. I want to live a life I'm proud of. If we walk away now that moment is gone."

To Cara's relief, both Janet and Julia agreed to play their assigned parts and once the wine was finished, and they had their notes detailing times and positions, the two women retired for the night, nervous at what was to come yet utterly determined to honour the lives of those taken too early, whether they be animal or friend.

Once the door closed behind them, Lillian went to the kitchen, brought out the brandy and poured a healthy measure into two glasses. Returning to the dining room table, she took the seat opposite Cara and placed the glasses in front of them.

"Are you sure you want to do this?" Lillian asked, again.

"Without any shadow of doubt," Cara replied firmly.

"It's not too late to back out."

"Only the weak back out," Cara said, employing the Romanian lilt of their lost friend. Lillian smiled before raising her glass.

"To Emilia and the Dromos Animal Liberation Front. One for all…"

"And all for dogs," Cara finished.

They then knocked back their brandies, held each other tightly, and called it a night.

Somewhere between breakfast and lunch, Special Constable Michalis Georgiou took a call from Cara because she couldn't get through to Antoni on his mobile.

"He is in meeting," Michalis told her. "Very top level."

Unlike the last time, when she was feeling slightly hysterical about things, Cara took Michalis at his word and left a sweeter message than the previous one she had left with him. An hour later, Antoni returned her call.

"Sorry," he apologised. "The big bosses are going crazy."

"What about?"

"You don't want to know," he told her, and he really meant it because, if he was right, they were going nuts about his girlfriend, which might prove to be awkward. "So, what can I do for you?"

"Actually, it's more what I can do for you. I thought I'd buy you lunch."

After cursing his bad luck in Greek, Antoni explained in English that it was unlikely he'd be able to take a break before 4pm; he was on the 2pm to 10pm shift. "I've been called in early because of office politics," he said. "The district police chief demands and the slaves in the provinces come running."

"Then let me buy you coffee and cake at 4pm."

"Do they do vegan cake around here?"

"Probably not. I'll buy you coffee and a carrot."

"Sounds delicious. See you at four."

Cara put down the phone feeling nervous, excited and not a little sad. She looked at Cooper and Peaches and grabbed their faces.

After kissing them both on the nose she collapsed onto the cool tiles and cried into their fur. Once the wave had passed, she took a deep breath and channelled the essence of Emilia by demanding she get her "shit together", which she did by going for a shower and making herself look as beautiful as any woman approaching middle-age can possibly be in 35°C heat. Finally, after sorting out some last-minute admin, she waited for the clock to tick its way towards 4pm. When it reached 3.50pm she got in the car, headed for the station and picked up Antoni.

Choosing the coffeeshop next to a charity shop, Antoni took a seat, feeling rather pleased with himself as he sat down. The morning's meetings had gone well, in as much as he had managed to calm everyone down and convince them that the animal rights extremists that had got everyone so agitated had made their point and, while he had no real proof, experience told him that their message had probably ended with the death of the woman at the racing yard.

"I'd be surprised if Emilia Branza wasn't involved in the Dromos incidents given the location of her death and the fact that she lived here. Besides, if you have to kill yourself to be heard then it would seem the battle is pretty much lost," he told Superintendent Constantino Parpis, who seemed to like the line even if he didn't totally buy it.

"Well, I for one, would be quite happy to see this problem disappear. It was bad enough when the politicians got involved, but now I've got the tourist board on my back," the Superintendent moaned in between pulls on his cigarette. Antoni whistled in response. In Cyprus – the Birthplace of Aphrodite – tourism was *il capo dei capi* of government departments thanks to the two million holidaymakers who arrived each year to add their hard-earned euros to the national economy.

Of course, it wasn't the satisfactory morning at work that had returned the spring to Antoni's step, but rather the fact that the woman he had come within an inch of losing was now sat opposite him paying for coffee and orange cake.

"I feel honoured," he said.

Cara smiled, melting a little under the warmth of his dark eyes. She leaned over to kiss him. To Antoni's surprise, she took her time letting go.

"You taste sweet," Cara said as she finally leaned back in her seat. Antoni was going to reply with something funny, and probably inappropriate, when he was stopped by a sudden unmistakable sadness in Cara's eyes. He remembered she was mourning a friend whose body had barely had time to grow cold. Even so, there was something about the look she gave him that troubled him. This feeling wasn't eased any by the kiss they later shared as she dropped him back at work. Maybe he was being uncharacteristically sensitive, but it felt like goodbye.

At 9pm, Lillian arrived at Cara's house, bringing Janet with her. After introductions were made to Cooper and Peaches, the women quickly got down to business. There were three numbers to call and they were all made on Cara's UK phone, which she still kept for emergencies and newspaper business. It was also handy for anonymous calls as it was programmed to 'private' on the Caller ID. It was Cara who volunteered to do the talking, all in English, trusting that someone on the other end of the line would surely know the language just like everyone else on the island under the age of 65. The first call she made was to the leading Greek-language newspaper, followed by the leading English-language newspaper and finally to the news channel of the country's largest television broadcaster.

"If you want to know the identity of the Dromos Animal Liberation Front, the group of animal lovers you commonly call the Dog Paw Gang, have a team at the Kings Avenue Mall car park in Paphos by midnight and await further instructions. We will need a contact number."

Naturally, there were a few questions and a healthy dose of scepticism, but Cara made it clear they would find all the answers they needed later that night, and if they didn't believe her, they could tell this to their editors the following morning when they explained how they missed the year's biggest news story. By the end of the calls, Cara had three contact numbers. She then turned to Janet.

"Thank you for doing this," she said.

"It's my pleasure," Janet replied. "Now, go and do what you have to do and I pray it all goes well. Don't worry about things here."

Janet bent down as best she could, given her lack of legs, and patted Cooper and Peaches on the head. When she straightened herself up, Cara moved forward and sank to her knees, taking hold of both dogs to hug them tight.

"I won't be long," she lied. Perhaps sensing she wasn't telling the whole truth, both Cooper and Peaches tolerated the embrace until Lillian gently informed Cara of the time. "Yes," she agreed, "we better get going."

At a little past 10pm, Cara and Lillian made their way to Julia's house. As they had a couple of hours to kill, further details to finalise and some serious dismantling to do when they got there, it was safe to say their minds were too preoccupied to notice the car that started following them at a safe distance. Once they parked up at the back of Julia's property, the vehicle behind them killed the lights and disappeared into a nearby field.

Twenty minutes later, sat in the dark and surrounded by banana leaves, Antoni started to feel embarrassed and not a little foolish. He wasn't sure what he was waiting for, but Cara's last kiss had been on his mind all day, so when he finally finished his shift, he decided to pay her a visit. As he turned into her street, he saw her reversing out of the driveway and heading the other way. Naturally, he did what any lovesick puppy with detective skills would do under similar circumstances, he waited a second before carefully following.

As Antoni sat in the car waiting for something to happen, all sorts of scenarios crossed his mind, but as the clock ticked steadily towards midnight, he pretty much came to the conclusion that he was stalking a girls' night out. However, just as he was about to drive away, he saw the lights of Cara's car come into view, followed by a lorry that looked very much like a horse transporter.

"Well, this is turning weird," he muttered, ducking down in his seat as they drove past. When he was relatively confident that he could follow without causing alarm, he turned the key in the ignition and set off after them.

As Cara drove, she was too sick with nerves to talk, so she reached for a CD in the side pocket of the driver's seat and fast forwarded it to track seven.

I have given to you, Jane
A torn and tattered love

"For the love of God, haven't you got anything more upbeat?" Lillian asked. "Who is this?"

"The Mark Lanegan Band."

"No George Michael, is he? Can't we have the radio on?"

Though Cara loved Mark Lanegan and felt at liberty to play whatever she liked as they were in her car, she acquiesced. Ejecting the CD, the first song playing on the radio was Hurt by Johnny Cash.

"Embrace the dark, Lillian," she said laughing. "We have the spirit of our girl with us tonight!"

Though Lillian covered her ears in mock horror, she thought Cara was probably right, and even though the song was unremittingly depressing, she felt oddly comforted by it.

As they reached the outskirts of Paphos, taking a short cut towards the highway, Cara's phone rang. It was Julia.

"I think we're being followed," was all she said.

Instinctively, Cara looked in the rear-view mirror, but all she could see were the headlights of Julia's horse carrier.

"OK, we'll take the next right, while you carry on and we'll meet you at the industrial estate as soon as we can," Cara replied.

"Roger that."

"What's going on?" Lillian asked as Cara put the phone on the dashboard.

"I don't know yet, but Julia thinks we're being followed."

"Oh God, no." Lillian crossed her chest before quickly reaching for the grab handle as Cara turned a sharp right and Julia went thundering passed them. "Where's she going?" Lillian asked, hearing the panic creep into her voice.

"To the industrial estate, we'll meet her there, if it's safe to do so. Ah, here we are." Cara glanced in the mirror to see two headlights turn in their direction. As it was dark, there was no way of seeing more of the car behind them, so she took the next left and carried on driving until she came to the Tomb of the Kings Road where there were plenty of street lights and plenty of traffic lights to stop at and take a look. It was at the second set of lights that Cara got her answer.

"Holy crap," she muttered.

"What?" said Lillian about to turn in her seat until Cara's hand shot out to stop her.

"Don't look! I don't want him to know we've spotted him."

"Him? Who?"

"Antoni."

"Your boyfriend?"

"Yes."

"The policeman?"

"Yes."

"Oh, Mother of God." Lillian crossed herself again. As the lights changed, she told Cara to put her foot down and "lose the bastard."

"The what?" Cara asked, half-laughing as she struggled with her own surge of adrenaline.

"The bastard!" Lillian repeated, holding onto the grab handle for dear life as Cara swerved right and then left before shooting up a one-way street the wrong way, taking another right, followed by another, until she spotted a large open driveway where she killed her lights, drove in and immediately switched off the engine. Two minutes later, Antoni's car went careering passed, closely followed by a set of blue lights. Cara glanced at Lillian who looked to the heavens, put her hands together and whispered 'thank you'.

After giving it a couple of minutes, Cara edged out of the drive-way and glanced left where she saw Antoni further down the road standing on the pavement having been pulled over by a patrol car. She shook her head in disbelief before laughing.

"Your Lord really does work in mysterious ways," she told Lillian, and they drove away at a more sedate pace to meet up with Julia, who they found ten minutes later, parked at the entrance of the industrial estate.

With a flash of headlights, Cara signalled that Julia should follow. They made their way along the battered tarmac road that skirted the boundaries of the industrial estate until they came to a right turning immediately opposite a huge concrete drain pipe. They followed this road for a few minutes more until the tarmac finally gave up any pretence of being a road and turned into a rubble track. Another right turning towards the end of it brought them to a stop in a large gravelled area.

"Kivotos," Julia whispered to herself from the cab of the horse box as her lights lit up a series of cages some 70 metres in front of them. She had heard about this place from the local Press and she was shocked to see how much of what she had read was true. There were clearly dogs there, but they appeared to be either too tired, too sick or too traumatised to kick up much of a fuss at the late hour of this intrusion.

"Okay babies," Cara said as she got out of her car. "Your life is about to get a hell of a lot better."

And with that they got to work.

Taking five 20 litre fuel cans from the back of Cara's car, they carried them over to the pens. By now most of the dogs had been roused from sleep, but they barely made a sound, and because they were in such a pitiful state, everyone tried to keep their eyes averted as they did what they had to do. Towards the back of the pens, next to some kind of outhouse, Cara found a number of old tyres which she stacked together. She then returned to the car with Lillian to fetch two 13kg gas cannisters that felt a hell of a lot heavier than 13 kilos. Placing them in the rings of two tyres, they stacked all the wood they could find around the cannisters along with anything else that might be flammable.

"Done?" asked Julia when they eventually joined her back at the horse box.

"More or less," Cara said. "Now, let's liberate these puppies."

After opening the side of the horse transporter and pulling down the ramp, the three women, armed with a number of collars, leads and wire cutters, finally walked over to the dogs. Some of their cages were bolted shut, others were padlocked, but they worked through them all systematically, from one end to the other, to make sure no dog was left behind. One by one they either led or carried those poor, painfully thin and petrified creatures over to the horsebox, inside of which were a number of blankets waiting, laid out on a bed of fresh hay. There were also bottles of water and bags of dog food in the lorry as well as a number of buckets that would be put to good use once they were safely away.

Once all 26 dogs were on board, the three women lifted the ramp, closed the horsebox and took a moment to say their goodbyes.

"Good luck," said Julia. "Emilia would have been beyond proud."

"I hope so," Cara replied.

Julia then stepped back to give Lillian and Cara the space they needed to say their farewells.

"It's not too late," Lillian whispered.

"I'm good with this, really I am," Cara replied, reaching up to wipe a tear from her friend's lashes. Stepping back, she shook her head, straightened her shoulders and smiled. "Right, I'll give you forty minutes to get as far as you can down the highway. Drive safely and, if your God wills it, I'll see you on the other side."

"One for all…" replied Lillian.

"And all for dogs."

Without another word, and half-blinded by tears, Lillian jumped into the passenger seat of Julia's horsebox while Cara walked back to her car where she opened the boot to retrieve a pair of overalls that had once belonged to Derek. Given their difference in size and gender, she found them overly roomy, but Lillian said they were standard safety issue from Derek's oil rig days and she insisted Cara wear them.

Maybe it was the adrenaline pounding in her ears, but Cara wasn't initially aware of Julia's lorry pulling away until the very last minute. She turned just in time to lock eyes with Lillian before she disappeared from view, leaving Cara in near darkness. After grabbing a torch from the car, she looked to the heavens.

"This one's for you, Emilia."

Cara got to work; dousing the outhouse, the rubber tyres, the gas cannisters and every last dog pen with petrol. When she was done, she looked at her watch, which showed there were still ten minutes to go. So, she returned to her car, fixed her hair, wiped the sweat from her face, powdered her nose and reapplied her lipstick before calling three numbers she had written on a piece of paper some hours earlier. As each person answered, she gave them the same directions.

"Stay at the entrance when you arrive, set up your equipment and all will be revealed."

Cara then took up position, holding an empty beer bottle stuffed with a petrol-soaked rag in one hand and a cigarette and lighter in the other. Though Cara hadn't smoked for almost seven years, the idea of starting again, albeit temporarily, pandered to her sense of theatre.

For more than an hour, Antoni drove around Paphos trying to find

Cara's car. He had to admit it; she had some impressive driving skills. He had been less impressed with his fellow law officers and got pretty close to losing it when they held him up for so long. But what could he tell them – that he was following his girlfriend because he suspected she was about to commit a crime and he wanted to stop her rather than arrest her? No, there was nothing he could do apart from apologise, make up some rubbish about being in a rush to get home and take the patronising lecture about 'setting an example' on the chin. By the time they were done, Cara was long gone and he couldn't even be sure she was still in Paphos. Even so, he wasn't prepared to give up so easily. After reasoning that he might stumble across Cara and her friends, as there couldn't be that many horse transporters cruising around the city at this time of night, he carried on driving, around and around, until his tank neared 'empty' and the clock on his dashboard read 3:00. But then, just as he decided to call it a night, he saw three vehicles turning out of the Kings Avenue Mall, all heading in the same direction, including one which looked very much like a TV van, complete with satellite dish attached to the roof. As this was no common sight in downtown Paphos at three in the morning, he followed.

At first, Antoni assumed they were heading for the highway, which panicked him slightly as he was desperately low on fuel, but then the three-vehicle convoy turned towards the industrial estate on the outskirts of the city. After turning right, opposite a large concrete ring, they followed the road until it disintegrated into a rough track and it was at that point that Antoni had a pretty good idea of where they were heading. What he lacked was any idea of what might be happening, what might have already happened or what was about to happen, and because he had no idea about any of those things, and he didn't want to be seen until he did have one, he parked up at the side of the track and followed on foot. He knew there was only one end to this road.

By the time Antoni reached the entrance to the Kivotos Dog Shelter, he saw eight people standing by their cars, apparently hanging around with nothing better to do. Two of them were holding notepads, suggesting they were journalists, two were carrying cameras around their necks, presumably photographers, and the others were congregating around a TV camera that had been set up in front of a row of kennels some 70 metres away. As Antoni scanned the area behind them, his eye was caught by the faint glow of what looked like a cigarette burning. He next noticed the incredibly strong and unmistakable smell of petrol in the air and he knew, with absolute certainty, what was coming next.

Antoni ran, as fast as his legs would carry him, but he didn't even reach the small bank of journalists before he saw a Molotov cocktail fly through the air. Almost immediately, the flame took hold and it spread with lightning speed backwards and sideways, climbing up the frames of a series of kennels and pens, along the ground and up the walls of a building at the back. As plumes of smoke rose in the air, like twisted ghouls fleeing the inferno, a shape could be seen moving their way. At first it was just a shadow, a dark silhouette walking towards them, and away from the orange flames, but as the fire grew in intensity the shape of a baggy pair of overalls became clear as well as the long hair playing in the breeze. As a huge explosion lit up the night sky, Antoni clearly saw her face.

"Cara!"

Chapter Twenty-Seven

Nicosia Central Prison was actually the only prison in the Republic of Cyprus whether it be centrally, easterly, westerly or southerly and it was home to 600-plus inmates who were mostly men, although there were a number of women also serving time behind the same bars, including Cara.

As one might expect, prison was no holiday camp, but once Cara managed to look past the towering walls topped with rolls of barbed wire, the place was more civilised than she would have imagined. Not that this was always the case. According to one long-timer on her block, the jail was pretty grim before the female governor took over, with 13 suicide attempts every month and daily incidents of self-harm. Nowadays, prisoners were more likely to kill themselves on release rather than during their stay.

In the first few weeks of her incarceration, Cara was pretty much terrified of pretty much everything. Still, she did her best to navigate prison life by not casting judgement, at least none that could be seen, as she mingled with an assorted crowd of petty criminals and hardened killers. Though she initially struggled to find sleep through the cacophony of angry screams and sobs of other inmates, she even got used to that after a while. And even though the accommodation was basic, her cell was one of the better ones because she had been gifted a place in the new €700,000 women's wing, along with 40 other female prisoners.

To her surprise, Nicosia Central looked more like a building site than an established prison as there was major reconstruction work on-going in order to provide more space for an ever-growing population, half of whom were foreigners, not unlike her. Among the new extras was a basketball court, which seemed very 'prison', and a spanking new visiting area, which was nice because during the course of her stay she had quite a number of people queueing up to see her. As Cara had become quite the cause célèbre on the island thanks to her antics and some fabulous Press overage, she found herself courted by British journalists looking for a scoop, animal welfare organisations looking for a mascot, politicians looking for votes and diplomatic staff looking for a way to engineer her early release, quietly.

As it transpired, Cara had been spot on about the impact her Messiah-like pose in front of the fireball destruction of one of the island's most notorious dog shelters would have. The image made front page news not only in Cyprus, but also in the UK, and the TV coverage of her 'sacrifice' was beamed across the globe. Unable to brush Cara's protest away, like they had successfully done with Emilia's, the authorities were forced to respond to questions about animal welfare on the island while rescue shelters reported a sud-den demand for unwanted dogs with many of them finding loving homes abroad. However, most satisfying of all was the demise of the hellhole that was the Kivotos dog farm. Thanks to the Dromos Animal Liberation Front, there would be no return to business once the current furore died down. The place had been blown to smithereens and there was even talk of erecting a statue upon its ruins, dedicated to every animal that had ever died a painful and unnecessary death at the hands of man. Meanwhile, the fate of the farm's former canine residents remained a mystery to everyone other than Cara, Lillian, Julia and Janet – as well as Janet's rescue contact in the east of the island who suddenly found herself ex-tremely busy in the days following Cara's arrest.

As agreed earlier, and though Lillian wasn't exactly happy about it, Cara had pleaded guilty to one count of arson and the theft of 26 dogs. She also asked the court to take into considera-tion a number of other crimes she had committed under the guise of the Dromos Animal Liberation Front. During the brief court hearing, she verified that Emilia Branza had been the only other member of the organisation until her tragic death to highlight the atrocities committed by some of the island's racing yards. At this point in the proceedings, Cara turned to the Press Bench and told them, "Take a look at how many foals are born each year and see how many make it to their fifth year. Your readers would be appalled." Of course, the prosecution went ballistic at this point and even the friendly judge reprimanded her for addressing the media directly, but during the days and weeks that followed, Cara was gratified to see the media respond with a number of sympathetic profiles of her friend, painting Emilia not as a depressed, disease-riddled misfit, but as a woman of rare warmth, good humour and an incomparable compassion for animals.

As Cara's story showed no sign of abating, the government finally responded to the growing clamour for animal welfare reforms. Of course, it might have been mere coincidence, but during her incarceration the President announced a number of new initiatives including the creation of an animal police unit plus harsher punishments for animal abusers. A new animal welfare department would also be managed by the government's veterinary services.

"The amount of coverage has been staggering and the knock-on effect unbelievable," Lillian breathlessly revealed during one of her weekly visits. "I think attitudes might really be changing. Really, I've never known so many people want to get involved; offering to feed the stray cats, volunteer at shelters and patrol the usual poison hotspots. My only regret is seeing you in here."

"Don't worry, it's not too bad," Cara assured her. "Not now I'm the governor's bitch."

"That's not even funny," Lillian replied, shaking her head while trying not to catch the eye of any 'real' criminals in the room.

"Lillian, lighten up. It's okay," Cara said, before asking the question she asked every time Lillian visited. "How are Cooper and Peaches?"

"They're good. They miss you," Lillian replied, as always.

"I miss them too."

"I know you do."

When Cara and Lillian originally came up with their plan for Kivotos, Cara had been surprised by Lillian's offer to take her pets while she was away, given Derek's allergy.

"He won't be coming back," Lillian informed her with no hint of drama in her voice before revealing the finer details of their separation.

Though Cara was shocked by the news, she also suspected Derek would eventually return. However, Lillian never mentioned any desire for reconciliation during her visits, not even after Derek revealed he'd had enough of his mistress. Three months into their separation, and about two months into Cara's incarceration, Derek made his first tentative steps towards saving his marriage. "I miss you," he wrote to Lillian via email. "I've been a fool and I am extremely sorry for hurting you and our children with my stupid, thoughtless, selfish actions. I know it may never be possible, but in time, I hope to make amends. I love you, Lillian. Please, I want to come home."

Of course, Lillian cried when she read the email, even though she had been expecting it; you don't live with someone for more than three decades without knowing how their mind works, unless they're a psychopath. And the truth was, she felt incredibly sorry for Derek. He had been an A-grade fool and yes, he had hurt her immensely, but unfortunately for Derek, the most stupid thing he ever did was give her the opportunity to taste another life. Where once Lillian might have crumbled under such a change in her fortunes, she actually felt liberated by the freedom, so much so she could no longer see a way back.

Derek and Lillian did meet up again – not in the house because Cooper and Peaches would have triggered Derek's allergy and Lillian thought he had suffered enough – but on a quiet stone beach, close to Paphos airport. With no one to watch their heartache, they clung to each other for a while as they cried for the kids they once were and the loss of a dream they once cherished. But Derek could tell there was no way back for him, at least not at that moment. Lillian had blossomed in his absence. In the end, they both agreed it would be best if they simply parted ways and began the sad process of an amicable divorce. As they each contacted lawyers, Derek made it clear that he didn't deny his wife anything she deserved, in fact he was prepared to be overly generous, and though Dan and Lucy tried to get Lillian to change her mind, she was adamant. She no longer wanted to share her life with Derek.

Ironically, while Lillian appeared to be streamlining her domestic arrangements, Cara found herself in the curious position of having a more complicated personal life inside prison than she ever did outside of it. Barely a fortnight into her six-month sentence, she was blindsided by a visit from Tom.

"If you wanted to get my attention you only had to call," he said, and Cara burst into tears when she saw him because he was as tall and funny and as handsome as she remembered him being, and she was also in prison.

It was the strangest feeling to suddenly have Tom sitting opposite her after an absence of nearly six years and though he was a little softer around the edges and his hair greyer than before, it felt like time had stood still during their years apart. It hadn't, of course, and they'd both moved on to other lovers, although Cara had shown far less haste than Tom in this matter. Maybe because she was still disappointed by this fact, it was perhaps inevitable that it would creep into their conversation at some point.

"What else could I do?" he asked.

"Join a monastery?"

"A possibility if I was living in 13th Century England, Cara. Anyway, I don't understand why you're so rattled. If memory serves, it was you who left me. I never wanted us to break up. That was your decision. But I have to say, it's clear you've flourished without me."

Tom held up his hands as he looked around them.

"Son of a bitch," Cara half-laughed before falling silent. She had never properly accepted that she had been the one to leave the relationship, possibly because she had spent so many years feeling like she was being pushed out of it. As if reading her mind, Tom reached across the table to take her hands.

"I never stopped loving you, Cara."

"I'm sure that must please your girlfriend," she replied, a little more bitterly than intended.

"To be honest, she was close to impossible to please. She also left me."

"Do you think there may be a pattern forming in your life?"

"I don't think so. As far as I'm aware, she hasn't morphed into a one-woman crime spree in a foreign country. I think she's dating an accountant in Walthamstow."

Cara smiled. Unable to help herself, she asked, "Did you love her?"

Tom's eyes flickered, and her heart plummeted.

"Yes," he eventually responded. "Yes, I did. But in a different way to you."

And because Cara was afraid to ask whether 'different' meant 'more', she stopped digging. She then stopped talking altogether, not because she was upset, but rather because she realised that she was still in love with this man from another time in her life. Perhaps sensing this fact, and just before his visit came to an end, Tom left her with another bombshell.

"I don't know what you plan on doing when you leave here, but I want you to know that I was a bloody fool to let you go, Cara. Look, I don't expect an answer from you now, or indeed anytime soon, but I was rather hoping that, if you don't become a career criminal in the near future, then maybe we could give our relationship another shot."

And having said what he came to say, Tom walked out of the room, leaving Cara reeling. Her confusion wasn't eased any when a few days later, Antoni came to visit.

"Let's get married," he said.

Cara looked at Antoni, lost for words. If she was brutally honest, she knew she loved him, even more so after she emerged from the flames of Kivotos. With gas bottles exploding in the background, Antoni had sprinted out of the dark to rugby tackle her to the ground so he might use his body to protect her from the burning debris raining down on them. It was an especially selfless act given the Press was on hand to record their every move, and Antoni's heroism subsequently made a two-page spread in at least two national newspapers in England, which took a lot of explaining back at the station.

"It has been awkward," Antoni confessed the first time he visited. "I've been suspended following an investigation into the matter."

"Oh God, Antoni, no."

"Don't worry. It's a formality," he assured her. "But with everyone looking, procedures have to be seen to be followed. Thankfully, most of my colleagues are willing to believe I was following you out of jealousy that night, not because I suspected you were going to set fire to half the town. The hearts of Cypriot men run wild like the bulls."

"Good to know," Cara said with a laugh, and when Antoni proposed two weeks later, she nearly said 'yes'. But then she recalled their conversation about kids.

Antoni wanted a family and Cara knew beyond doubt that this was something she couldn't give him. Having been in a similar situation with Tom, she wasn't sure she could rob Antoni of that dream simply to satisfy her own needs. And then there was Tom. The cloud that had hung over her for the past six years. In all the time they had been apart, his reappearance had revealed how little she had actually moved on. And if her feelings remained that strong, how could they be wrong? But then, when her life was potentially in danger, it was Antoni who had launched himself in harm's way to protect her. Hard as she tried, she couldn't imagine Tom being so selfless, or agile.

Clearly sensing her hesitation, Antoni sighed before asking her "to think about it." And because Cara did love him, and she wasn't as self-reliant as she liked to imagine she was, she told him she would.

Knowing she would have to make a choice sooner or later, Cara chose the 'later' option not only because it was easier, but also because, if only for a short while, she wanted to enjoy the uncommon occurrence of having two men profess their love for her. Then, towards the end of the second month of her incarceration, and after much lobbying by diplomats and a couple of minor British celebrities who like animals, Cara was released from prison under special dispensation of the President. As she had served only a third of her sentence, it was suggested to Cara that she might want to quietly disappear. She was assured that the government was determined to change the fate of animals in the country, but with another holiday season fast approaching the tourist board would prefer to have the island associated with sun, sand and sea rather than poisoned dogs and butchered cats. Naturally, Cara was happy to comply. As far as she was concerned, she had done her bit and served her time and all she wanted was to be reunited with her dogs. As a consequence, when the day of her release came, there were no newspapers or welcoming committees to greet her. Cara simply collected her personal belongings, which didn't amount to much, and walked out of the prison gates and into the open air where she found a solitary car waiting for her.

Cara smiled and paused to breathe in the air of freedom, knowing she had made the right decision. The Dromos Animal Liberation Front had left its mark and it was time for a new beginning. As Cara crossed the asphalt parking area, she saw the driver's door open and she immediately fell to her knees as Cooper and Peaches came running, whimpering and thrashing their tails in her face as they competed to shower her with kisses.

"Oh my God, I missed you like you wouldn't believe!" she told them, crying tears of joy.

"And they missed you too," a voice informed her. Cara looked up to find herself half dazzled by the huge smile waiting for her.

Wiping tears from her face, she got to her feet to meet the embrace coming her way.

"Lillian," she said.

"My dear Cara. Good to see you back on the outside."

"It's good to be here."

Taking hold of the leads that Lillian held, she clipped them onto the collars of her dogs who were starting to notice there were other, more interesting smells, than Cara in the area. They then walked back to the car. After settling Cooper and Peaches on the back seat, Cara joined Lillian in the front.

"Did you get everything sorted?" she asked, and Lillian nodded. "So, what now?"

Reaching into the glove box, Lillian pulled out two plane tickets, two EU passports and two pet passports. Cara inspected the tickets.

"Spain," she said, nodding her approval.

"I hear there are dogs there that could do with our help," Lillian replied.

"Then we best not disappoint them," Cara responded.

Lillian paused for a second and smiled. She then turned the key in the ignition, conducted a three-point turn and set off in the direction of Larnaca airport.

The End

ACKNOWLEDGEMENTS

In 2005, I moved to Afghanistan where I found one of the great loves of my life, my rescue dog, Blister. Following stays in Pakistan, Qatar, Austria, Croatia and France, Blister now lives with me in Cyprus, along with five more dogs that we picked up on our travels.

During our 15 years together, Blister has been my loyal friend and longsuffering companion, and perhaps unsurprisingly, she is one of the main inspirations behind this book. The other inspiration is my horse, Achilles.

Achilles died in 2015, three years after he entered my world. His loss was huge, but his ultimate gift to me was the secret of happiness. Today, horses are the great passion of my life. Naturally, they are also a constant source of worry and learning, so it's fortunate that I have had fantastic support throughout this journey from Caroline Scambler. As my friend and trainer, there is much of Caroline in this book and even more of George's Ranch, the equestrian centre she built and nurtured over two decades, and the place where I keep my horses today. Special mentions also go to fellow horse lovers Leah and Hannah, Nicole, Debbie, Anne-Marie and Ella, Maria and Irina, Eva, Lynne and Lana, Elise, Jay C and Jay M, Lou and Leah, Chanchal, Thilina, Asanka, Irene Ierides and anyone I may have forgotten who fed me during the lean years, took photos of my progress, even when there was none, and basically had my back during the regular existential crises that come with horse ownership.

Special thanks also go to John Kelly and Andreas Koutsides for their detective knowledge, my cousin Stephen Coates for his DIY know-how, Simon J Hilliard who helped with the nuts and bolts of my criminal activities, and the heroes from QAWS, PAWS, Tigger House, Cyprus Love Dog Rescue, Stray Haven, OnlyVets and Judy Mitra who have all helped me in some way over the years whether it was with my own dogs or dogs I have found.

As ever, my mum, dad and sister worked as my trusted first-draft readers, with Janey Harvey, Sarah Dean Kelly, Hélène Collon, Ali Rhind and Teresa Tyler casting their careful eyes over the second draft.

And last but not least, there are two more huge inspirations behind this story – my wonderful friend Vaia Konstantinidi who guided me with strength and good humour through the challenges of MS, and Fabiola Lubita who carried the weight of the world's animal abuses on her shoulders and who sadly disappeared from my radar as the years passed by. If you ever read this, Fabi, I hope you are happy.

ABOUT THE AUTHOR

Andrea Busfield is a former News of the World reporter who moved to Kabul some years before the paper shut down. It was a life-changing experience in many ways and when she returned to Europe, she brought with her a street dog called Blister. Fifteen years later, Blister lives with Andrea in Cyprus – along with five more rescues.

As well as having her own pack of strays, and a number of feral cats, Andrea has found homes for nine other dogs that wandered into her path over the years.

While she considers her dogs to be 'part of the family', her great passion in life is horses and in 2012 she fulfilled a childhood dream when she bought a four-year-old thoroughbred stallion named Achilles. Sadly, Achilles passed away three years later and Andrea took on a retired racehorse called Lucky Star. Despite some challenging moments, this sweet-natured horse mended a very broken heart and reignited her passion for riding. So much so, Andrea bought a second horse in 2017 – a six-year-old Andalusian mare called Mina – and in 2021, a Hanoverian warmblood foal called Sundance. In between writing, Andrea now spends her time working out how to feed them all.

Andrea has written three novels: Born Under a Million Shadows; Aphrodite's War; and The Silence of Stone. She also continues to work as a freelance journalist.